DEATH
OF A KING

ANDREW H. VANDERWAL

TUNDRA BOOKS

Published in Canada by Tundra Books,
a division of Random House of Canada Limited,
One Toronto Street, Suite 300, Toronto, Ontario M5C 2V6

Published in the United States by Tundra Books of Northern New York,
P.O. Box 1030, Plattsburgh, New York 12901

Library of Congress Control Number: 2012947607

Library and Archives Canada Cataloguing in Publication

Vanderwal, Andrew H.
Death of a king / Andrew H. Vanderwal.

ISBN 978-1-77049-398-8. – ISBN 978-1-77049-399-5 (EPUB)

1. Scotland – History – Wallace's Rising, 1297-1304 –
Juvenile fiction. I. Title.

PS8643.A69D43 2013   JC813'.6   C2012-905813-0

We acknowledge the financial support of the Government of Canada
through the Canada Book Fund and that of the Government of Ontario
through the Ontario Media Development Corporation's Ontario Book
Initiative. We further acknowledge the support of the Canada Council
for the Arts and the Ontario Arts Council for our publishing program.

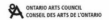

ONTARIO ARTS COUNCIL
CONSEIL DES ARTS DE L'ONTARIO

Edited by Sue Tate and Kelly Jones
Designed by Kelly Hill

www.tundrabooks.com

Printed and bound in the United States of America

1 2 3 4 5 6   18 17 16 15 14 13

For Annette, who bought *The Scottish Chiefs* classical comic book for me on one of our many walks to Frank's, the local variety store.

With special thanks to all the readers of *The Battle for Duncragglin* who encouraged me to write this companion book: Reid, for the valuable feedback on an early draft; Eric, Graham, and Jan, for their advice and edits; and Ronnie, for giving me a true introduction to his magnificent country and for telling me – back when we stood as unruly young men at the edge of a cliff near his home in Kinghorn – that, a long time ago, a king died here.

Quhen Alexander our worthi king had lorn,
Be awentur, his liff besid Kyngorn,
Thre yer in pess the realm stude desolate;
Quharfor thair raiss a full grewous debate.*

Words spoken by a blind minstrel in 1477, which roughly translate as

After good King Alexander died on his way to Kinghorn, without leaving an heir to the throne, things went down the toilet for Scotland – big time.

Or, if you prefer a somewhat more literal translation

When Alexander, our worthy king, had lost,
Became cold, his life beside Kinghorn,
Three years in vain the realm's study [for a successor]
    desolate;
Therefore there raised a very grievous debate.

What an understatement that was!

---

* Henry the Minstrel, *Wallace; or, The Life and Acts of Sir William Wallace, of Ellerslie*, published from a manuscript dated M.CCCC.LXXXVIII (Glasgow: Maurice Ogle & Co., 1869).

Contents

PROLOGUE

THE NINETEENTH DAY OF MARCH IN THE YEAR OF OUR LORD MCCLXXXVI (1286)

The torch cast a flickering light over the coarse stone walls as the squire hastily led a man and a woman up a spiral staircase. He checked to see no one was about and then directed them across a tapestry-filled room to a curtained recess, where they would be secluded.

The squire held out his hand. "Show me the money," he demanded.

The man held up a gold coin.

The squire snatched the coin, turning to hold it to the light. "Whose face is this?" he asked suspiciously.

"A great queen who reigned in another time."

The squire pointed to the date. "And what does this signify?"

"That you're an idiot," the man snapped. "If you don't want it, hand it back."

The squire quickly pocketed the coin. "The audience ye seek is very hard for me to secure, sire. Perhaps if I had a few more of these . . ."

"More! How many? Hurry up, man, I haven't got all day."

"Well, Sir William Douglas le Hardi is in chambers with King Alexander the-now, together with the king's advisers. They contemplate important matters of state and willnae wish to be disturbed. But if I gave two of these to the court magistrate, I think he could be persuaded to ask M'Lord Douglas to step out for a moment. And then if Lord Douglas was offered ten, he might – just might – be inclined to hear your case."

"Ten coins!"

The squire shrugged. "Lord Douglas doesnae do anything for a pittance, sire. Ten may not even be enough."

"Very well." The man counted out twelve coins and dropped them into the squire's outstretched hand. "But bring me Lord Douglas, or I'll have your head."

The squire bowed and backed from the alcove. As soon as he was past the curtain, he turned and ran.

"You would 'have his head'?" The woman stifled a nervous giggle. "Where did that come from?"

"I don't know. It sounded good, though, didn't it?" The man straightened his robe and thrust out his chin. "Aren't you glad I brought these royal garments? It makes me look like I just might have the authority to carry out a threat like that, don't you think?"

The woman didn't seem convinced. "More likely that's the last we've seen of that fellow *and* our money. It cost us a lot to buy all those gold coins."

"He'll deliver . . . if he can. People in this time really *are* concerned they might lose their heads."

"George, do you really think we should be doing this? Shouldn't we go back? What about our son? What if something happened to us . . . ?"

The man put his arm around her. "I know it's hard, Marian, but after coming all this way, we have to see it through. We're almost there. Just think of all the lives that are at stake. So many of our ancestors killed, murdered by King Edward, that bloody Hammer of the Scots, and for what? Imagine what could have been. . . ."

Marian adjusted the edges of his robe to cover the jacket he wore underneath. "You're right." She took a deep breath. "Very well, but promise me, this is our last attempt. After this, we go home, back to our own time."

"I promise."

The curtain burst open, and a bearded, heavyset man stormed into the alcove with the squire.

"Who is it that dares to disturb me when I'm with the king?" he demanded.

George bowed. "The matter is of great importance, M'Lord," he said, speaking carefully rehearsed words. "The kingdom's future depends on what we do tonight."

Lord Douglas glared at his squire. "Ye had me leave the king to hear this drivel?" He turned to leave.

"Wait," Marian called out. "King Alexander must not ride tonight. If he does, he will die!"

Lord Douglas paused, his hand still clutching the curtain. He cocked his head. "How do ye ken the king planned to ride tonight? It was a decision he made but minutes ago."

"All that matters is that he stays here tonight," George added hastily. "Think of what would happen if King Alexander dies. He has no successor. His third and last child, Alexander, Prince of Scotland, died two years ago."

Lord Douglas shrugged impatiently. "If King Alexander died, it would be a sorry state of affairs. But ye are wrong. He has a successor: his granddaughter, Margaret —"

"A three-year-old who lives in Norway!" George interrupted. "M'Lord, please consider: King Edward has crushed Wales, and castles are being built for English nobles to occupy and rule that once-proud country. With each success, King Edward's ambitions become greater."

Lord Douglas's eyes narrowed. "If ye are implying that King Edward would turn on Scotland, ye are making a very serious accusation. People lose their heads for less. King Edward is King Alexander's trusted and respected brother-in-law —"

"M'Lord," Marian interjected. "What makes you think King Edward would stop at Wales? Imagine what he would do to Scotland if given half a chance."

Lord Douglas regarded them curiously, gold coins slowly trickling from one hand to the other. "The clouds portend a great storm this night," he said finally. "King Alexander would be well advised to stay here until the morrow."

Marian clasped her hands. "Thank you, M'Lord."

"But before ye go," Lord Douglas held up his hand, "I will need to hear how ye knew that he plans to ride tonight and why ye're convinced he is to die." He signaled his guards. "Take them to the bell tower."

"M'Lord, no!" George cried in dismay as the guards approached. "There is somewhere we urgently need to be."

"Your affairs will have to wait. With apologies, M'Lady." Lord Douglas gave Marian a slight bow. "But I think ye'll find the bell tower has all the comforts ye'll require. Many a noble has spent time there. I look forward to a full explanation, but first I'll have a word with my king." With that, Lord Douglas pushed aside the curtain and left.

The squire listened to Lord Douglas's receding footfalls and shook his head. "Oh, my. Ye'd better come up with some good explanations . . . or Lord Douglas will have your heads!"

———◆———

"I dinnae give a damn about the weather," the king thundered, his robe billowing as he rose from the head of a long oak table. He flung up his arm. "Assemble the men and prepare the horses. I wish to see my queen *tonight*."

"King Alexander, Your Grace, with all due respect," Lord Douglas began. "Queen Yolande is safe in Kinghorn. Surely there is nothing that is so urgent that requires your royal presence on this miserable evening."

With a tilt of his head, the king gave Lord Douglas a one-eyed squint. "Ye ken fully well that the king has no issue," he growled.

Lord Douglas nodded respectfully.

"Tonight I seek to rectify that," the king added with a hint of a smile.

"Oh, for God's sake." Lord Douglas thumped the heavy table. "Can Your Grace not think of more important matters?"

The king's advisers glanced nervously at one another, but the king merely laughed.

"What can be more important," he said, clapping his arm about Lord Douglas's shoulders, "than to have an heir? I willnae live forever, and I wish to leave the kingdom in good hands."

"Your Grace," Lord Douglas said quietly, "if I may have a private word."

King Alexander gave a nod and looked pointedly at his advisers. They hastily left the room.

"This evening I met with two people, a man and a woman. They spoke strangely and were hard to understand, but appeared sincere. I have no reason to believe they did not speak the truth as they know it."

"Get to the point, man," the king grumbled good-naturedly. "Out with it."

"They said that if Your Grace rides tonight, you will die."

The king threw back his head and laughed. Giving his eyes a wipe, he said, "Oh, Lord Douglas, with stories like these, I have no need for jesters."

"There's more, Your Grace," Lord Douglas continued.

The king stared back with a mocking frown. "What more can there be to this ludicrous tale than the death of a king?"

"King Edward will invade Scotland."

King Alexander froze, the smile fading from his lips. "*That* is not amusing."

"Nor is it meant for amusement," Lord Douglas said.

"I wonder how they know I contemplated riding tonight," the king thought aloud.

"That remains a mystery, but I intend to find out."

"Excellent. Do that. And should I die, as they predict, on my ride tonight . . ."

"Yes, Your Grace?"

"Kill them."

King Alexander stepped purposefully onto the wharf, glad to be off the ferry's pitching deck. It was a bad night for traveling. The black waters of the Firth of Forth were more menacing than he had ever seen before.

He took a deep breath to quell his lingering seasickness. He was resolved not to display weakness, not ever, and certainly not because of a bobbing boat. Even as he had thrown up over the side, he had made it appear as if it were merely a minor annoyance.

The horses had not liked the crossing one bit and were letting their handlers know. They fought the reins, stamping and rearing. Only when back on solid ground did they allow the men to stroke their necks. Eventually the whinnying and tossing of their heads lessened, and they ceased to snort. A few treats were nuzzled from their handlers' hands.

Distant thunder rumbled as the men prepared to ride.

"We'd best be quick if we're not to be caught in a downpour," said the captain of the guards.

The king agreed.

The wind whipped overhanging branches and swirled leaves about them as they rode hard and fast along the winding and hilly road from North Queensferry to Kinghorn.

The rush of the wind in the trees sounded like the continuous crashing of surf on a shore, but when they were halfway to Kinghorn, they clearly heard a voice calling from the darkness.

"King Alexander, where do ye ride tonight?" the voice moaned through the wind.

The king felt the hairs on his neck rising as he recalled Lord Douglas's warning.

The captain of the guards signaled for his small company to halt and take up positions about the king. "Who's there?" he demanded. "Reveal yourself."

The guards shifted nervously in their saddles, their swords ready. With the roar of the wind, it was impossible to tell where the voice had come from.

Another voice groaned above the din. "King Alexander, King Alexander . . ."

And yet another goaded, "Your queen . . . your queen awaits."

"My God, the devil is out tonight," a guard muttered, quickly crossing himself.

The captain's arm shot up to signal his men. "Your Grace, we must be away with haste. I fear an ambush."

"Wait!" King Alexander shrugged off his robe and flung it at an astonished guard. "Put that on and ride as if ye were king," he said. "I will slip away at the next bend and ride unnoticed along the cliff trail that follows the shore. If there is an ambush, they will have missed their prey."

"Your Grace!" the captain cried. "We cannae leave thus."

"It is my command. Go!"

The captain's arm dropped, and the guards spurred their horses into a gallop. Around the next bend, as planned, the king veered his horse onto a side trail. The dark woods closed in around him.

The king smiled at his own cleverness. No one could have seen his maneuver in this darkness. His assailants would find, to their dismay, that the king's guard had naught but a guard for a king.

Familiar with the terrain from his childhood years, the

king guided his horse through the twists and turns of a narrow trail that came perilously close to the drop down to the shore. King Alexander loved the view over the Forth from the top of these cliffs, particularly on a clear day when he could see all the way to the Bass Rock and to where the saddle-shaped hills of Arthur's Seat overlooked Edinburgh Castle.

Lightning flashed, illuminating the frothing crests of waves breaking over rocks far below. King Alexander kept up a hard pace, knowing he was near Kinghorn Castle. He wanted to be comfortably within its secure walls before the rain came pounding down.

There was another explosion of light and the king's horse reared. In that brief moment, King Alexander saw that the trail was blocked by a hooded figure.

"Stand aside," the king commanded angrily, his sword instantly drawn.

The only reply the figure gave was to thrust his long, crooked staff up high. A sheet of lightning crackled across the sky, revealing a pale, hollowed face with blood-red eyes.

Terrified, the king's horse bucked, launching the king from his saddle. The last thing the king heard as he tumbled over the edge of the cliff was an echoing laughter.

Moments later, the king's broken and mangled body lay shattered on the rocks far below.

1

THE PROFESSOR'S VISIT

A car pulled off the lane next to a farmhouse, its wipers slapping back and forth. A plump middle-aged man popped open his umbrella before getting out. Slamming the door behind him, he hurried for the shelter of the farmhouse porch. After pausing to pass a comb through his sparse, windblown hair, he pushed the doorbell. No one answered, so he tried knocking.

From far within came the call: "I'll get it."

The door cracked open, and a teenage girl with long brown hair peered out.

"Professor Macintyre!" She flung open the door. "What a surprise!"

The professor smiled warmly. "Good to see you, Annie. I hope I didn't come at a bad time."

"Of course not. We're always glad to see you."

"The weather has been nasty, hasn't it?" He gave his loosely collapsed umbrella a shake and stepped into the house. "How's your mum?"

"Oh, about the same." Annie smiled sadly, hanging the professor's coat on a rack. "She seems happy enough."

"Who's there?" A stout man peered into the dark foyer. "Oh, Professor Macintyre," he said without enthusiasm. "Do come in." He turned and called in the direction he had come. "Put on the kettle, my dear. We have company."

"Mr. McRae, I don't want to be any trouble." The professor wrung his hands. "It's just that –"

Annie's father cut him off with a wave. "No trouble. Come in."

Annie ushered the professor into the sitting room and offered him a seat. Her father went to find his wife.

A boy not much younger than Annie came into the room, frowning with concentration as he stirred a brimming glass of chocolate milk. He froze as he saw the professor, and his frown turned into a scowl. He took a quick gulp of milk and marched straight through the sitting room and out a door on the other side.

"Don't mind him," Annie said, shifting uncomfortably. "Willie likes to pretend none of this ever happened."

"That's understandable. It must have been hugely traumatic for your brother to have been almost hanged, all the bloodshed . . ."

"It's more what he's endured since being back," Annie said. "His classmates are so cruel. They taunt him, saying he's as crazy as his mother."

"He really shouldn't have told anyone about the time travel." Professor Macintyre shook his head. "It's not surprising no one believes it."

"It was wee Craig who talked about it mostly," Annie

said. "He wants so much to go back in time again. Now everyone thinks our whole family is crazy."

Mr. McRae came into the sitting room, balancing a tray with three cups of tea. "Please pardon my wife," he said. "But she's no' in a frame of mind for company the-now."

"But of course." Professor Macintyre had to listen carefully to follow Mr. McRae's northern Scottish dialect. "I understand."

"Truly?" Mr. McRae asked sharply. "Do ye ken what it's like to live with someone who doesnae ken what time she's living in, no' even what century – someone who's afraid of her own shadow?"

"It's not the professor's fault that Mother is the way she is!" Annie protested. "You should be thankful for everything he did to bring her back – and us too!"

"Thankful, aye," Mr. McRae said bitterly. "I'm so thankful for everything these days. My wife comes back to me as mad as a hatter after a year's absence; that boy Alex, who came from Canada for his summer holidays, is lost and is presumed to have been swept out to sea by the tide; the townspeople regard us as the crazy farm folk; and my children all speak of ludicrous time travel. To make matters worse, there's a distinguished archaeology professor from the University of Edinburgh who appears to be humoring them, coming to my house and feeding into their tales of nonsense."

Professor Macintyre opened his mouth, but Mr. McRae cut him off.

"Dinnae tell me it isnae rubbish. If it wasnae, why are no' your learned colleagues all over this? Why do I no' see it in the papers?" Mr. McRae's teacup trembled as he raised it to his lips.

"It's as I said before," Professor Macintyre replied gently. "This matter is too explosive to make public, or even to share with my colleagues. Just imagine what would happen if eager scientists started making all kinds of forays into the past. They might completely change what happens, and it could be even worse once the government got their hands on this. They might try to change history so that Great Britain doesn't lose past battles. The world as we know it would cease to exist."

"And it's such a great world we have the-now?"

"It has its problems," Professor Macintyre acknowledged. "But it's what we have. Each of us can only do what we can to make it better."

"Better? Well, we can hardly make it worse." Mr. McRae stole a glance at his watch and gulped the last of his tea. "Will ye look at the *time*! If I dinnae milk the coos, there'll be chaos in the barn. Please excuse me, Professor."

Mr. McRae put his cup on the tray. "Dinnae get up on my account," he said, waving the professor back into his seat. "Finish your tea. Annie will see ye out."

Annie waited until the side door slammed shut behind her father before eagerly turning to the professor. "So?" she said. "What did you find out?"

Professor Macintyre held up his hands apologetically. "Not much – not even with the help of leading historians and biographers. If Alex survived, he didn't do anything to merit an entry into a chronicle or text. There's only one thing of note that I've discovered, and it probably has nothing to do with him."

"What is it?" Annie was on the edge of her seat.

"There was an earl called John de Warenne, the sixth

Earl of Surrey, who was in charge of an English army when it was crushed by the Scots. They had made the mistake of crossing a narrow bridge where they were vulnerable to attack. It was called the Battle of Stirling Bridge. It was one of William Wallace's greatest victories. When King Edward heard about the debacle, he was furious."

"What's that have to do with Alex?" Annie asked.

"Earl Warenne had said the battle was lost on account of a boy with a strange manner of speech."

"Alex!" Annie exclaimed. "It must have been him. No matter how long he stayed back in time, he would never have been able to completely get rid of his accent. But what did he do? What else did Earl Warenne say?"

"That was all. King Edward did not want to listen to excuses, particularly one that blamed the defeat on a boy."

"But if Alex did have something to do with the English defeat, wouldn't Earl Warenne or King Edward have tried to have him captured or killed?"

"Well, yes . . ." The professor stared down into his teacup. "I suppose they would."

"Was he . . . tortured . . . killed?" Annie asked hesitantly.

"Annie, believe me," the professor pleaded. "I tried to find out, but I couldn't locate any further reference to him anywhere."

"Did you learn anything else?" Annie asked, her voice shaking.

Professor Macintyre put his hand on Annie's arm. "You have to let it go, Annie – whatever else happened to Alex in the past has happened. It's over – done. We have no way of knowing."

"He should have come back with us." Annie started to cry. "He stayed behind because he wanted to keep looking for his parents, but it was hopeless – who knows what could have happened to them? They might even have gone back to a different time." She took a deep breath and settled back in her chair. "Whatever happened to him back then," she said, biting her lip, "I just hope he didn't suffer too much. . . ."

2

September MCCXCVII (1297)

Rain fell steadily on a man and a boy who were leading a big ox down a winding coastal road. The ox pulled an empty two-wheeled cart, its iron rims clattering over rocks embedded in ruts. After all the bad weather the past few days, the road was a mess.

They came to a stone house up a slope from a pier. The cart driver pulled up the ox, gave the lead to the boy, and rapped on the door. A shuffling noise came from within.

"What do ye want?" a muffled voice called out.

The cart driver frowned at the door. "The ferry to South Queensferry. What else would I want?"

A peephole slid open and a wrinkly eye peered out, darting from man to boy.

"Who are ye?" quavered an old man's voice.

The cart driver removed his cap. "Donald Dundonnel's my name," he said with a slight bow. "I'm known by my friends as Don-Dun. I'm a produce merchant seeking passage to the farmlands south of the firth. The dumb lad next to me here is my distant nephew, Alex."

The old man eyed them suspiciously. "Is there anyone else with ye?"

"Only my trusty ox, Rhua –" Don-Dun tilted his head inquiringly. "What is it, man? Ye're acting strangely."

The peephole slammed shut. There was a thump as a bar slid back, and the door creaked open. A bent, toothless man stuck his head out.

"There's no ferry today," he announced.

"No ferry?" Don-Dun exclaimed in dismay. "When will it sail next?"

"Come." The old man shuffled out of the house. He led them around the corner and used his cane to point down to the pier. "Do ye see the top of a mast sticking up from the water? That's the ferry."

Don-Dun's jaw dropped. "What happened?"

The old man gave a furtive glance. "It was horrible. . . . Inhuman, they were."

"Who?" Don-Dun snapped. "Speak, man, ye're making no sense."

The old man fixed him with a beady eye. "Seven days ago, the ferryman gave passage to four men – nae, not men, monsters. Why he agreed to take them I dinnae ken – it was a bad night for crossing. When he brought them to this side, they hit him over the head, hauled him up by the neck, and threw him overboard. I watched it all from my window. They took their horses off the boat and then sank it."

"Have ye found your ferryman?"

"Good God, man." The old man pressed his hands to his chest. "Look at me. How am I to trek about these shores? He's gone, and now I need a new ferryman – one that is skilled at repair." He paused, giving Don-Dun a hopeful, appraising glance. "By chance, can ye fix a boat?"

"No!" Appalled, Don-Dun squinted through the rain to see if he could spot the ferryman's remains along the shoreline. "Have ye reported this terrible crime?"

"And to which authority am I to make this report? King Edward's men no longer rule this country. We live in chaos. Everything was better before that brigand William Wallace started stirring up all this trouble."

"Who was it who murdered him?" Don-Dun persisted. "Can ye describe them at least?"

The old man regarded him coldly. "They were the Four Horsemen of the Apocalypse, mark ye my words. Laugh not!" He waved his cane. "Those men were not from this world!"

Don-Dun grimaced. He had heard enough. The old man was obviously not of sound mind. He pressed a few coins into his hand. "Here, this is to help with the repair. . . . Yes, I insist. And I hope ye find a new ferryman soon."

The old man tucked the coins away. "God bless," he murmured.

Don-Dun led the ox back onto the road. With the ferry-house receding behind them, the boy, Alex, gave Don-Dun a scowl.

"When you introduce me, will you please say I'm *deaf* and dumb? Otherwise, people will get the wrong impression."

Don-Dun raised an eyebrow. "Do ye mean, the *wrong, wrong* impression?"

"Exactly. We don't want people to hear my strange accent and wonder where I'm from. But just saying I'm dumb doesn't cut it. Dumb people still speak – take you, for instance."

"Watch it," Don-Dun growled, raising his hand, "or I'll box your ears so hard, ye'll be deaf and *numb*."

Alex skipped to safety on the other side of Rhua. He glanced back at the stone house. "What was that old man saying about things being 'better before'? Doesn't he know William Wallace is fighting for freedom and liberty?"

Don-Dun pointed across the firth. "See that? Miles and miles of the best farmland around. The folk over there are well fed and want no part of Wallace's war."

"How could they not?" Alex asked indignantly. "Don't they want King John Balliol to rule over a free Scotland?"

Don-Dun snorted. "Freedom's all well and good, but having a roof over your head and food on the table comes first."

Alex studied the lush rolling hills on the far side of the firth – so near and yet so far. "How will we cross?"

Don-Dun shrugged. "We either find another ferry or seek farms on this side that have fresh produce for sale. This might no' be the way we were planning to go, but we're here the-now, so we'll carry on. Sir Ellerslie will no' be pleased if we return to Duncragglin Castle without any fresh greenery."

Alex lapsed into silence, mud sucking at his boots. It all seemed so futile. Despite having been back in time for over a year, he had yet to find his parents. His friends – the cautious and caring Annie, wily Willie, and that daredevil, pain-in-the-butt little Craig – were back in the twenty-first century. They had gone "up the spiral," as the professor had put it. "Consider time as something that spirals between two equal but opposite singularities" is what he had said. "Through the time chamber, we leap from one spiral to another."

None of that made any sense. All Alex knew was that his friends were gone and his parents were still missing.

As he leaped to clear a large puddle, Alex's foot skidded and he fell into the mud. Don-Dun rounded the cart and extended a hand, his face contorting in an effort not to laugh.

Alex waved him away and got up on his own. Great – now he was wet *and* covered in mud. He scraped a clump off the back of his elbow and flicked it at Don-Dun.

"Stop that," Don-Dun said, laughing and ducking. "Dinnae blame me. It was ye who asked to come."

It was true. This soggy venture had been his idea. "Take me with you," he had pleaded when Don-Dun prepared to leave on a produce-gathering excursion. "I'll pretend to be your deaf and dumb nephew from up the coast. No one will know I'm not from around here." He had hoped to find something that would show his parents had been here – anything that might lead to them. Now it all seemed so futile. Sir Ellerslie was right. If his parents were around, word would get back to Duncragglin soon enough. Strange-sounding people wearing odd clothes would not make it far unnoticed.

Don-Dun gave Alex a concerned glance. "Cheer up, laddie. It cannae rain forever."

Alex turned away. He was tired. Sleeping under the cart had been almost impossible these past days. The cart kept off most of the rain, but the cloak he used as a blanket was soaked. He had lain awake shivering most nights, just waiting for the break of day.

Head down, he forced himself to put one foot in front of the other, over and over again. Cold, wet, and hungry, down the misty road he squelched, hoping the rain would stop.

"Well, lad," Don-Dun began, his eye on the unrelenting clouds, "Sir Ellerslie gave us some extra coin, so how about we spend a night indoors? But dinnae think I'm going to make a habit of this," he added hastily. "Never before have I afforded myself such luxury."

Alex raised his fist and allowed himself a small whoop of joy.

3

THE SPRAY BOMBER

"Hey, Willie, is this your mum?" A red-haired boy smirked as he held up a book and pointed to a picture of Mary, Queen of Scots. He showed his friends. "She looks like her, don't you think?" he asked. They all laughed.

"Leave me alone, Stephen." Willie scowled. He bent over his schoolbook, trying to block them out and concentrate on his history assignment.

"Where's your mum going next, Willie," the boy taunted, "back in time to see some cavemen for a little fun?"

"More likely she'll be seeing your daddy, Stephen," another boy chimed in.

"No way. My daddy's got more class than that." Stephen laughed. "He wouldn't be interested in that old nutter. But maybe that sister of his, what's her name? Annie? Though she's kind of flat –"

Willie threw his book and hit Stephen squarely on the side of the head.

"Willie!" the teacher snapped. "Outside!"

"But he –"

"I don't want to hear it." The teacher stormed over to position herself between the boys. "Down to the principal's office – now!"

Willie stood, trembling with rage. He flung his school notes to the floor and stepped on them on his way out.

———•◆•———

"So, what are you here for?"

Willie regarded the burly, bristly haired boy in army fatigues sitting next to him with suspicion. Alan was older, having repeated a grade or two, and was not known for being especially friendly.

"Hitting Stephen Newland in the head with my history book," Willie replied.

"That English prig?" Alan nodded approvingly. "I hope you got him good."

"How about you? What did you do?"

"Oh, the usual." Alan shrugged. "Just told the teacher to bugger off."

"Who?"

"Truscott."

"What, that English prig?"

Alan broke into the glimmer of a smile. "Did you hear the one about wee Johnnie in history class?"

Willie shook his head.

"Well, the teacher was asking who knew who said what, and anyone who got it right could leave class early. So the first question was, who said 'Ask not what your country can do for you . . .' Johnnie knew this one, so he shoots up his hand and says, 'Me, me, me.' But the teacher points to this little, prissy English girl, who gives the answer."

"What was it?" Willie asked.

"Think *I* remember? Anyway, the girl gets to leave, and the next question was, who said 'Blah, blah, but we will never surrender.'"

"Let me guess. Johnnie knew the answer."

"Aye, he was bouncing out of his seat, waving his hand to get the teacher to pick him, but instead she points to a proper-looking lad, who answers in a snobby London accent."

"So the lad gets to leave?"

"Aye! Well, by now, Johnnie's pissed. He thumps his hand on his desk and says, 'Just what are all these bloody English doing here?' The teacher spins around, real furious-like, and says, 'Who said that?' So little Johnnie pipes up and says, 'William Wallace! Can I go now?'"

"Alan!"

The boys looked up, startled. The principal was standing at his door.

"Come here, please."

Alan mockingly held his wrists together as if handcuffed. He gave Willie a nudge. "How about we meet after school? I have plans. . . ."

———◦•◦———

Willie waited in front of the school, his hands in his pockets to keep them warm. He had picked a spot where he could see everyone come out the front door, but by now, just about everyone had left – and there still was no sign of Alan. Maybe the principal had sent him home early.

"Hello, Willie."

Willie jumped. Someone was in the shadows behind him.

"Alan! Er, hi. How did you get on with the principal?"

Alan shrugged. "'What are we to do with you, Alan?'" he growled, mocking the principal's artificially low voice. "'You seem like such a promising young lad. But if this continues, we'll have no option but to have you removed from this school.' Blah, blah, blah." Alan turned his head and spat. "The bastards are all the same."

"Who?"

Alan motioned for Willie to follow. He threw out his arm. "Look around you, Willie. What do you see?"

Willie peered past the school and down to where the road curved and joined the high street. Beyond the town hall clock tower and clay tile roofs, a tanker ship sat on the edge of the horizon. He saw nothing out of the ordinary.

"Pretty, isn't it?" Alan commented. "But if you look closely, you'll find it isn't Scots anymore. Sure, there's more Scots about than anyone else, but we're not the ones with the jobs – at least none that matter. Who runs the big supermarket out on the edge of town, the one that's bleeding all the business out of the high street? Who runs the garage that fixes silencers, the bookstores, the big-box stores? Who runs the fast-food places?"

"Well, last I saw, it was a Pole –"

"I'm not talking about the chip wagon!" Alan snapped. "Well, seeing how you're so dense, I'll give you a clue: it's not us Scots. We don't own or run anything around here anymore. All we do is stand behind the counters and serve."

"I thought the Poles did that."

"You're right!" Alan exclaimed. "Not only do we not run things, we don't even get the crap jobs anymore. So where does that leave us, sonny boy? Well, let me tell you: on the dole – that's where – living on other people's handouts, like my dad does."

"How about your mum? Does she have a job?"

"What mum?" Alan retorted angrily. "I had one once, but she's gone off to London to live with some English prig." Alan kicked a stone. It clattered down the road and pinged off the side of a parked car.

Willie glanced about nervously, but no one seemed to pay any attention. It was as if the passersby were deliberately looking away.

"Do you know what I think the problem is?" Alan asked as they trudged past the parked car.

Willie looked to see if there was a chip in the paint. He had no idea where Alan was leading him.

"Everyone blends in," Alan went on. "It's hard to see who's a Scot and who isn't, which business is owned by a Scot and which is not. If fact, it's even hard to tell which *car* belongs to a Scot."

"So what?"

"So what!" Alan was astounded. "That's how we are defeated, that's what. If we can't tell who's us and who's them, then we can't see what's being done to us. Well, I plan to fix that, Willie-boy. See here." Alan opened his jacket. Poking up from his large inner pockets were the tops of aerosol cans. "When I'm done, it will be clear who and what does not belong."

They came to the corner store and went in to buy something to drink. Alan stopped to flip through a magazine off the top rack while Willie kept browsing. Rounding an aisle, he came upon a few boys from his class and stopped short.

"Hey, Willie, what's the big idea throwing that book at me, eh?" With a jerk of his head, Stephen Newland motioned for his friends to block Willie's retreat. "See that red mark?" He tilted his head and parted his hair. "That was not very nice."

"What do you want?" Willie asked, hoping Stephen couldn't hear the tremor in his voice.

"I think you need to learn some manners." Stephen stepped up very close and crumpled a fistful of Willie's jacket. "Outside."

"What color do you think he should be, Willie?"

Stephen spun about. "Alan! What are you doing here?"

Alan opened his jacket again, flicking his fingers through the aerosol cans in his inner pockets. "Red . . . purple?" he muttered. "No, wait. Here it is!" His face brightened and he pulled out a can. "Yellow. Perfect!" He grinned at Stephen.

Stephen paled. He looked quickly for his friends, but they had faded away. He licked his lips nervously. "Don't do anything you'll . . . regret."

Alan gave him a humorless smile. "I never do." He grabbed Stephen's jacket and spun him around. There was a brief struggle and a fizzing sound before Stephen broke free. Stephen sprinted from the store, the bright yellow stripe on his back bobbing as he ran.

"What's that you'll be having, Alan?" the proprietor asked warily.

"Two IRN-BRU." Alan tossed down a magazine. "And these English girls."

4

AUNT FIONA

Annie eyed the weedy front gardens, broken stairs, and trash that littered the road. She checked the address on her scrap of paper once again. Yes, strange as it might seem, this would appear to be the right house.

She double-checked the number and rang the bell. Tapping her foot, she stared anxiously at the door. It had taken her a long time to get to Edinburgh by bus, then another hour to find her way here. She was about to ring again when the door snapped open.

"I don't want any," a gray-haired elderly lady said.

"Mrs. Murray?" Annie said uncertainly.

"Nor do I wish to take part in surveys." The lady started closing the door.

"Are you Alex Macpherson's aunt Fiona?" Annie asked quickly.

The lady stared. "Who are you?"

"I'm Alex's friend. He was staying at our farm last summer when he disappeared."

"That's nice. What do you want?"

"I, um . . ."

"Come now, spit it out. I havenae got all day."

"I need to know about the disappearance of his parents." Annie folded her hands imploringly. "I think it might explain what happened to Alex. Please, Mrs. Murray!"

Mrs. Murray paused. "Well, I cannae be standing here yammering all day," she said, stepping aside. "Come in, if you must – just for a moment, mind." Mrs. Murray headed stiffly down the narrow hall, her bony shoulders lurching from side to side. "Make sure you close the door tight behind you," she called over her shoulder. "Would you like tea and a biscuit?"

"No, thank you. I don't want to be any trouble."

"It's too late for that. But I was just going to have some myself anyway." Mrs. Murray pointed Annie in the direction of the sitting room and shuffled away.

Annie had a quick peek around. The room was cluttered with knickknacks and ornaments. A ceramic cat's sad eyes pleaded from a china cabinet in the corner. Another shelf displayed plates decorated with painted scenes of Edinburgh. One depicted the Scott Monument along Princes Street. Another was of the Golden Mile, looking up toward the castle.

Annie examined a buffet cabinet lined with framed photographs. She picked up one of a balding, big-bellied man grinning for the camera, with billowing mist over a huge waterfall in the background. Annie figured it was Alex's uncle Larry standing before Niagara Falls.

Her eye fell on a picture of a woman pushing a stroller past the Straith Meirn town hall. Picking it up to examine it more closely, she saw that the stroller's clear plastic rain-shield was pulled back. Inside was a small child clutching a toy rattle.

Mrs. Murray's voice came from behind Annie. "That's my niece, Marian, Alex's mum."

Startled, Annie almost dropped the picture. "You're not Alex's aunt?" she asked, quickly returning the picture to its spot on the buffet.

"Oh, no, of course not, although he called me Auntie – that's easier for a child than Great-Auntie." Mrs. Murray bent awkwardly to place a tray on the low coffee table. "His dad's the man next to the stroller, the one staring up at the clock tower. He was always looking off somewhere – never paying attention to the present – at least not when I was talking to him. Whenever we met, he treated me as if I weren't even there."

"What kind of work did he do?"

"Pilot, if you could imagine that." Mrs. Murray plopped herself down on the settee. "I wouldn't want to be in any airplane he was flying, that's for sure."

"And Mrs. Macpherson?"

"Nurse, and a good thing too, seeing how reckless that man was." Mrs. Murray raised the lid of a small ceramic pot and dipped in a teaspoon. "Sugar?"

"No, thank you. Just a spot of milk, if that's all right," Annie replied.

Mrs. Murray tipped in a bit of milk and slid the teacup and saucer over to Annie. "He was always embarking on adventures, hiking through the Himalayas in his youth, sky-diving, hang gliding, karate, rally car racing, caving – you name it, he did it – even after he started raising a family. Terribly irresponsible, he was." Mrs. Murray took a sip of tea.

"What is caving?"

"Oh, I hadn't heard of it either until that dreadful man explained it to me one day. It's where you go into caves and crevices and find your way deep underground. Apparently there are entire societies devoted to this kind of behavior. It's just so silly – grown men and women crawling about in underground grottoes like little children." Mrs. Murray sniffed.

"Did he find any caves around here?" Annie asked eagerly.

"Oh, probably." Mrs. Murray gave a vague wave. "Like an unruly child, he was, forever keeping an eye out for something to explore. Marian and I just couldn't take a quiet walk along the shore with that man. He would always have to scamper over the rocks, looking for God knows what."

"Was he interested in something in particular?"

"That man was interested only in himself – and all things medieval." Mrs. Murray smoothed her skirt. "He was always going on about historical battles and such dreadful things. When the movie *Braveheart* came out, he saw it at least five times and then had the audacity to complain about how inaccurate it was."

"So he had an interest in the time of William Wallace?" Annie was suddenly on the very edge of her chair.

"That, he did. He went on and on about what could have been. If only this, if only that." Mrs. Murray stirred her tea vigorously. "How many times did I have to hear about how different things would have been if King Alexander hadn't managed to throw himself off a cliff back in 1286."

"Throw himself off a cliff?" Annie echoed, puzzled. "Did he commit suicide?"

"Och, no, he went riding through a storm in the dead of night to see his queen – probably just overeager to get there. He was likely riding recklessly fast along the cliff tops when his horse stumbled – or something – and he fell to his death. That husband of Marian's was convinced he was assassinated, even though there isn't a scrap of historical evidence of such a thing. He was sure that King Edward, that nasty Hammer of the Scots, was behind it somehow. He would go on about how many of our own ancestors wouldn't have been slaughtered and about how the entire history of Scotland would have worked out for the better if King Alexander hadn't gone over that cliff."

Mrs. Murray picked up the photograph of her niece.

"Well, if only that man wasn't such a fool," she added bitterly, "Marian might still be with us today."

"Can you think of where Alex's parents might have gone?" Annie asked timidly.

"No, I cannae."

5

THE CRAWFORD INN

A thatched cottage materialized from the thick gray mist. Next to it was another, and then another. Alex's spirits soared. With so many cottages about, they *had* to be entering a village.

Alex knew not to expect much of remote villages, and this one was no exception. Small shops lined the main square. Balconies transformed the alleys that led off the square into dark tunnels. But there *was* a place to stay. Carved letters on a sign hanging from a beam proclaimed a two-story building to be the Crawford Inn. Don-Dun wound Rhua's lead about a post and looked the timbered building up and down.

"Shall we see if they have a room?" he asked teasingly.

"Sure, why not?" Alex did his best to sound nonchalant. "It must be hard on your old bones to be bedding off the side of the road each night."

With the glimmer of a smile, Don-Dun pushed the heavy door open and ducked under its low frame. The swinging door struck an overhead bell, letting out several clangs.

Don-Dun removed his dripping hat and ran his hand up his forehead to get his wet hair off his face. A girl about Alex's age appeared, standing expectantly with her hands behind her back. Reddish-brown hair stuck out from under her cloth cap.

"Afternoon, miss," Don-Dun said pleasantly. "Bonnie day, is it no'?"

"If ye say so, sire." She bent her knees in a quick curtsy, holding her knee-length dress out with one hand.

"And if I say it is raining too hard for even a duck to be out?"

"Then that it be, sire."

"So be it then, miss. In fact, it's so miserable we are seeking a room for the night."

As suddenly as she had appeared, the girl was gone, leaving Don-Dun and Alex in the alcove, dripping onto the flagstones, with Alex staring wide-eyed.

Don-Dun gave him a nudge. "Dinnae forget yourself," he growled.

A man appeared, wiping his hands on a dishcloth as he squinted at them from under bushy eyebrows. The girl peeked out from behind him.

"Good day." Don-Dun inclined his head in greeting.

The man tucked the cloth under his apron string. "What's your business?"

"We're looking to hire a room for the night," Don-Dun replied politely.

"I asked 'What's your business,' not 'What ye'd be wanting.'"

Don-Dun paused. "Merchant of hay and greens," he said, pulling out a coin.

The innkeeper eyed him suspiciously. "How does a merchant of hay 'n' greens come to be staying at an inn?"

Alex glanced apprehensively from the innkeeper to Don-Dun. Try as he might, he couldn't suppress a long hacking cough.

Don-Dun put his arm about Alex's shoulders. "I have to get this lad out of the rain," he said. "He hasnae been well. He's a rather frail dumb *and* deaf boy. I'm afraid I'll lose him one of these days."

Alex obligingly let out another cough, this time doubling over and turning red.

"All right, all right, ye c'n have a room, but keep him quiet. I dinnae want him disturbing other guests." As the innkeeper snatched Don-Dun's coin and gestured to a room beyond the alcove, the girl quickly disappeared through a door. "Have a seat," he said. "We've got some mutton stew to warm ye while we get your beds ready."

Don-Dun and Alex barely had time to hang their dirty wet cloaks on pegs and get seated before the girl was back, balancing a tray on her left arm, steadying it with her right. On it were two mugs brimming with froth.

It was an awkward way to carry a tray. Alex tilted his head and noticed with surprise that the girl's left sleeve was sewn shut.

Frowning with concentration, the girl set the mugs before them on the uneven table. Without waiting for acknowledgement, she was gone.

Alex elbowed Don-Dun. "Don't forget to ask."

"Ask what?"

"About whether they've seen two strangers who talk

funny, of course! How am I to find my parents if I'm not to speak and you don't ask about them?"

"Shush, they'll hear ye." Don-Dun raised a finger to his lips. "I'll ask, dinnae worry."

Alex blew on the frothy drink and sniffed. Wrinkling his nose, he had a tiny sip of the yellow liquid. He screwed up his face. "Horse piss," he muttered, wiping the foam off his nose. "Can you ask them for some water instead?"

Don-Dun shook with laughter. "Nae, all this rain will have dirtied up their well. It's either this or muddy water that'll make ye sick."

Tipping back his mug, Don-Dun took a big gulp. He banged it down on the table, smacked his lips, and let out a satisfied sigh. "That, lad, is a fine ale. True, it's no' the finest I've had, but it's better than naught. Drink up. It'll do ye good."

The girl returned, carrying a tray with two steaming bowls of thick brown stew. When she bent to place the bowl in front of Alex, he became acutely aware of the freckles on her cheek and the upturn of her nose.

"Tell me, lass," Don-Dun began. "Have ye seen two strangers come through here, a man and a woman?"

The girl looked puzzled. "This is an inn," she replied. "Just about everyone that we see is a stranger."

"Aye, but I'm thinking of strange strangers. Folk who talk in a peculiar way that ye will never have heard before. And they might be dressed in outlandish garb."

"Not that I've seen, sire."

Alex was struck by her eyes. They were such an unusual green, with a hint of amber about the pupils.

"Meg!" The innkeeper stood glowering in the doorway. "Dinnae disturb the guests."

The girl gave Alex a curious glance as she backed away. The innkeeper cuffed her when she squeezed past him, then turned and followed her to the kitchen.

Alex stared angrily after the departing innkeeper. It took a while for him to notice the rich meaty smell wafting up to his nose, but then his mouth started to water and his eyes dropped to the chunky stew. It smelled delicious.

Raising the bowl to his lips, he slurped in a few pieces. Some were chewy, even gristly, but he didn't mind – he was used to that. He felt the warmth course through him as he alternated mouthfuls of stew with sips of ale.

Alex began feeling light-headed and cheery. It was *so* good to be out of the rain. Soon he would be curled up under a warm blanket on a straw mattress. His damp clothes would be dry by morning.

The bell clanged as the door burst open. Four large men came stomping in.

"Innkeeper!" one of the men bellowed. They shrugged off their drenched cloaks and shook them briskly. Swords and daggers bristled from their belts. They spread their cloaks out over the pegs, dropping Don-Dun's and Alex's cloaks to the floor.

Don-Dun's lips tightened, but he continued to eat his stew as if nothing had happened.

The tallest of the four men turned his long hooked nose toward Alex and Don-Dun and stared with black, expressionless eyes as he slowly removed the longbow he kept slung across his back.

Next to him, a thin gaunt man stood on Don-Dun's cloak and wiped his feet. He twitched his sparse, stringy whiskers with an ill-concealed smirk.

Don-Dun kept his eyes on his stew. Alex bent over his bowl and did the same, taking a mouthful that suddenly had no taste.

Alex was relieved to see the innkeeper appear from the kitchen, but now that the innkeeper was in the same room as these four men, he somehow seemed a lot smaller.

"What's taking so long?" the gaunt man demanded. "Bring us some food and drink, man, and lots of it."

The innkeeper stood rubbing his hands with his dish-cloth. Alex held his breath, wondering what the men would do if the innkeeper asked them to leave.

Gesturing for them to sit, the innkeeper then ducked away.

Alex could feel the men stare as they moved toward a table. A big-boned, beefy man with a protruding jaw bumped their table. Don-Dun clutched his wobbling mug of ale and glanced up.

"What?" the man demanded, thrusting his jaw out even further. "What do ye want?"

"Nothing," Don-Dun mumbled, looking down into his ale.

The man gave their table another bump. Getting no reaction, he let out a snort and swaggered off to join his friends. They laughed and talked, paying no further attention to the very quiet Don-Dun and Alex.

The innkeeper returned with food and beer.

The tall, hook-nosed man dropped some coins on the table. "Make sure we can never find the bottom of these mugs," he rasped. His companions nodded approvingly.

The innkeeper scraped up the coins. "So, where would ye men be headed tonight?" he asked with forced enthusiasm.

His question was met by four silent, hostile stares.

The fourth of the group, a thin hooded man, spoke for the first time. "We'll be staying here," he stated flatly in a cold harsh voice.

The innkeeper spread his hands apologetically. "Sorry to say, we have no beds."

The men chuckled. One slapped the table, threw back his head, and laughed.

The hooded man gave the innkeeper a cold smile. "I'm sure ye can find us beds if ye try hard enough."

The innkeeper wrung his cloth. "I dinnae ken how. There simply arenae any more beds – the last were hired but minutes ago."

"To them?" The hooded man jerked his thumb in the direction of Don-Dun and Alex. "How much did they pay?"

"A penny. But –"

"And ye have a bed, and the girl too, do ye not?"

"My bed isnae for hire!"

The hooded man reached his long bony fingers into his pocket and pulled out two halfpenny coins. With a flick of his wrist, he sent them flying through the air. They rang on the stones near Alex's feet.

Don-Dun motioned for Alex not to move.

The men resumed their conversation. It was as if Alex and Don-Dun were no longer there.

Catching Don-Dun's gaze, the innkeeper motioned to the door with his eyes.

"Come, lad," Don-Dun said loudly. "It's far too bonnie a night to be spending it indoors. Let's be off." He picked Alex's muddy cloak off the floor and passed it to him. "Ye shouldnae leave it on the ground like that," he admonished. "It'll never dry out that way. Ye'll catch the death of cold."

The bell clanged on their way out. The roars of laughter from within were soon drowned out by the rain.

Alex put his wet cap back on. Cold water trickled down his neck. It was hard to believe it could rain for so long. Alex bitterly suspected it had stopped for those few minutes they were inside, only to start up again in time for them to come back out.

It was dark as well as wet and colder than ever. Had they not stopped at the inn, they would have found a spot to set up camp by now. Don-Dun would have selected a high bit of ground and found wood to light a fire that, while small, would have been enough to warm up by while Don-Dun heated some dinner. All this would be hard to do now that night had fallen.

Rhua was where they had left him. There was no sign of where the men may have tethered their horses, but Alex doubted they traveled on foot. The men had most likely stabled them nearby.

"So, that's it then?" Alex snapped. "You let them have our room, just like that."

"Do ye have a better suggestion?" Don-Dun stroked Rhua's neck and unhitched the rope from the post.

"You could at least have told them what you think."

"I did."

Alex frowned. "How?"

"I left the two halfpence on the floor."

Alex thumped his forehead in disbelief. *Some gesture!*

6

NIGHT SPORT

Don-Dun coaxed Rhua onto a bridge. The ox clopped quickly to get off the echoing planks.

Now that they were away from Crawford's few lights, darkness surrounded them. Alex didn't know how Don-Dun managed to stay on the road. It seemed Rhua was leading the way.

They had not gone far when Don-Dun silenced Alex with an urgent gesture. He reached for his lance. From behind, a voice was hailing them.

Alex was still fumbling to remove his crossbow from its hiding place under the cart when an outline materialized.

Don-Dun lowered his lance. "Why, if it isnae Meg, the girl from the inn! Just what are ye doing out on a night like this, lass?"

The girl held up two halfpence. "Ye left this."

"Bless ye," Don-Dun said softly. "But ye shouldnae. Your father probably is expecting to keep that."

"He's no' my father!" Meg exclaimed, sounding annoyed. She paused, then lowered her voice. "Those four men were speaking after ye left. One said he thought they had met the deaf and dumb lad before. The others were no' so sure. Then they saw ye left these two halfpence on the floor, and they became right agitated, they did. One said their money wasnae good enough for ye, and another said this was a fine night for making sport. They talked of waiting for ye to get out of town, then hunting ye down. But, from what they said, it seemed the lad is the one they really want. They had much merriment in their speech, sire, but I believe what they said was no' in jest."

Don-Dun stared off into the darkness. He gave a resigned shrug. "We'd best leave the road and find a place to hide."

"There is a trail ye can take just a short way back," Meg suggested. "It follows the river downstream."

Don-Dun considered this. "Very well then," he said. Hiking up his lance, he turned Rhua around and carefully guided the ox so that the cart's wheels followed the same ruts they had made on their way out of town.

Alex stepped on the bow of his crossbow and pulled up sharply on the drawstring. It hooked on a catch, and he inserted a bolt.

"Should he be using that thing?" Meg asked Don-Dun apprehensively.

"What, the bow? Aye, dinnae worry. He's been practicing with it this past year, and he has no' had an accident with it yet."

"Yet!" Meg waved for Alex to keep the bow pointed in another direction. "The innkeeper didnae have an accident with his ax either, until my hand got in the way!"

"He cut off your hand?" Don-Dun asked, aghast.

"It was a long time ago, when I was just a little girl." Meg looked away. "Maybe he was right. I shouldnae have been playing in the woodpile when he was chopping." She led them off the main road onto a narrow track between two stone dwellings.

Leaving Rhua's lead with Alex, Don-Dun circled back and trampled the mud to obscure the cart tracks from the point where they turned.

"I want to thank ye for all your help," Don-Dun said to Meg. "Ye very likely saved our lives . . . but it's time ye headed back."

Meg looked dismayed.

"Ye cannae come with us, lass," Don-Dun said quietly, "or the whole village would join those four men in hunting us. It's best ye stay with your family."

"I havenae got a family," Meg cried. "They died years ago. I was taken in by that innkeeper, and I dinnae want to stay with him anymore. I'm just his servant."

"Aye, innkeeping's a lot of work," Don-Dun said, nodding. "But it's got to be done. Ye cannae just run away from the man who has been your benefactor all these years."

"But he would sell me too, sire." Meg sounded close to tears. "He would sell me to service the patrons. He told me he would as soon as I was old enough. Those men tonight were asking if they could buy me, and he didnae say no!"

For a long moment, there was nothing to be heard but the pattering of raindrops in the mud.

"It's against my better judgment," Don-Dun said, his voice sounding tired. "But ye can stay with us the-now." He took up Rhua's rope. The cart lurched behind him, and they plodded down the trail in silence.

Alex kept glancing back, disturbed that those men thought they knew him. He was sure he hadn't met them before. They were not the kind of men he would forget.

The trail ended abruptly at a flooded riverbank.

"Best get in the cart," Don-Dun suggested. Walking ahead, he guided Rhua into the water. It got worryingly deep, but never deep enough for the cart to float or for Rhua to lose his footing.

Once they reached the other side, Alex leaped off the cart and glanced back over the flooded section. Surely the men would not follow them through all that? He wondered if perhaps they were not being pursued at all. Maybe Meg made it all up just to get them to allow her to come along.

Then he heard voices.

Don-Dun turned Rhua off the trail and hitched him to a tree. He gently stroked the ox's neck. "We have to be hiding in the woods the-now, but we'll be back soon," he murmured. "Just ye wait here, old boy."

Leaving Rhua looking forlorn, the three ran up a wooded slope and climbed the rocky banks of a creek that trickled down the hillside. They came to a crest, and Don-Dun paused to gather his bearings. He took them to the shelter of large pine trees with sweeping boughs.

"We'll hide here for the night," he whispered, sliding into a spot where he could watch for the men.

Alex curled up in a nook under a bough while Meg settled in a dry spot near the trunk. He remained silent, not wanting Meg to find out he wasn't so deaf and dumb after all. Fortunately, the rain had let up. Alex listened, but all he heard was a faint buzzing in his ears. Dead-tired, he felt as if a weight were pressing on him.

When Alex opened his eyes, much to his surprise, it was light. He peered down the slope. It was too misty for him to see very far. A form suddenly emerged. Alex snatched up his crossbow – and then saw it was Don-Dun.

"You scared me," Alex said irritably.

"Sorry." Don-Dun shrugged, knotting his trouser cord. "But some things cannae wait."

"Those men wouldn't still be looking for us, would they?"

"It's no' likely. We'd best be quiet, though, just in case."

Meg lifted her head, her eyes wide with astonishment. "He *can* speak!" She pulled her tangled hair back from her face. "I knew it! But what strange manner of speech is that?"

Alex scowled, annoyed at having forgotten to stay silent.

"He's from far away, lass," Don-Dun said. "Let's leave it at that. We would be grateful if ye wouldnae tell others. Ye ken how suspicious folk are these days."

"Who would I tell? I'm coming with ye, am I no'?"

Don-Dun said nothing. He jerked his head for them to follow him.

They quietly slipped through the chilly mist, heading downhill to the river. Alex held back, watching as Don-Dun and Meg dissolved into the whiteness ahead. Beyond his small bubble of hazy visibility, he could see nothing. It was eerie. There could be anything out there, and he wouldn't know it. Moreover, it could be quite close. Alex quickened his pace.

A sudden shout froze Alex in his tracks. It sounded like Don-Dun.

Blood pounding in his ears, Alex fumbled with his bow. Having no time to think, he rushed toward the cries, crossbow ready, come what may.

He couldn't see what was before him until he was almost upon it. Rhua lay in a puddle of blood next to the overturned cart. Don-Dun was on his knees, holding Rhua's head. The gentle beast's throat was slit from ear to ear. Don-Dun touched his forehead to Rhua's cold snout, his face contorted with grief.

"Who did this?" Alex asked, stunned.

Meg looked at him as if he were stupid. "The men who were following us – who else?"

"But why?" Alex asked.

"Because they couldn't find us," Meg replied. "That's the kind of men they are."

His arms covered in Rhua's blood, Don-Dun got to his feet and grabbed his discarded lance. "Back to the hiding place – both of ye," he snapped. "I'll be back soon."

"I'll come with you," Alex said.

Don-Dun dismissed him with a flick of his wrist. Then he disappeared into the mist, leaving Alex and Meg alone with the dead ox.

7

A BEGGAR'S WELCOME

Their sack of provisions lay ripped open next to the overturned cart, its contents strewn about. The money that had been hidden under a plank was gone.

Alex and Meg gathered up precious bits of dried beef and bread from the mud and returned to their hiding place.

The sun broke through, and Alex shrugged off his cloak, his clothes still damp from last night's rain. Deciding he didn't care what Meg thought, he also took off his tunic, shirt, and socks, and he spread them all out to dry.

Meg carefully hung her cloak and outer garments from a branch. She wore a sleeveless wool undershirt, her white arms poking out. A dirty handkerchief was tied over the end of her left arm, where her hand should have been.

The sun rose higher. Alex nibbled distractedly on some bread, worried about the many bad things that could have happened to Don-Dun.

Finally it was too much. Alex reached for his damp shirt.

"What are ye doing!"

"Going to help Don-Dun."

"What do ye think ye can do?"

"I'm going to do whatever I'm going to do." Alex threw on his cloak and slung his quiver over his shoulder.

"But . . . I cannae go back there." Meg's voice shook.

"Wait here then." Alex snatched up his crossbow and left.

———◆·◆·◆———

The warmth of day steamed the remaining dampness out of Alex's clothes. Being dry and warm made no difference to his mood. Everything would have been all right now, had it not been for those four men. He would have had a good night's sleep and would have been continuing his search for his parents. Instead, Rhua was dead and everything was in ruins.

Thinking about Don-Dun made him sick with worry. What if he was too late? What if Don-Dun was dead?

Alex left the path to avoid seeing Rhua.

"Laddie! Get over here," someone called from afar.

Startled, Alex spotted several men further upriver. He was relieved to see that they were not the men from the inn.

Ignoring their persistent calls, Alex hid his bow under a bush. He picked up several sticks. The men would have seen that he carried something, and he hoped they were sufficiently far away to think it was just these sticks.

The men came angrily leaping through the heather. Alex held up his sticks in a cross as if to ward off their approach.

"Laddie, answer me!" One of the men grabbed the front of his tunic.

Alex shook his head and let out a strange moaning noise.

"Have ye seen a girl? We think she might have been

taken by a man who is traveling with a boy." The man gave Alex an impatient shake. "Tell me!"

"Tsk, tsk," tutted one of his companions. "Hold on, there. Can ye no' see the lad's dumb?" He shouldered his friend aside and knelt next to Alex. "What are ye doing here, laddie?" he asked gently.

Alex gestured in the direction of the distant cart and Rhua's carcass.

The man shaded his eyes and squinted. "What's over there – where the laddie's pointing? See where the birds are circling?"

"Something's on the ground," another said.

"What is it?"

"Cannae tell."

"Let's go," urged another.

The kneeling man reached into a pocket, drew out a coin, and pressed it into Alex's hand. "Get something to eat," he suggested kindly. He pushed Alex to get him moving and then joined the others heading for the carcass. Alex waited until they were quite far away before turning back for his crossbow.

Reaching a rise in the trail, Alex saw the village in the distance. He was surprised how far they had traveled the night before.

Before crossing the bridge into town, Alex hid his bow under another bush. The sticks he carried with the bow might disguise it from afar, but they wouldn't fool anyone up close.

Keeping a wary eye out for the four men, Alex slipped from building to building until he reached the village center. Seeing no sign of Don-Dun, he plopped himself down outside the town's only general store and scratched about in the dirt, watching as people came and went. He decided to keep up his deaf and dumb act so that the villagers wouldn't become suspicious over his strange way of speaking.

No one paid him any attention, and he didn't overhear anything of importance in the conversations of passersby.

Alex got up and entered the general store. Its shelves were filled with sacks, farming tools, ropes, and building supplies. Sticks of bread and pots of dried vegetables and fruits lined a counter.

He sidled up next to two chattering women and heard them complain about how expensive things had become on account of all the fighting, and how the hills were full of dangerous men – like the wild one who had come running through town with his spear this morning, looking to kill some travelers who had stayed at the inn this past night. . . .

"Get out!"

A round-bellied shopkeeper stomped out from behind the counter. Startled, the women turned and stared as he dragged Alex by the back of his muddy cloak and flung him out the door.

"That is no way to treat man or beast!" one woman exclaimed. "Why, he was holding a penny to buy something to eat, and all ye do is throw him out. How can ye live with yourself when ye treat the less fortunate so?"

"I cannae have beggars in my shop," the shopkeeper growled. "He'll bring in fleas and foul odors."

"Och, ye bring in enough foul odors of your own," the other woman said, laying a coin on the counter. "Here, this is to buy some bread for the lad."

"All right, all right," the shopkeeper said. "Keep your coin. I've got some scraps in the back."

"Scraps? Save them for your pigs. The lad's entitled to something decent once in a while." The woman tucked some strips of dried meat into a round flatbread. "There, that'll be a fine treat."

"Right then. I'll no' make ye ladies pay this time." The shopkeeper wagged his finger. "But if more beggars come around, I'll show them the way to *your* doors."

The women smiled.

"Bless ye," the first one said. "I'm glad to see ye have a heart in there somewhere. Ye just might live a good and full life."

"I doubt it," the shopkeeper muttered.

Alex went back to poking about the dirt with his stick. The women exited the shop a few moments later, each with a basket under an arm. One gingerly tossed him the flatbread roll on her way past.

It had occurred to Alex that the wild man the women spoke of could have been Don-Dun. He hurried after them, hoping they would say more.

They turned to look at him with alarm. "Go away," one demanded. "Dinnae follow us – we havenae got any more."

Alex held back until they resumed walking, and then he shuffled after them again.

Exasperated, the women turned back to the general store.

"Shopkeeper," one called, holding open the door. "Would ye please get rid of this little brute for me?"

"Oh, so he's a little brute the-now?" The shopkeeper peered smugly out the door at Alex. "What happened to the poor, unfortunate lad ye spoke of earlier?"

"Enough of that. Just get rid of him for us, would ye, please?"

"I can have him locked up in the miller's cellar with that wild man," the shopkeeper offered. "That'll teach the pesky beggar to be harassing townsfolk."

"There's no need to be so harsh," the woman admonished. "The lad's not much more than an animal. He doesnae ken what he's doing."

"I'll just drive him off then, shall I?"

The woman gave a reluctant nod. "Be gentle," she pleaded.

Moving quite quickly for a big-bellied man, the shopkeeper stormed out of the store, a riding whip in hand. Alex ran, but he was not fast enough to avoid a stinging lash across the shoulder.

"I'll have my son and some other village lads keep an eye out for him," the shopkeeper said, giving the women a satisfied smile. "They'll make sure ye're no' bothered again."

Excited, Alex ran for the bridge, convinced that the wild man they had captured this morning and locked in the miller's cellar was Don-Dun. He wondered how he was going to find this cellar.

Alex stopped. Crossing the bridge was a group of men pushing a heavy cart that was loaded with fresh cuts of meat. The men from the inn were not among them. Nonetheless, Alex backed warily into the shadow of a building. The man who had given him a coin hours earlier was guiding the cart from up front. As Alex suspected, the cart was Don-Dun's. Trailing along behind was Meg, her head hanging down miserably.

Alex watched as the men brought the cart to a butcher

shop. A man wearing a blood-smeared apron greeted them enthusiastically. He went around to the back of the cart, slid a heavy hindquarter onto his shoulder, and staggered into his shop – soon to reemerge for another.

The head was last to be unloaded. Two men each took a horn and pulled. The back of the heavy head thumped onto the dirt and was dragged indoors.

That was the last Alex saw of Rhua. The beloved beast was gone . . . for good.

"There he is!"

Alex turned toward the voice, startled. Three boys were coming his way. One was pointing.

"There's that beggar-boy my father told us about!"

Not liking the look of this, Alex got up and walked away.

"Hey, beggar-boy, where are ye going, beggar-boy?" called one of the boys. He was bigger than Alex and carried a stick.

Alex quickened his pace, his mind racing. He had to get away from these boys, but how? The boys were spreading out to cut off his escape. One threw a stone. It didn't miss by much.

"Rude little beggar-boy, isn't he, lads? Doesnae answer when he's called."

"Maybe he hasnae got a tongue," another responded.

The bigger boy tossed up a knife and caught it deftly by the handle. "He won't when we're done with him."

Alex sprinted for the general store in the hope that someone there would help him. A boy stood in his way. Alex made as if to pass him on one side, and then he skipped past on the other. Bursting through the door, Alex startled the shopkeeper into dropping a parcel. A few townsfolk turned to stare.

"Out, out!" The shopkeeper grabbed Alex and threw him out of the store. Alex lay sprawled in the dirt at the feet of the three boys. "I told ye lads to get rid of him, no' bring him to my shop!" The shopkeeper shook his fist. "Make sure he doesnae come back."

"Dinnae worry." The bigger boy grinned. "He's no' coming back."

Alex looked up pleadingly, but the shopkeeper went inside his store and slammed the door. The bell hanging over the door tinkled, and all was still.

"Ye're coming with us, beggar-boy."

Hands clamped onto Alex, and he was brought to his feet. A stick jabbed into his side. Flung forward, Alex staggered and fell. Amused, villagers stopped to watch as if they thought this was all just harmless fun.

He was pulled back up to standing. Again, they pushed him forward. This time, Alex tried to run, but his feet were kicked out from under him and he sprawled headlong into the dirt. Several smaller boys had joined in, and Alex was now in the midst of a pack. The hands hauling him up also grabbed his hair. Sticks stabbed him from all sides.

Singing "Na-na, na na-na!" the laughing mob dragged him down the road, the younger boys jabbering gleefully.

It seemed they were going to take Alex back over the bridge, but at the last moment, they veered off the road, yanking him down an embankment to a secluded bend in the river.

Alex lost all hope that someone would intervene.

He pulled and twisted with all his strength, but it was no use – there were too many of them, all pushing, kicking, and jabbing him to the water's edge. Alex was sure they meant to drown him.

Before Alex had a chance to take a breath, one of the large boys forced his head underwater. Alex writhed and fought. The fist holding his hair pulled his head back out of the water just long enough for him to take a gasp before he was thrust under again. He felt a searing pain in his chest, and his world blackened.

Hacking and retching, he vaguely realized he was no longer underwater. He rolled his head in the mud, trying to breathe normally. The boys were standing around him, laughing and joking, waiting for him to recover sufficiently for the games to resume.

Right in front of him was the river, its swirling current still high from the recent rain. Miraculously, there was no one between him and the water.

Alex leaped and dove.

As the water closed in over him, he heard shouts. The water was muddy, but he stayed under, kicking as hard as he could to put distance between himself and the shore.

His cloak weighed him down, so he shrugged it off. Short of breath, he had to come up. When he broke the surface, he took in quick gasps of air. Stones splashed down near him. The current was taking him toward the bridge. Several boys had sprinted up ahead, clambering onto the bridge to wait with their rocks for when the current brought Alex within range.

But, unlike these boys, Alex could swim.

Much to their surprise, he broke into a front crawl, which took him directly across the current to the far side. The boys scampered over the bridge and ran up the opposite shore to intercept him.

Alex scrambled ashore and frantically beat about the bushes looking for his crossbow. The boys were closing in fast. Just when Alex thought he'd best leap back into the river, he found his crossbow. He fumbled to load and tension a bolt. Straightening, he raised his crossbow and sighted.

The look of astonishment that spread over the leading boy's face was almost comical. He skidded to a halt, the others piling in behind, tripping over him. They fell in a panicked heap, struggling to their feet to run back to the bridge.

Alex turned the crossbow to the boys across the river. As one, they fled up the embankment and back toward town.

Triumphant, Alex trained his bow onto the boys sprinting back across the bridge. He didn't mean to squeeze the trigger, but somehow he did. The string twanged and the bolt shot. Dismayed, Alex watched it soar. Then the bolt struck with a sickening thud.

8

THE PAYMENT

Convinced he would be pursued, Alex ran as fast as he could. He looked back and saw that his footprints stood out clearly in the dirt, recent rains having blurred everything else.

His bolt had hit the bridge, not his tormentor, but he knew the villagers would be after him regardless. They would not take kindly to a beggar-boy who shot at one of their own.

Hoping to lose his pursuers, Alex headed into the woods and doubled back to the river. To confuse them further, he decided to swim back toward the bridge. The villagers would not expect that. They would be surprised he could swim at all, much less swim upstream. They'd more likely assume he crossed the river and scour the banks on the other side.

Alex sidestroked, pushing his crossbow ahead with his lead arm until the bridge came into view. There was no one on it. Alex strengthened his kicks and struggled against the current. His progress was slow. By the time he reached the darkness under the bridge, he was exhausted. He pulled himself up out of the water and onto the bridge supports, still hidden from view.

Hearing voices, Alex scrambled higher, until he was tucked directly under the boards.

"Is this no' just a waste of time?" one of the voices said, footsteps reverberating on the bridge. "In the hopes that he can starve the advancing English army into turning back, Wallace will soon be coming through here with his men, destroying the harvest that we Scots have worked so hard to produce . . . and yet here we are, chasing about the country-side looking for some beggar-boy."

"That was my son he very nearly killed," another voice replied. "I want him caught."

The footsteps on the bridge were joined by the clopping of horses' hooves. Alex heard a babble of other voices: "Bolt struck here" and "How did the beggar get his hands on a bow?" and "Maybe he's still nearby." Alex was terrified they would check under the bridge.

"There go his tracks," someone said. "Let's make haste."

The footfalls ended and the voices faded.

Alex headed back into the current and continued upstream, keeping close to the shore. He tried walking where his feet could touch bottom, but that stirred up a cloudy muck that Alex feared would give him away.

The riverbanks became increasingly wooded. He heard an odd flapping sound. Rounding a bend in the river, he saw a large rotating wheel protruding from a tall stone founda-tion. Above, a chute poured water into catch basins.

A *mill!* Excited, Alex crawled out of the water, staying on his knees to pull off his tunic and wring it out. The breeze gave him goose bumps. He put the tunic back on wet, but at least no longer heavy and dripping.

As he climbed the wooded embankment, Alex heard the groaning and creaking of wood shafts and gears turning within the stone foundation.

Up at the top, bushes opened into a clearing, where a pair of tethered oxen chewed contentedly alongside four unusually large horses. Inside the mill's open loading bay, men tossed sacks onto a wagon. Others emerged from the mill's front door.

Alex shrank back further into the bushes, his heart pounding. The gaunt man first out of the door was the one who had wiped his feet on Alex's cloak at the inn. Next was the big-boned man who had bumped their table and the tall, hook-nosed one with the longbow. The man with the hood came out behind them.

The thin man handed a pouch to a fifth man, the last to exit the mill. "Your payment, miller. Our master, Earl Warenne, will be grateful."

The miller carefully thumbed the coins from hand to hand, his lips moving silently. "Thirty," he affirmed with a nod.

The hook-nosed man clapped the miller on the back. "Aren't ye glad we came? Ye're a rich man now."

"I just hope Wallace doesnae learn of this."

"Ha! Wallace is the least of your worries." The big man leaned in close. "King Edward is the man to fear. He is so *angry* over Wallace's rebellion that he has ordered Earl Warenne and his treasurer, Hugh de Cressingham, to lead their forces into Scotland to crush it."

"Their armies will need to be fed," added the thin man, "and if our master doesnae find the food he has paid for . . ." He scratched the wispy whiskers under his chin as he searched for words.

"Ye will come to an unspeakably slow and horrible end," the hooded man said matter-of-factly.

The hook-nosed man smiled. "Now, it is true that Wallace is doing his best to turn back the English army by destroying all the food in its path. Yes, his men are sweeping through the countryside, viciously putting a torch to the hard work of one Scottish village after another. But when they come here, what will they find?"

"Nothing?" the miller offered.

"Only enough to be convinced they have it all. The rest we will have carefully hidden." The man swung up onto his horse. "Just make sure the remainder is shipped by nightfall."

The four men spurred their horses into a gallop. Within seconds, they had passed Alex's hiding spot and disappeared down the road.

The loading done, the miller ordered his men to hitch the oxen to the wagon. One shouted and flicked his switch. The oxen extended their necks and got the heavy load moving.

The miller pinched the bridge of his nose and squeezed his eyes shut. With the sound of the hooves fading, he turned and disappeared into the mill, leaving the loading doors open.

Alex scampered out from the bushes and ran towards the mill, stopping to peer into the dark loading bay. No one was there. Along one wall stood large sacks of flour.

He slipped inside. When his eyes adjusted to the dim light, he tiptoed up to a door at the back and pressed his ear against it. He heard creaking and rumbling, but no voices. Alex lifted the latch and cracked open the door. Ghostly structures rotated within the gloom. With a clattering and occasional groan, horizontal and vertical cogs meshed as they turned large gears. It looked like the inside of a huge windup clock.

Carrying his crossbow about was a nuisance, so Alex searched for a hiding place. It would be useless until it dried anyway, its wet drawstring far too loose. As he tucked the bow behind a sack, he spotted a hole in the floor, with a ladder leading into the darkness below. Alex quietly climbed down the rungs, feeling safer once he was out of sight.

The only light entering the lower room came through the cracks in a closed shutter. A shaft entered through one wall, turning a set of gears larger than the last. Alex figured the waterwheel must be on the other side of the stone wall. He was definitely in the cellar. Crates, tools, and clay urns littered the dirt floor. To one side was a pile of thick spokes that looked like spare cogs. On the other side was a door barricaded with a beam. At first, Alex thought it led outside, but then he realized that it was on the side of the cellar that led into the embankment.

Alex crept up to the door, knelt, and peered through a hole near the bottom. He couldn't see anything.

"Don-Dun?" he whispered fearfully. "Are you in there?"

"Laddie! Good God! Have they got ye too?"

Alex leaped up to lift the beam, but stopped as he heard footsteps above. Feet appeared on the ladder, stepping down one rung to the next. Diving behind a crate, Alex made himself as small as possible. Not daring to look, he stayed still as someone trod across the floor.

"Pass out your buckets," a man demanded loudly. Alex recognized the miller's voice.

"The laddie! What have ye done with the laddie?" Don-Dun roared.

The miller stood silently for a moment. "Dinnae be daft, man," he said. "Pass out your buckets."

"Ye ken fine what I speak of. If ye hurt that laddie, so help me God!" Don-Dun pounded on the door.

"Get a grip on yourself. There is no laddie here," the miller said. "Ye're just losing your mind, that's all. Pass out your buckets the-now or ye'll get no food."

Don-Dun fell silent. Alex risked a peek around the edge of the crate and saw the miller pull a bucket out from a hatch in the door. When the miller straightened, Alex ducked. Footsteps sounded across the floor, up the ladder, then over-head. The miller was finally gone.

Alex rushed to the door and heaved the heavy beam out of its brackets. He pulled the door ring, and the door slowly swung toward him. Don-Dun stood hunched in the cramped space.

"Laddie? I cannae believe it! The miller's right – I must be going mad."

Don-Dun stepped forward and stumbled, grabbing the wall for support. Alex steadied him as he came through the door.

"I'll be all right. It's just my leg – sound asleep, it is."

"There's no time for that," Alex said anxiously. "We've got to get out of here."

"Aye, that we'll do, laddie." Don-Dun slapped the side of his leg. "It's better already."

With Don-Dun in the lead, they climbed the ladder and crossed the floor of the upper room. Through a crack in the door to the loading bay, they saw another wagon, parked in the same spot as the first. It was larger, almost filling the opening. The miller's men were tossing in sacks of flour, cream-colored dust puffing from the seams when the sacks landed.

Alex and Don-Dun waited for them to finish, watching as they covered the load with a tarp.

"Make haste in your return for the next load," the miller said. "All this must be gone by nightfall."

The miller and the men squeezed past the wagon and left the loading bay. Outside, oxen snorted and stamped their hooves.

Don-Dun dashed through the empty loading bay to the back of the wagon. Fumbling quietly, he loosened the tie-downs at the end of the tarp.

Alex snatched his bow from its hiding place and ran to where Don-Dun was holding up the tarp, waving impatiently. Alex climbed onto the back of the wagon and wriggled between the sacks as Don-Dun squeezed in and lowered the tarp over them.

The wagon jiggled as the men climbed onto the riding-board up front. Alex heard a shout, and the wagon lurched forward. The men were talking, but Alex and Don-Dun could not hear a word over the creaking and clattering of the wheels.

Alex did not dare even a whisper to Don-Dun. They rode for over an hour, it seemed, and Alex grew increasingly nervous that when they arrived at their destination, the men would throw back the tarp and find them.

There were sudden shouts from up front, and Alex felt the wagon turn. It lurched from side to side, the wheels bouncing over ruts. Don-Dun gave Alex a nudge, squirmed backward, and slid out from under the tarp. Alex followed, silently dropping to the ground next to him.

They watched the wagon list and heave its way up the steep trail, the men shouting to the oxen and whipping their backsides.

"What a strange place to be bringing so many sacks of food," Don-Dun said as they watched the wagon disappear. "I wonder where on earth they're headed."

"They're hiding it," Alex said. "I saw the men from the inn paying the miller. They bought the food to feed an army that King Edward is sending into Scotland to put down Wallace's rebellion."

"Of course!" Don-Dun smacked his fist into his palm. "We have to tell Wallace."

"Let's get Meg and head back to Duncragglin," Alex urged. "She'll be safe there. And Sir Ellerslie will know how to get word to William Wallace about the hidden food. Then I can go back to looking for my parents."

"Get Meg?" Don-Dun snorted. "We shall do no such thing. We must warn Wallace straightaway so he can destroy this food. Maybe then we can get your Meg."

Alex felt his face grow red. "She's not *my* Meg. The inn-keeper is going to sell her. If we don't get her now, it might be too late. It's not far – Crawford is just over those hills."

Don-Dun gripped Alex by both arms and stared him

straight in the eyes. "Perhaps ye dinnae understand," he said slowly. "This is no time to be trying to rescue a damsel in distress or to be searching for missing parents. The entire fate of Scotland might hang in the balance. If the English army gets its hands on this food, it will be able to advance further north. Many will die."

Don-Dun turned to head north, for Duncragglin.

Alex hesitated. He thought of Meg being sold by the innkeeper. That decided it.

9

THE SCOUT TROUPE

Not long after Alex left Don-Dun, the woods gave way to cultivated fields, where men and women bent to hack at the soil. Alex felt sorry for these Scottish farmers. They had no idea that William Wallace was going to destroy their crops. Come winter, their children would be hungry. *Surely Wallace would allow them to keep some food – as long as they kept it from the English?*

His crossbow tucked under his arm, Alex struck out across a field.

"Ahoy!" A farmer waved.

"Which way is Crawforrrd?" Alex asked, doing his best to roll his r's.

He headed in the direction the farmer pointed and found himself on a trail between cultivated plots. Climbing on top of a stone wall for a better view, he saw thatched roofs off in the distance, the familiar bridge barely visible on the far side.

When Alex reached the village, he slipped through an alley and came upon a lane. An open sewer ran down the middle.

The shutters of a second-story window banged open, and with a cheery "hi-ho," a woman flung out the contents of a chamber pot. Alex raced to get out of the way, the vile deluge splattering behind him. Laughing, the woman slammed her shutters shut.

Alex knew he had reached the back of the inn when he found the stables. He tried a door, but, as he feared, it was locked. Cupping his hands, he called Meg's name.

A few faces peered at him from behind neighboring shutters. Then the door flew open, and an arm grabbed the front of his tunic, pulling him inside.

"Just what are ye doing here?" Meg hissed, lowering a beam across the door.

"I've come to get you, of course." Alex shrugged. "Didn't you want to come with me and Don-Dun?"

"Ye've come to get *me*?" Meg said. "I dinnae need your help to run away – I'd be better off doing that all by myself. Then I wouldnae have nearly so many coming after me. Ye've got half the village up in arms. Did ye really think ye could come back here without anyone seeing?"

Alex opened his mouth, but no words came out. Despairing, he realized what would happen if word of his whereabouts reached his pursuers.

"Quick," Meg said. "If we're lucky, they didnae see ye come through this door. Ye can hide in the attic for a while, and maybe they'll think ye escaped into the countryside." She pulled him up a set of stairs to the second floor. "Up there." She pointed to a small hatch in the ceiling of a linen closet. "Stay on the beams or ye'll fall through." She closed the closet door behind him and was gone.

Careful not to step on the neatly folded linens, Alex slung his crossbow across his back and climbed into the low attic. Toward the middle of the space, he found a few loose boards spread across the beams.

With nothing to do but wait, he lay down, folded his hands over his stomach, and stared at the rafters. *Things aren't so bad,* he thought. *Once everyone's asleep, I'll find a way out.* He knew which road Don-Dun was taking. If he ran fast enough, he would catch him eventually.

It grew cooler. Alex closed his eyes and listened to the sounds of lodgers settling into their rooms. Soon it would be time for him to escape.

Suddenly he awoke to a hand shaking his shoulder.

"Shhh. It's me," Meg whispered.

"What time is it?" Alex asked.

"It's well past midnight. The village men have been out lookin' for ye and Don-Dun all this time. It's worse than I thought – much worse. They're madder than hell. I dinnae understand why – Don-Dun's just a cart driver, and ye're just a boy."

Alex thought back to their escape. With a sinking feeling, he realized that they'd left the tie-down ropes loose when they slipped off the back of the wagon. The men would have been able to see that he and Don-Dun had hidden aboard, and they would fear that their stowaways would know where the food was hidden.

Alex told Meg what he knew.

"The English are invading Scotland?" Meg gasped. "And men from the village are hiding food to help them? If that's true, they'll kill ye for sure, just to keep ye from talking."

"If they catch me, you mean." Alex prepared to leave.

"Ye cannae go out there," Meg cried, taking hold of his arm. "They're everywhere! Ye'll never get past them."

All of a sudden they heard voices and the stomping of many boots charging about the corridors below.

"Meg, we know ye're up there," the innkeeper called from below. "Come down, lass, and nothing will happen to ye. It's the laddie we want."

Alex looked at her expectantly, but Meg shook her head. "It makes no difference," she said, resigned. "I'd just as soon let them come and get me."

His hands shaking, Alex tensioned the bow. These men were going to kill him. Knowing he had nothing to lose, he decided to shoot if given the chance.

A gloved hand pushed up the hatch. Alex raised his bow and sighted. His heart was pounding madly.

Meg and Alex heard shouts, some from as far away as the street. The hand disappeared and the hatch fell back into place. Sounds of running down corridors, clomping, and stamping reached them, followed by yells, then silence.

Confused, Alex lowered his bow. He and Meg glanced at each other. Heavy footsteps bounded up the stairs, stopping somewhere below.

"Alex! Are ye up there?"

Don-Dun?

Alex and Meg heard a clattering in the linen closet. The hatch was knocked open, flying out of place, and Don-Dun's head popped up.

"Point that thing somewhere else," he demanded. "Let's get moving – there's no time to waste."

Immeasurable relief flooded through Alex.

"Hurry!" Don-Dun shouted.

Alex and Meg scrambled after Don-Dun all the way down to the street, where a half dozen armed men on horseback were holding back a crowd of angry villagers. Meg was hoisted up onto the back of a horse, behind one of the armed men. Don-Dun leaped onto another horse, yanking Alex up behind him.

Alex spotted someone training a bow in their direction. Aiming the best he could from the back of a horse, Alex shot his own crossbow. His bolt struck a shutter next to the archer, startling him into missing his target.

The riders spurred on their horses, and the villagers scattered out of their way. They galloped well out of town before slowing to give the horses a rest.

"Anyone get hit?" A heavyset rider trotted his horse up past the others, looking everyone over.

"Not me," sang out one.

"Nor me," added another.

"That archer had his sights on me. Too bad ye missed him, laddie."

"He was one of the four English agents I spoke of," Don-Dun said, speaking loudly for all to hear, "the ones who are paying the villagers to hide the food."

Alex started to relax, leaning back to place his hands on the horse's swaying hindquarters. "Was I ever glad to see you," he said to Don-Dun. "Who are these guys?"

Don-Dun shot him a withering glance. "For such a foolish lad, it seems ye have luck on your side," he said. "These men are a scout troupe of Wallace's. I talked them into going into the village for ye. I told them that Wallace knew ye personally and wouldnae be pleased to learn ye were left to your fate."

"So where are we going?"

"We're going south toward the borderlands. Once we find the English, we're to report their numbers and location back to Wallace."

"Won't they kill us if we do?"

"Not if they dinnae see us."

Alex thought about leaving the riders and heading back to Duncragglin, but traveling alone wasn't terribly appealing. For one thing, the riders did not have a spare horse to give him. For another, the bands of thieves living in the hills preyed on anyone who traveled alone. It was better to stay with the scout troupe, he decided. At least they were going back to see Wallace once the scouting was done.

The group left the road and headed up a trail. With unerring accuracy, the horses picked their way over the rocky terrain.

Stopping only for short breaks, they rode all day and well into the night before settling to sleep. By mid-afternoon the next day, Alex's muscles ached. Getting off the horse and walking was not an option: the horses were going too fast for him to keep up.

The group skirted a large town, the turrets of its imposing castle keeping a watchful eye over the surrounding countryside.

Rounding a bend between low hills, they saw a long marshy valley stretched out before them, a river meandering down its length. Stone huts dotted the slopes of distant fields.

Alex pointed to a long narrow bridge that cut straight through a marsh, crossing a river to reach the foothills on the other side. "Will we be crossing?" he asked.

"Nae, Stirling Bridge leads to the north," Don-Dun replied. "We need to continue further south to find the English."

"Stirling Bridge?" Alex exclaimed. "Is that *the* Stirling Bridge, the one over the River Forth?"

"There's none other."

"Has there been a battle here between the Scots and the English?"

"I dinnae ken. The English have invaded our lands so often."

"No, I mean, a *big* battle with thousands and thousands of troops?"

Dun-Dun shrugged.

"If, for some reason, you see Wallace before I do, tell him to keep an eye on this bridge," Alex said excitedly. "Would you do that please? This is important."

"Watch the bridge? What's the point in that?"

"The English army will cross this bridge. Wallace needs to be ready for them."

Don-Dun snorted. "The English will send their army across this narrow bridge?"

"They will." Alex nodded vigorously. "Just tell him, would you please?"

"Fine." Don-Dun shifted in the saddle and raised a finger to his lips. "But from here on, try 'n' keep a still tongue in your head. If there's an army about, it will have its own scouts, and we dinnae want to blunder into them."

The group took a trail that led south, away from the valley. Trees closed in around them.

10

LORD CRESSINGHAM

It was the leader of the scout troupe who first noticed something was wrong. No birds chirped, none flew overhead – there was only a deathly quiet. It felt as if all of nature were holding its breath.

The scout leader drew up his horse, raising his hand to get everyone's attention. He cocked his head to listen, and the other men did likewise.

Don-Dun shifted in his saddle. "Get down for a moment, laddie – ye also, Meg. Find a place to lie low."

Alex pulled his crossbow from the saddle sling and leaped down.

The leader conferred quietly with his men. They separated, with Don-Dun and three men riding up the wooded incline to the left and the leader taking two others with him to the right.

Meg motioned toward a dense thicket.

Within the bushes, they found a trickle of water too small to call a creek. Curious to see where Don-Dun and the others were headed, they followed it upstream, remaining well hidden within the thick bushes along its sides.

The bushes thinned. Alex and Meg crouched to remain out of sight as they climbed higher. Leaving the cover of the bushes, they slipped from tree to tree until they reached the top of a ridge.

On the other side, row upon row of tents stretched out for miles. A smoky film from hundreds of cooking fires hung over the fields, the setting sun giving it a rosy glow. A massive army was settling in for the night.

Each tent looked like it could hold about twenty-five people. Dozens of men were about each one, so that calculation seemed about right. Alex also saw bigger tents, with banners flying from their peaks. Those were probably for the officers or nobility. *Surely* they *don't sleep crammed together*. He wondered if King Edward was there, somewhere.

Alex counted the tents that spread out over about a quarter of the camp, multiplied that number by four, then by twenty-five men to a tent. *There can't be that many in each tent*, he decided. *If there are, that means there are over fifteen thousand men down there!*

"Allo, allo, who 'ave we 'ere?"

Alex jumped. Two armored English sentries with drawn swords stood right behind him and Meg.

"Give me that. There's a good lad." A sentry snatched the bow from Alex's grasp, raising his arm to stay the sword of the other sentry. "Just 'old on with 'at."

"What? Stand aside, man!" The other sentry glared. "We're under orders to kill any we encounter – not capture them."

"Aye, but that command wasn't for *children*, ye shtupid twit. Besides, we're due to be relieved, and these two can be

put to work. I'll tell the captain about them on my way in
and send up the relief to get ye."

"The captain won't be pleased," the other retorted.
"We're to kill *everyone*. That means men, women, *and* children! Those are our orders."

"We can always kill them later, after they've done their
work. And if the captain wants them killed, he can kill them.
Right there – on the spot. So there's no problem, all right?"
Not waiting for an answer, the sentry slapped Alex with the
flat of his sword. "Get moving," he barked.

Alex stumbled down the hill, shooting glances back at
the trees along the ridge. There was no sign of Don-Dun
and the men, only more sentries – a lot more. He realized it
was too late to expect any help. The sentries were patrolling
the outskirts of their camp in groups of two, each within
shouting distance of the next. An alarm would raise hundreds of men within seconds.

Alex and Meg were marched through a maze of tents
surrounded by dirty, tired-looking soldiers who glanced at
them disinterestedly.

"Captain." The sentry saluted a gaunt man sitting on a
log before a fire, his thin splayed legs stretched stiffly before
him.

"Uhh," the captain grunted, glancing up. His hollow,
unfocussed eyes seemed to stare through the sentry. "Find
food?"

"I was on sentry duty, captain. Not scouting."

"What good are ye?"

"I've caught these two spying."

"Kill 'm."

"Right 'ere, captain?"

"Uhh, why not?"

"The bodies would mess up our camp. We'd be tripping over them the whole time."

A soldier sitting on the other side of the fire piped up. "Maybe we could eat 'm."

"I get a leg," said another eagerly, his sleeve sliding down his thin arm as he waved it in the air.

"A leg! What are ye thinking, man? Those two are tiny!"

"Aye, ye're right." The soldier lowered his arm. "They're only children –"

"Ye can't have a whole leg to yourself – we've got to share, right?"

The men burst into guffaws, slapping the dust from their knees and giving each other a shove. One fell over sideways, continuing to laugh even as he lay in the dirt.

They had a *very* hungry look in their eyes. Even the men in the nearest tent were showing interest, their big grins gleaming in the darkness.

A soldier arranged skewers by the fire, carefully laying them side by side. Another slowly drew his sword. The captain's lips twisted into a half-smile. He turned away and said nothing.

Alex felt a chill. His legs trembled. These men were not joking.

"Folk from my village have hidden lots of food," Meg said abruptly. She pointed over the hills to the north. "It's that way, less than a day's ride."

"Food?" The captain stared at her coldly, his face contorted. "If ye speak falsely, a horrible and slow death awaits ye."

"But I dinnae speak falsely, sire. It's from my village. Ye can ask Earl Warenne's men. They paid for it."

"Warenne's men?" a soldier repeated, aghast.

"Uhh –" the captain began.

"They've been keeping it from us," said another angrily. "I knew it!"

"I thought his men looked better fed than ours."

"Let's take our share!"

"Quiet!" Clutching his knees, the captain stood. "Earl Warenne has joined forces with our Lord Cressingham to help us put down the Scottish rabble. His food is our food. Let's go talk to the lieutenant and get this sorted."

The captain took the lead, keeping a tight grip on Meg's arm. A company of twenty followed, Alex shoved along in their midst. As they wound between neighboring camps, word of Warenne's treachery rang out: "Warenne's men are hoarding food" and "The pigs!"

Their ranks swelled as company after company joined the captain. Men stood aside as the group passed, then filled in behind, trampling smoldering fires in their wake. It wasn't long before they became a band of hundreds of noisy, hungry men who were shaking fists, waving weapons, and clamoring for what was rightfully theirs. News of their march spread through the camp in a wave.

From up ahead came a shout: "What is the meaning of this?"

Men from between the larger tents came running. Soldiers led horses forward and helped knights wearing long, flowing garments into saddles, hastily handing them shields and swords.

"Halt, and announce yourselves." The command came from a fat man who rode toward the crowd, no sword in hand, his eyes scanning the gathering. Mounted knights quickly followed, as did soldiers on foot.

"Kneel! Kneel before Lord Cressingham, treasurer of the king of England," the knights called out.

The men grumbled, but their shouts of defiance died away. The captains dropped to one knee, followed immediately by their men. To do otherwise could mean death. Alex dropped, not wanting to be the only one left standing in a sea of kneeling men while the fat man looked for a culprit. He slid behind a soldier to be out of Cressingham's sight.

"Who leads here? Speak or die."

"Uhh, it is I, M'Lord," the captain said, letting go of Meg to raise his arm.

Cressingham glared at the trembling captain, scorn on his face. He turned to his knight. "Who is this idiot?"

"I have no idea, M'Lord," the knight replied. "One of our many captains, it would appear."

"Why do ye lead the men thus?" Cressingham demanded. "Explain yourself, man, and be quick about it!"

"W-w-w-we, uh, have, uh, l-l-l-learned of a large hidden store of food, M'Lord."

"Excellent! Ye were right to hasten to tell me, though ye need not have brought so many with ye. Now, where is this food?"

"I-I-I-I-I —"

"Out with it, man!" Cressingham shouted, his jowls jiggling.

The captain shook. "I d-d-d-don't know, M'Lord. B-b-but these children –"

"Ye don't know!"

"The ch-ch-ch-children know, M'Lord."

"Children? I have been roused from my bed on account of the tales of children?"

The captain was incapable of further reply. He had bowed so far forward, his face was almost pressed into the dirt.

"Where are these children?"

Not daring to raise his head, the captain awkwardly flapped his arm toward Meg, who had shuffled sideways to be next to Alex.

"Step forward."

Alex and Meg rose and picked their way past the kneeling men to stand before Cressingham's large horse. Alex felt very small.

"Where is this food?" Cressingham demanded.

Meg looked around, trying to get her bearings. She pointed west.

"No, that way," Alex said, pointing north.

Meg shot him a confused glance. She raised her arm to point west again. Alex frowned and pulled her arm down.

"That way," he insisted, pointing north again. "The bridge is that way."

"Bridge?" Meg repeated.

"The way to the hidden food is over the long bridge," Alex stated, doing his best to warn her with his eyes.

"They'll kill us," she whispered.

"Shhh," he hissed back.

"Bah! This is naught but the babbling of children." Cressingham shifted to face his knights. He pointed to Alex and Meg. "Kill 'm and be done with it."

"M'Lord," Alex called desperately. "The food from an entire valley has been stored in a cave – the whole harvest – enough to feed an army. It is just over a bridge –"

"We cannot ignore this talk of food, M'Lord," a knight said. "The men are hungry. They have risen up with arms. Their discontent will be hard to contain."

"What bridge is this?" Cressingham demanded. "Who knows of it?"

"I do," said another knight. "It cuts across a bog to the east of Stirling. In the middle, it spans a river that feeds the Firth of Forth."

"But we're advancing west of Stirling," Cressingham said.

"The bridge gives us a much shorter route to the north," another knight piped up. "We'll rout Wallace that much sooner."

"And there's food on the other side," said another.

"Ye would have our entire twenty-thousand-strong army cross a long narrow bridge?" Cressingham was astounded. "What of Wallace and his men?"

"We can send an advance troop to secure the far end," a knight said. "The rest can pass in safety."

Cressingham nodded slowly, his gaze shifting from the knights to the kneeling men. It settled on Alex.

Alex lowered his head and wondered if he should go back to kneeling. He wished the earth would swallow him up.

"Where are ye from?" Cressingham demanded.

"Far away, M'Lord" was all Alex could think to say.

"I know that, ye idiot," Cressingham snapped. "Answer my question."

"I don't know, M'Lord. I came by boat with my parents." Alex lied, not knowing what else to say. "We were, er, separated, and now I'm trying to find them. Have you, by any chance, heard two people who speak like me? They might be wearing strange clothes with tiny metal clasps that close up the front –"

"Silence!" Cressingham roared, spittle flying from his mouth. "But for our need for ye to lead us to the food, ye'd be dead right now."

"M'Lord?" The captain looked up fearfully from his prone position. "The lad has said Earl Warenne knows of this supply of food."

Cressingham turned to Alex in fury. "How do ye know this?" he demanded. "Mind, if ye make false accusations, your death will be very slow."

"Four men were helping the villagers hide the food," Alex replied. "They said Warenne paid in gold."

"Describe these men."

"Well, the tall one with the longbow has a hooked nose and black eyes, and black eyebrows too. They come up in a peak." Alex crooked his fingers over his eyes to demonstrate. "I think he was the leader. But the thin one was the scariest; he looked like a walking skeleton with skin stretched over his bones –"

"I know of these men," a knight interrupted. "They're Warenne's men, all right."

Cressingham stroked his chin. "Well, lad, lead us to this food and maybe, just maybe, I'll tell ye more about the special guest King Edward keeps in Hog Tower. I've heard he has a garment with the mysterious clasps ye speak of."

"Does he have a strange way of speaking?" Alex asked, unable to contain himself.

Alex did not see the blow coming until it was too late. A knight smacked him off his feet with the end of his lance. "Impertinent youth!" he growled. "Do not speak unless spoken to."

"Men!" Cressingham spoke loudly so that his voice would carry over the crowd. "Arise. At first light on the morrow, we advance north and cross at Stirling Bridge. By nightfall, we feast."

The troops stood, cheered, and waved their weapons.

Cressingham motioned for silence. "Get some rest," he ordered. "Come morn, there will be much to do." Cressingham turned his horse, not waiting to see if he would be obeyed – that was simply taken for granted. "Keep those two safe," he ordered a knight. "They will lead us to the food . . . and then they will get their reward."

11

STIRLING BRIDGE

The knight guided Alex and Meg to a large tent that was partitioned into sleeping quarters, each strewn with bedding. In the center was a common area with chairs.

The knight dropped into the tallest backed chair. "Raulf," he called, raising a foot.

A scraggy, stooped man hastened to pull off the knight's boot.

"Tie those two," the knight ordered, lifting his other foot. "Cressingham would not be pleased if they escaped and there was no one to show our men where Warenne has hidden the food."

"Can anyone tell me where Hog Tower is?" Alex asked.

"Shut your mouth or we'll gag it." Raulf roughly tied Alex's hands to the center pole. He puzzled over what to do with Meg, finally deciding that tying her one hand to the pole would suffice.

Raulf and others of lesser rank pulled out blankets and arranged themselves about the common room while the knight and his entourage flopped down behind their partitions. A knight threw a blanket at Alex and Meg to share.

The tossing and grunting of the men soon turned to snorts and snores.

"We're in big trouble once they find there's no food on the other side of that bridge," Meg whispered. "Ye ken fine my village is the other way."

"Don't worry," Alex said quietly. "I know what I'm doing."

"How is it ye think ye're so smart when ye dinnae ken about one of King Edward's favorite places for keeping prisoners?" Meg asked.

A stone hit Alex on the shoulder. Raulf glowered at them, a finger pressed to his lips.

"You mean, Hog Tower?" Alex said eagerly, ignoring him. "Where is it?"

"Have ye heard of Berwick-upon-Tweed, the town near the English border where King Edward had everyone killed – every last man, woman, and child?"

Alex nodded, feeling a rising sense of dread.

"There."

———◆◆———

Morning came with a great bustle of activity. An army of twenty thousand does not pack up quietly. They slurped down cold watery gruel for breakfast and licked the bowls clean. Tents were taken down. Mule trains snaked through the camp, stopping to load tents and bundles left by soldiers who did not wait for the loading to be done. With the mist still hovering in the fields, the army was on the move.

Alex marveled at what a great army it was. He saw hundreds of light-armored men on horseback and dozens of heavily armored men on huge iron-clad horses. Behind them were so many foot soldiers that they blotted out the earth and turned the hills into a moving mass of men. They marched in formation, shoulder to shoulder, each company of one hundred led by its captain, each captain following banners held aloft by the standard-bearers.

Standing awkwardly on a stool, with plated armor covering every inch of his large body, was Cressingham. Alex recognized him because he had not put on his helmet.

It took the help of a squire and a few others to get Cressingham onto his warhorse. The big horse skittered sideways. Bringing it under control, Cressingham advanced the animal at a brisk walk. Riding with him were knights of high rank wearing crested surcoats and carrying large, colorful banners.

Raulf was ordered to take Alex with him on his horse and to stay with the knights who rode with Cressingham. Meg rode nearby, sitting captive before a knight.

"It won't be long before I get to kill ye," Raulf murmured cheerfully, reaching around Alex to take up the reins.

It was a chilly morning. Low dark clouds rolled overhead, punctuated by shafts of sunlight. The wind picked up, blowing away the remaining mist. Banners fluttered on their long staffs.

Breaking into a slow trot, Cressingham and his entourage pulled out in front of the main force and met up with another group of knights on horseback. Riding among them was an older man, gray-haired and lean, with a deep blue cape fastened over his crested surcoat. He wore only light armor, polished chain mail gleaming at his neck and on his arms.

"Earl Warenne." Cressingham nodded sourly in greeting.

Warenne jabbed his finger to the north. "Why are we advancing in this direction?" he demanded. "Our plans have us passing Stirling Castle to the west."

"Aye, but the men are hungry, and there is a large hidden store of food to be had to the northeast of Stirling," Cressingham replied. He sat back and squinted, watching for the older man's reaction. "I think ye know of what I speak."

"I know of a hidden store to the west," Warenne replied, "not one in this direction."

"And why do I not know of this hidden store to the west?" Cressingham demanded.

The older man's bushy eyebrows bunched into a frown, his eyes sweeping over Cressingham's entourage. "So that is what this is about," he said angrily. "Ye trust me not. Very well, continue with your folly. Your men can lead the way."

"That is precisely what I had in mind."

Tightlipped, Warenne turned his horse and led his knights away. The call went out for his men to hold back and let Cressingham's troops advance.

Cressingham's entourage continued forward, cresting a ridge. Behind them, marching men in armor filled the slopes. In the valley ahead, advance troops were already stationed next to the long, low bridge that Alex had seen when he was with Don-Dun. It jutted straight across the bog-filled lowlands, arching to cross a river at the center. On either side, pockets of shallow, reedy water glistened between scruffy bushes and tall grasses.

Approaching it from this new angle, Alex was struck by how narrow it was. No more than four horses would be able to ride side by side, and the arch in the center would constrict them further – to only two. It would take hours for so many thousands to cross.

Riders came galloping back from the advance troops, hastily drawing up their horses before Cressingham.

"This may not be a good time to cross, M'Lord," one called. "There's a force on the other side."

"Number?" Cressingham snapped.

"Can't tell, M'Lord," the rider replied. "We sent some emissaries across, offering to spare their lives if they gave us unfettered passage, but our emissaries have been rebuffed. It appears that the Scots are preparing to do battle. We've seen only a few hundred moving about, but there could be several thousand more behind the hills, for all we know."

"Not too bloody likely," Cressingham grunted scornfully.

"Even a small number could make the crossing difficult, M'Lord. Our men will be in a very thin line."

"Fools! Who's leading them?"

"William Wallace, M'Lord."

"That brigand!" Cressingham snorted. "Well, that accounts for their stupidity. The Scottish nobles would have had more sense."

"He has some nobles with him, M'Lord. Sir Andrew Moray, for one."

"Sir Andrew Moray! That Scottish noble from the northeast? And he lets Wallace lead?"

"So it would appear, M'Lord."

Cressingham shifted in his saddle and beckoned for a knight to approach. "Bring up the longbow archers," he ordered. "Line them up as far into the bog as they can go. They're to fire over the river and drive the Scots back until our men have secured the other side."

At first, Alex did not see anyone on the opposite hill-sides. Then he caught flashes of sun reflecting off armor. Straining, he noticed specks, dots, moving across the slopes. The number of Scots was a far cry from the mass of men and horses marching up behind him.

Cressingham summoned his senior knights. "Have our light cavalry cross in the advance force. Once we hold the opposite side, Wallace will flee. We must be ready to move quickly and give chase." Cressingham sat back and smiled. "King Edward will be very pleased if we capture Wallace today."

It gave Alex a chill to hear the trumpets sound and to watch so many cavalry and foot soldiers begin their march across the bridge. Archers standing in the bog let loose volley after volley, driving the few hundred Scots back up the far hill. The bridge landing was clear. Half of the archers joined the crossing, their green doublets easily spotted between the companies of foot soldiers. The lead cavalry stepped off the bridge onto the opposite side unimpeded. They fanned out into a defensive arc as hundreds of foot soldiers and archers filled in behind them.

Several quiet hours passed as thousands of troops marched over the wooden structure. About half of the men had crossed when Cressingham beckoned for his helmet. He put it on and lowered his visor. Now entirely encased in armor, he was impervious to arrows and swords – not that either was expected; the Scots were to be crushed before he reached the battle.

Cressingham smiled at the thought of King Edward's praise. "*Ye brought me Wallace's head, did ye? Crushed the Scottish rebellion? For these good deeds, I grant ye the lands of . . .*" Cressingham wondered whose estates those would be. With the deaths of so many from King Edward's battles in France, there was an abundance of land available.

Cressingham kicked the ribs of his armored horse and gave the signal to cross. His knights followed.

Hooves thudded on the bridge like a heavy rain. The timbers shook. Horses snorted through the nostril holes of their metal face shields. Sunshine pierced through gaps in the dark clouds, lighting whole sections of the landscape where, on the other side, a few Scots on horseback sat motionless high up the opposing slope, well out of range of the archers.

Alex wondered which of these solitary figures was Wallace and what was going through his mind as he looked down the valley to the overwhelming enemy forces below. Alex could not imagine how anyone could muster the resolve to stand up to such overwhelming might.

Packed uncomfortably close on the narrow bridge, the knights and their men rode in pairs. Raulf, with Alex in front of him, rode next to the knight with Meg. Raulf was silent, concentrating on keeping his lance from prodding the horse in front and from catching the rail posts.

Cressingham rode up ahead. The standard-bearer at his side held aloft a large and splendid royal blue flag depicting two golden lions that supported, between them, a red cross.

They had traversed the arch at the center and were nearing the end of the bridge when Alex heard a commotion from behind. He couldn't see around Raulf, but he heard shouts warning that a short section of the bridge had collapsed just past the arch. No one could turn around because their horses were shoulder to shoulder, nose to tail. Knights removed their helmets in an attempt to see behind them.

"How big a section fell?" one called, frustrated that the view was impeded.

"How many went in?" asked another.

Several knights cursed the bad luck of having the structure fail at this critical juncture. Foot soldiers were dispatched to run back and get answers. They had to squeeze past the packed horses, sometimes finding it easier to crawl under the horses' bellies.

Answers soon came, passed forward from soldier to soldier. "Four went down with the timbers. They're up to their necks in mud, their horses too."

"They'll have to strip their armor to climb out." Raulf slapped his thigh and laughed. "What a sight that will be!"

The knight next to him chuckled. "They'll be cursing, right enough. No one likes to bare their backside in front of the troops. But don't let 'm hear ye laugh, or ye'll make them furious!"

"The bridge will be back up in an hour or so," a knight behind them predicted. "A few lashed timbers, a row of boards, and they're done."

"They'll miss all the fun," Raulf said. "We'll have finished routing the Scots by then."

Alex glanced about nervously. If he was not mistaken, the fighting would start soon.

The command rang out for those beyond the break to continue crossing. The painfully slow stop-and-go shuffle started up again.

12

Lady Fortune

Because Alex did not wear a helmet, he was among the first to spot the Scots rising up from the marsh. He heard no signal, yet they came leaping and hollering through the muck as one, heading straight for the bridge, where the immobilized knights sat watching, dumbfounded.

Commands were shouted, and the English archers unleashed a hailstorm of arrows. Many found their mark.

Horrified, Alex watched as men went down. Some curled up under their shields, an arrow sticking out from some part of their body. Others writhed, twitched, and then lay still.

Alex felt sick. He heard screams from both men and horses, but he could not see what was happening with so many knights blocking his view. It seemed the Scots who had leaped up from the muck were attacking the bridge somewhere behind him.

Raulf let out a torrent of curses, but neither he nor any of the nearby knights on their heavy warhorses could turn or do anything to help those behind.

A crier called, "Foot soldiers are needed. Tell Cressingham."

The cry was repeated up the line.

"The knights who fell into the bog wouldn't have had a chance," the knight next to Raulf said. "They were half out of their armor."

"They're attacking where the timbers gave way," someone behind Alex shouted. "Bring foot soldiers . . . now!"

"Hurry up, men!" Raulf called as soldiers came tramping down the bridge from the far side, pushing their way past nervously stamping horses. "Get those damn Scots!"

"They'll take care of that rabble in no time," a knight predicted confidently.

"We should take some alive and make an example of them," another suggested.

"How long will we have to sit 'ere?" complained another. "Why isn't anyone moving?"

A distant roar caught everyone's attention. From over the ridge came a wave of Scottish warriors. They leaped and shouted and hurled taunts, stopping their advance just out of range of the English archers.

A further movement caught Alex's eye. A column of Scots sprinted from behind a hill, heading straight for the bog. Archers fired at them, but they kept coming.

"They've caught us in a bad way," a knight called in dismay. "The men behind us will be no help at all, and we're stuck on this damn bridge."

"Not to worry," another scoffed. "We have enough men landed on the far side to hold off these savages."

Alex sensed that the tenor had changed. This was turning into a real battle.

The Scots kept coming. The ones in the lead reached the bridge at the far side, shouting and hurling spears and rocks at the armored knights perched on their horses. Weighed down by their armor, foot soldiers clustered in the fringes of the shallow mud, reluctant to go into the deeper bog where the more nimble mud-covered madmen would have an advantage.

The knights jabbed with their lances. The Scots ducked and weaved. When one succeeded in grabbing hold of a lance, others helped pull the lance from the knight's hands. Each captured lance was turned against the knights. Legs were jabbed and horses collapsed, the knights crashing down with them.

Alex could no longer see what was happening up ahead, but he could hear the huge commotion of clanging metal and screams. It was as if all hell had broken loose.

Raulf and the knights around Cressingham were holding their own against the Scots in the bog, although the glorious banner was swaying precariously.

Alex could only sit and watch, sickened as Raulf impaled a Scot with his lance. Raulf yanked his lance out of the first Scot and stuck it into the shoulder of another. A few more jabs from Raulf and they both went down, their mouths gaping in agony.

Foot soldiers hurried back to assist the knights, squeezing between the big warhorses and stabbing their swords at Scots who came close to the bridge. By sheer weight of numbers, some foot soldiers were forced off the edge and into the bog to fight the Scots deep in the squelching muck. Swords clashed. Gashes appeared where men were struck. A severed arm lay in the mud. Stabbed men doubled over, fell, and the fight continued on top of them.

Alex watched as some not yet dead were trampled, their shrieks ending suddenly when they were pushed under the wet brackish mud.

Cressingham's horse let out an awful scream and buckled. To Alex's astonishment, William Wallace sprang up from under the horse and buried his dagger deep into the slit of Cressingham's visor. He twisted the dagger with both hands before pulling it out with a spurt of blood.

The terrified standard-bearer leaped off the far side of his horse. The glorious flag he was carrying fell into the mud.

Raulf thrust his lance toward Wallace's unprotected back. With a shout, Alex grabbed hold of the lance and dropped off the horse. Moments later, a suit of armor came crashing down next to him. It was Raulf, his vacant eyes staring at nothing.

Alex was suddenly hoisted into the air. In a blur of wind, screams, and clashing metal, he saw that Meg was pressed against him, her cries merging with his own. Wallace held them both with one arm as he fought his way out of the thick of battle with the other. The sounds receded, and they were dropped unceremoniously onto the ground. Wallace stood panting heavily.

A Scottish noble wearing light armor under a flowing cape came striding up to them, guards at his side.

"Why must ye persist in plunging into the midst of battle?" he asked Wallace irritably. "As a leader that Scotland can ill afford to lose, ye are to direct the fighting, not take part in it."

Wallace grinned. "Aye, Sir Andrew. I cannae argue with that, but old habits die hard. And besides, wherever I go, someone always seems to watch my back." Wallace clapped Alex about the shoulders, almost knocking him over. Bending down, he added, "Thanks, laddie, that lance almost got me."

Bending down to Alex's eye level probably saved Wallace's life. An arrow flew overhead and struck Sir Andrew instead. Heads turned to find its source, aghast that the enemy had managed to get so close. An archer was spotted. Appearing to be in no hurry, he turned and loped away, disappearing among the Scottish fighters.

Alex felt his blood run cold. It was the bowman of Warenne's four agents, the hook-nosed one who attempted to shoot at Wallace's scout troupe as Alex and Meg were being rescued from Crawford.

Wallace's face twisted in fury. "Get him!"

Men sprinted after the archer. Sir Andrew remained standing despite the arrow protruding from his chest. His eyes were locked on the battle below. "How bad is it?" he asked calmly.

Wallace glanced over the field. "Actually, it's going well – unfolding just as we planned."

"I mean, the arrow, ye idiot!"

Wallace stooped to examine it. "Well, it hasnae gone in too far. Here, allow me." Wallace grasped the arrow and gave it a swift tug. It came out easily, the metal arrowhead remaining stuck in the links of the chain mail.

Sir Andrew grimaced but did not cry out. He spat, and a squirt of blood splattered over the stones at his feet. "Bah.

Ye go into the thick of the battle, and it's me who catches an arrow."

Wallace pushed a cloth under the chain mail and pressed it over the wound. "I think it's best if ye oversaw the rest of the battle while seated," he said, easing Sir Andrew down onto robes his attendants had laid out on the ground. "I'm going to take a few hundred around Stirling and attack the English on the other side. It will take me about half a day to get there. By then, your men will have secured the bridge."

Sir Andrew waved his arm to fend off the assistance. "Good God! There are more English on the other side than there are here –" He broke off and coughed, his face twisting in pain. The cloth over his wound turned red.

Wallace watched sympathetically as Sir Andrew's men eased him against a hastily erected backrest. "Aye," he said when Sir Andrew recovered, "but they will be in a bad state, having just watched thousands of their brethren die on our side without them being able to help. It is my hope that they will scatter and we will have the opportunity to pursue their leader, Earl Warenne."

"Ye are the most audacious fool I have ever met, Wallace." Sir Andrew sent him a weak, wry smile. "But Lady Fortune smiles upon ye in ways the rest of us can only dream of. Go! We will finish the job here and await your signal."

Wallace gave orders and horses were gathered. Calls rang out for men to assemble and prepare to ride. Alex ran to where some abandoned horses were pacing and kicking about in a state of panic, hemmed in by fighting on one side and the river on the other. After a few failed attempts, Alex finally caught the reins of a horse. He brought it around and swung himself into its saddle. The terrified horse bolted past the fighters.

"Quick, Meg, climb on the back," Alex panted as he brought the steaming horse under control. "Wallace and his men are already far ahead."

"There are injured here who need help," Meg said, ignoring Alex's outstretched hand.

"But Wallace is heading south toward Berwick. That's where my parents are," Alex said. "Let someone else care for the injured."

"Who?" Meg looked around.

"I don't know. . . . Those that are less injured, nearby villagers –"

Meg shook her head. "Good luck in finding your parents," she called. "Hurry, or ye won't catch Wallace!"

Feeling torn, Alex turned away. He had to leave Meg. If he didn't ride with Wallace's men now, he had no way of making it south to Berwick.

13

LEFT BEHIND

Alex pushed his horse to overtake the group. He received angry stares and sharp words as he squeezed past men already riding as many abreast as the trail would comfortably permit. It took a lot of nudging and maneuvering, but Alex finally reached William Wallace.

A scowling guard with a matted beard positioned his horse to block Alex. "What's your business here?" he growled.

"I'd like to speak with William Wallace."

"No one gets to speak to the Wallace without a good reason," the guard snapped.

"Well, look who's here!" Wallace's voice boomed over the drone of many clopping hooves. He waved for Alex to come and ride alongside. A man with a neatly trimmed beard and expensive armor leaned forward as Alex approached.

"Who is this lad?" he asked Wallace.

"Sir John de Graham, this is Alex, a lad who keeps the strangest company I have ever encountered." Wallace paused. "If I were to tell ye all of it, ye'd think I was mad."

"But I do think ye're mad," Graham stated matter-of-factly.

Wallace laughed. "Ye dinnae ken the half of it! What if I told ye that this here lad is a traveler of time who comes to us from the future?"

Graham glanced sympathetically at Alex. "Does he truly believe that to be the case? He seems all right in every other respect."

"Not only does he believe it," Wallace went on, "but so do I. Just the other day, one of my scout troupes reported to me that this lad foretold of a great battle where the English would cross a narrow bridge –"

"A soothsayer!" Graham examined Alex with renewed interest. "Rarely do we hear of one so young."

"And this lad was with a number of others who went into the caves beneath Duncragglin Castle and disappeared." Wallace snapped his fingers. "Just like that."

"Wizardry?" Graham looked troubled. "Do ye think there's devil worship going on?"

"Nae, there's no sign of that. Worry not, M'Lord, he's just an innocent lad who has come to us from another time, that's all." Wallace gave Graham an exaggerated wink.

Alex stared at the trail ahead, horrified that Wallace was so casually revealing his time-traveling past. He knew what happened to people who were suspected of worshipping the devil, and it wasn't pretty.

Wallace reached over and clapped Alex's shoulder. "Relax, young lad, ye're with friends. And now that ye're here, do ye have any further words of wisdom for me?"

"How about invading England?" Alex suggested brightly.

Graham roared. "Oh-ho, that is excellent. Now I've heard everything!"

Wallace gave it some thought. "Actually, that's a brilliant idea," he declared. "How better to teach King Edward a lesson than to bring the battle to his own lands? There has been enough bloodshed in Scotland. Each time they come to fight us, the farms of good Scots are overrun and we are left bereft. As a result of today's battles, the people of Scotland will go hungry again. I say we go down there, take what we need from English farms, and bring it back to Scotland."

Graham was stunned. "Ye're not serious," he said quietly.

"I'm not suggesting we attack London." Wallace laughed. "Maybe down to Newcastle – or thereabouts. King Edward is in France the-now. He would be caught totally by surprise, and there would be no one to oppose us."

"Wallace, come to your senses," Graham pleaded. "Just think of what King Edward would do in retaliation."

"Is it anything he wouldnae do anyway?" Wallace retorted angrily. "He's killed every last Scot that had the misfortune of living in Berwick; he's invaded our lands and proclaimed himself Lord Paramount of Scotland. It's not enough to repel an attack, as we have just done. We must show him what we're capable of! Maybe then he will learn to leave Scotland to Scots."

"We'd need more men."

"Aye, once we're done here, we'll regroup. Then we'll pay them a visit they will never forget."

Graham snapped a long twig from a tree as he brushed past. *Scotland invade England?* The idea was more audacious than anything he had ever heard. He thrust the twig down the back of his armor to reach an itch.

"Sir Wallace?" Alex said politely.

Wallace leaned in to listen.

"Lord Cressingham told me that King Edward has a prisoner in Hog Tower who has a garment with tiny metal clasps."

"Oh-ho," Graham laughed, still giving his back a scratch. "And now the lad is telling us he's had an audience with Lord Cressingham? That's a good one. Next he'll tell us he directed Cressingham over the bridge."

Wallace silenced him with a stare. Leaving Graham shifting uncomfortably in his saddle, he turned back to Alex. "Go on," he said gently.

"That prisoner might be one of my parents."

"Ah." Wallace looked sympathetic.

"If those clasps are what I think they are, they're part of something called a zipper. They won't be invented for a very long time."

Graham spoke up. "I've heard of this garment. It has a sliding mechanism that brings the tiny clasps together to –"

"Yes, that's it!" Alex exclaimed.

A dark look spread over Graham's face.

"Apologies, M'Lord," Alex mumbled, bowing his head.

"I would be very surprised if the man I heard has this garment was your father," Graham said coldly, urging his horse to pull forward from the group.

"Give us time, lad," Wallace said quietly. "Berwick is one of the places we'll conquer on our way into England. We'll find out who's in Hog Tower."

Up ahead, Graham stood in his stirrups, shielding his eyes to see in the distance. "There's a remnant of the English army," he said, pointing to a small band of foot soldiers. "They're running for England."

Wallace motioned for Alex to fall back. He surveyed the surrounding hills and sent a few scouts up either side. Finally satisfied that they were not being lured into a trap, he signaled his men to charge.

Seeing that there was no place to run, the English foot soldiers flung away their weapons and dropped to the ground. The Scots ran among the prone English soldiers and snatched up their swords and shields. They soon had the English stripped of every scrap of armor and were arguing over who got what.

Wallace shouted over the bickering and ordered the men to assemble the English soldiers.

The captives clutched one another as they stumbled into position.

"Even though death is what ye deserve for invading our lands," Wallace called down to them, "today, ye will be spared. What ye will do is go straight back to England, stopping nowhere and rejoining no army. And when ye get home, ye will tell your families and everyone who will listen that the good people in the kingdom of Scotland are to be left alone!"

Wallace motioned for his men to step away from the captives. The English soldiers warily backed down the hill. Once clear of the surrounding Scots, they turned and ran.

Sir Graham watched, bemused, as the English sprinted over the rocky terrain, their undershirts flapping in the breeze. "Do ye really think they'll tell anyone that we're merciful folk who are to be left alone?"

"No, of course not." Wallace laughed. "But they'll spread terror among the English far better than a few silent dead."

They rode until near dark, the Firth of Forth occasionally visible on their left. Wallace chose a dale where they would be hidden while resting, and he signaled his men to stop.

"Post sentries on those hills," he ordered, pointing to strategic points around them. "There are large bodies of the English army still about, and I dinnae want them stumbling upon our camp, understood?"

Exhausted from a long day of battle and hard riding, the men thankfully reined in their horses. They dismounted to find places to tether them.

Alex untied his horse's saddle and slid it from the horse.

"Look after your horse, and your horse will look after ye," the man next to him quipped as he brushed his horse. He stopped to take a bite from a strip of dried meat.

"Where did you get that?" Alex asked, his hunger pains too strong to ignore. It had been many hours since he'd had a small bowl of watery gruel with the English soldiers.

"If ye havenae brought your own, that's your problem," the man said, turning his back.

The men around Alex were quickly spreading out their saddle blankets to claim the best spots on the bumpy ground. Alex dropped his blanket in what looked to be a reasonably flat hollow.

"Away with ye, laddie." A man waved dismissively. "That's my spot."

"I don't see your name on it," Alex protested.

The man grasped a corner of Alex's blanket and flung it away. "Begone," he growled.

Outraged, Alex went to retrieve his blanket. The man spread his blanket over Alex's spot and laughed with his friends.

Alex glanced around. Not far off, Wallace was conferring with his lieutenants. Alex thought about complaining, but he realized how ridiculous he would sound. With a sigh, he trudged away. It wasn't until he reached the edge of camp that he found a place to lie down.

Alex curled up on one half of his blanket and pulled the rest over him. Too exhausted to care about the rocks digging into his side or the scratchy wool that reeked of horse, he was asleep in minutes.

———◆◆◆———

Alex was awoken by voices in what felt like the dead of night. Lifting his head, he saw shadowy figures stepping between the sleeping men.

"Time to ride. Up ye get," they called. A boot crunched next to Alex and he felt a sharp prod in his side.

There was a dim red glow in the sky. Dawn was not far off. Throughout the camp, men were shaking out their blankets and getting their horses ready.

Alex rose to his feet, hoisted his blanket over his shoulder, and made his way into the pack of men. His horse was not where he had left it tethered, and he didn't see the saddle. With increasing concern, he broadened his search.

He saw a horse that looked like the one he rode yesterday, but a friend of the man who had tossed his blanket was already saddling it up. Although Alex had ridden the horse a good part of the previous day, he had not paid too much attention to its markings. Nor did he know the horse's name.

Men were mounting their horses when Alex finally spotted his saddle. It was not where he had left it. Nearby was a horse that no one was tending. It was the only unclaimed horse left, and it definitely wasn't the one Alex had ridden the day before. It stood with its front leg slightly bent.

Suddenly Alex knew what had happened. He ran through the crowded pack until he found the men from the night before. "Hey, give me back my horse!" he demanded, grabbing the reins of the one he was now sure was his.

The man pulled back sharply on the reins. The skittish horse pranced sideways, and the man gave Alex a kick that sent him flying.

"Dinnae touch my horse again." The man raised his whip. "Stop makin' a fuss and get on your own horse . . . that is, if ye ken what's good for ye."

Alex scrambled back from the hooves trampling all around him. The men were starting to leave. Alex ran to find Wallace, but he had long since mounted and was too far ahead to hear his shouts.

He watched helplessly as the men rode past, none stopping to ask why he wasn't on a horse, no one offering to have him ride behind them.

Alex made his way over to the lame horse and stooped to examine its front leg. As he suspected, the knee was badly swollen. The horse must have twisted it the day before, and it had stiffened up overnight. There was no way it could carry a rider today.

Looking up, Alex saw that he was on his own. The last of Wallace's riders were rounding the bend, disappearing from view. He did not know where he was – just that Edinburgh was somewhere east.

There was no point standing around. Even if Wallace were to learn he was missing, Wallace wouldn't turn around and search for him. He had far more important things to do.

Alex coaxed the horse to hobble to a nearby stream. He knelt down and took a long drink. It lessened the hunger pains in his stomach. He rubbed water over his face and around the back of his neck. He had to find something to eat – and soon.

After giving the horse a farewell pat, Alex set out in the direction of the rising sun.

———•◆•———

The sun was overhead, emerging now and then from between low-lying clouds, when Alex came upon a village that was little more than a few dwellings clustered about an intersection. It lay in a valley with large plots of blackened, scorched crops.

Alex hurried to catch up to a man who was crossing a field, with a hoe over his shoulder. "Pardon me, sire, but would there be any work I could do in exchange for a meal?" he asked hopefully.

The man shot Alex a withering glance. "Look at this," he answered with a wave of his bony arm. "All my crops have been burned to the ground. What am I to feed my bairns? Go ask someone else. There's nothing for ye here."

Dismayed, Alex sought out other farmers, but everywhere he turned, it was the same. The only food that was left was hidden by villagers or still in the ground.

That gave Alex an idea. Looking about to make sure no one was watching, he ducked behind some bushes and climbed over a low stone wall. The crops in the fields may have been burned before the English came, but there must be something left worth eating.

Alex knelt to examine the blackened stalks. He had no idea what they were, but he tried nibbling on one anyway. It tasted terrible. He picked up a stick and hacked at the damp, clumpy soil to see if perhaps its roots were edible. Up came a small tuber. Alex knocked the dirt off and took a quick bite. It was hard and crunchy. He wolfed it down and dug up another, hoping they wouldn't give him a bellyache. It was a chance he had to take.

Alex wasn't aware of the farmer approaching until he was grabbed from behind.

"Come with me, thief." The man yanked Alex to his feet.

"But, sire, the crops are burned – they are of no use to anyone," Alex protested, trying to squirm out of the man's grasp.

Keeping a firm grip on Alex's shirt, the grim-faced man marched him into the village. People came out of their houses to watch as Alex was dragged into the town square and thrown sprawling to the ground.

"First we had to endure our fields being burned by our own Scottish countrymen," the farmer announced loudly, keeping Alex pinned to the ground with his foot. "Next the

English invaders came through our town, abusing our women and stealing our food. And now we have thieves coming to scavenge what little we have left."

"But I see just the one," a woman called out over the ruckus.

"Aye, one the-now, but do ye really think he's alone? There will be many more out there just waiting for us to be weak. We need to make an example of this one so the others will stay away."

Angrily muttering their agreement, men thumped the ground with the ends of their digging forks.

"Off with his head," one suggested. Others murmured their approval.

"What kind of example would that be?" countered the man who had captured Alex. "Even if we took his head, stuck it on a pike, and displayed it outside of town, it would be for naught. The crows would be on him straightaway, and he would be unrecognizable within an hour. The other thieves wouldnae have any idea who we put out there or why. Nae, I say we cut off his hand and send him back out to them as a warning. They'll see we mean business once he shows up with his bloody stump."

The villagers argued among themselves. Horrified, Alex realized they were split between beheading him and cutting off his hand. No one suggested he be let go.

"Make way. Coming through!" someone called.

The circle parted to make room for a man rolling a tree stump. He had an ax tucked under his belt. He set the stump upright next to where Alex lay pressed to the dirt and gave it a twist to fix a wobble.

"Right then," he said, swiveling his shoulders. "I'm ready! Which is it going to be, his head or his hand?"

Dizzy with fear, Alex looked at the faces around him. There was not a sympathetic glance to be found. Children peered wide-eyed from around their mothers. Older boys and girls wriggled between one another and argued over who got to sit in the best spots. The villagers chatted happily.

"We'll start with the hand then, shall we?" the axman said.

A hush fell over the crowd as Alex's violently shaking arm was held forcibly over the stump. The man held his ax at arm's length to gauge the distance.

A voice called from afar, "Pardon me, good people, but could someone tell me which road leads to Haddington?"

The villagers turned to see a black-robed priest on horseback clopping toward their gathering. Not far behind was an entourage that included an armed guard and a covered carriage drawn by two horses.

The axman paused. Straightening, he pointed to the far end of the village. "Take the fork to your left; it's past the next bend."

"Anyone in need of last rites?" the priest asked.

"There's no need," a farmer replied. "We're only taking off his hand."

"Only his hand?" The priest sounded disappointed. "Are ye sure his offense wasn't greater?"

"Well, perhaps." The farmer looked uncertain. "He did steal food from our fields . . . but we want to make an example of him, and it's best if the example wanders about and shows himself to would-be thieves. Otherwise, what would be the point?"

"Indeed." The priest nodded gravely.

The man with the ax glanced about impatiently. Seeing a nod from Alex's captor, he raised his ax and aimed carefully.

To Alex, the villagers seemed to be spinning in a sea of dark spots. Voices faded in and out, and he no longer understood what was being said. He heard shouts off in the distance, and then everything went dark.

14

BLACK DOUGLAS

"Happy birthday, King Alex."

Alex watched his smiling father place a paper crown on his head. Someone dimmed the lights. His friends, seated around the table, chattered excitedly.

A chocolate cake, lit with five candles, was held up by his mother. "Happy birthday to you," she sang, and everyone joined in. A friend sang, "You live in a zoo." Someone else put in, "How old are you now?" and "You look like a cow." Giggles erupted all around.

"Blow them out!" a little girl called as his mother lowered the cake.

"Make a wish!"

Alex squeezed his eyes shut. What should he wish for? *A new game? More building blocks?* His friend Marty had a remote-control car that could do flips and keep right on going. He'd wish for one like that. Alex took a breath and blew hard.

His mother handed out paper plates and napkins. Everyone cheered.

"Cut the cake, cut the cake, cut the cake," the children chanted, pounding time on the table.

———•◆•———

"Yes, cut me a piece of that cake, would ye, my dear?"

Alex felt himself rocking from side to side, a scratchy blanket tucked under his chin. He was in a carriage – that much he knew. *But what carriage? And whose?* Alex quickly felt under the covers. Thank God: both his hands were still there. Wait, was he dreaming? Or was his birthday a dream? No, that had really happened. He remembered being crowned King Alex during a birthday party before his parents disappeared.

"Oh, look, he's waking up. Do something with him, would ye, Isabelle?"

"Yes, M'Lady."

Alex felt a damp cloth pat his forehead. He struggled to sit up but was dizzy when he moved. A young lady peered anxiously into his face.

"Careful. Ye're very weak the-now. Here, try having a sip." The young lady pulled the stopper from a clay jug and tipped some water into a goblet. "Not too much."

"Is he ready to leave the carriage yet?" asked the other lady, who Alex saw was clearly pregnant. She sat on the padded bench opposite him, nibbling a piece of cake and cupping her hand underneath to keep crumbs from landing on her fine dress.

"It will likely take a bit longer for him to gather his strength, M'Lady," Isabelle replied. "Not only has he had a terrible shock, he's suffered quite a stomach upset from whatever he ate last."

"Well, as long as he doesn't do any more of that moaning and carrying on in that strange dialect of his. Oh, that was *dreadful* to listen to."

"Yes, M'Lady. I think he's past that the-now."

"Good." She turned her attention to the goings-on outside the carriage, her interlaced fingers resting on her enlarged belly. "Surely it must be time for us to stop for tea. I'm famished."

Alex managed to sit up. He took the goblet Isabelle offered into his trembling hands and had a sip. The water settled in his stomach.

"That's enough," Isabelle said firmly. She tugged the goblet from Alex's hands and held it out of reach. "Give it a few minutes."

Alex licked his dry cracked lips. His head was starting to clear. "Where am I?" he croaked.

"Ye are in the company of the Douglas," the older woman said. "Ye have had the good fortune of having caught the attention of our young bishop, William Lamberton, who seems to forever be interfering in the lives of others." She sniffed and resumed her gaze outside.

"By 'interfering,'" whispered Isabelle, "Lady Eleanor means 'saving.'"

From outside the carriage came calls of "easy, easy." The wooden brake creaked and groaned. The carriage jiggled a few more times as it rolled over uneven ground, then stopped.

Alex expected the ladies to do something, but they remained still. Moments later, a quick rap sounded on the carriage door and it swung open.

"Teatime, M'Lady," a squire said with great flourish and a bow.

Lady Eleanor took his hand and stepped from the carriage. Remarkably, in the short time they'd been stationary, the men had made the semblance of a camp, with a table covered in a fine cloth held down in the breeze by neatly arranged clay goblets and baskets of food.

Holding her skirts up just enough to keep them from getting snagged, Lady Eleanor headed over the rough ground to a tent erected not far from the carriage. Isabelle followed a few steps behind.

Alex's legs shook as he stepped from the carriage's riding board onto the stool that had been placed there for the ladies.

There was a joyful cry. "Alex!"

"Meg?" Alex's jaw dropped. "How . . . what?"

And then he was wrapped in Meg's big hug. "It's so good t' see ye looking better," she beamed.

"But, but, but . . . ," Alex spluttered. "Weren't you helping the injured?"

Glancing around, he saw men tending horses, one building a fire, others emerging from behind shrubs still adjusting their tunics – none appeared to be recovering from any wounds.

"Aye, that was before the very kind Bishop Lamberton saw to it that the injured were cared for," Meg replied happily. "And when I pleaded to come with him, he said I could as long as I would assist with the ladies." Lowering her voice, Meg added, "It seems that properly caring for the ladies can be a bit of a struggle for these men. Ye'll have to pardon me the-now, but tea *must* be ready when they return from their toilet." Meg opened a basket and began arranging plates and cutlery on the table.

"Over here, lad."

Alex turned. A man in his mid-twenties, with thick hair shaped into a bowl cut, beckoned for Alex to join him and his gathering of guards. Alex approached, and the man thrust a cooked pigeon breast into his hands.

"Last I saw, ye were quite the center of attention. It cost us several loaves to convince the villagers to hand ye over – that and a solemn promise to administer proper justice."

"Are you Bishop Lamberton?" Alex asked cautiously.

"Aye, that's what they call me," the man grimaced, "although I've yet to be consecrated by the good Pope Boniface. For now, I am merely the humble chancellor of Glasgow Cathedral." He nudged Alex. "Eat up, lad – ye need to get your strength back."

Alex sank his teeth into the pigeon. Its meager strips of meat soon gone, he cracked the greasy bones to suck out the marrow.

"Here, have more." Bishop Lamberton passed him a pigeon leg, complete with claws. "It's not as if ye've been raiding *our* larders lately." He shot an exaggerated wink to the nearby men.

"I wasn't raiding," Alex protested. "The villagers' crops were destroyed by William Wallace's men to keep food from the English. I was just, um . . . finishing the job."

"Perfect!" Bishop Lamberton laughed. "And, as ye were merely continuing the work of Wallace, who in turn was acting on behalf of our exiled King John Balliol, that means ye are innocent of any wrongdoing, is that what ye are saying?"

"I think so. . . ."

Bishop Lamberton turned to the men who were eating
nearby. "What say ye? Innocent?" He gave a thumbs-up. "Or
guilty?" He gave a thumbs-down.

The men answered with a half-interested thumbs-up,
mostly to follow the bishop's prompted example.

"Well, then." The bishop smiled. "I have fulfilled my
word. Justice has been served. Ye are hereby declared an innocent man, er, boy, and are free to go. However, ye're welcome
to stay with us a bit longer – if ye care to go to Berwick."

"Thank you, Sir!" Alex nodded. "That is where I'm
headed."

"Lord," the bishop said quietly. "Ye're to call me Lord,
not Sir."

Thank you, Sir Lord Bishop – I mean, Bishop Sir . . .
Lord."

The guards burst out laughing. Flustered, Alex felt the
color rise to his cheeks. He busied himself with eating.

"Soup's ready," called a guard who doubled as a cook.

The men got out their bowls and stepped up for a ladle-
ful. They sat about on the ground, slurping contentedly. No
one had a spoon.

The soup smelled delicious. Alex watched them eat.

A guard threw his head back for one last slurp and then
held out his bowl. "Here," he said gruffly, letting out a burp
against the back of his hand. "Give it back when ye're done."

A boy's cry came from Lady Eleanor's table. "No, I
willnae!"

Heads turned. A scowling boy, perhaps a year or two
younger than Alex, stood shaking his long black hair back
and forth, his arms folded across his chest.

Her face flushed with irritation, Lady Eleanor was pointing emphatically for him to sit next to her.

With hidden smirks, the men looked back to their soup. None wanted to catch the wrath of Lady Eleanor.

"Ye cannae be telling me what to do – ye're not my real mother!" The boy's bottom lip protruded defiantly. "I shall eat with my men. If ye need me, that's where I can be found."

They glared at each other for several moments before Lady Eleanor waved him away. She dabbed her lips with a napkin and snapped for Meg to refill her glass.

The boy strode over to where the guards were finishing their tea. Catching sight of Alex, he stopped short.

"What are ye staring at?" he asked.

Alex took a sip of his soup, his fingers prodding a few chunky bits along to the edge of the bowl.

"I am James Douglas, son of Sir William Douglas le Hardi!" the boy squeaked. "And I demand an answer. Now, who are ye?"

Putting down his bowl, Alex stood and drew himself up to his full height. "I am Alex Macpherson the First, traveler through time from hundreds of years from now, friend and battle companion of William Wallace," he said as importantly as possible.

"Excellent!" the boy said. "I suspect we will get along very well, for I am otherwise known as Black Douglas, soon to be a great knight in the War of Scottish Independence."

The men tipped up their bowls to hide their smirks – including those who had finished their soup. Future commanders were known to have long memories.

The cook handed James a bowl of soup.

"So, what brings ye here?" James asked Alex.

"I'm looking for my parents," Alex replied. "They've come from the future, like me. I'm headed for Berwick because I've been told they might be in Hog Tower."

"Hog Tower!" James lowered his soup in surprise. "Why, that's where my father is!"

"What's your father doing there?"

"King Edward was angered to learn that my father supported William Wallace, so he's locked him up once again," James said proudly. "My father's been in Hog Tower so often, they've started calling it Douglas Tower."

"If King Edward knows your father has fought against him, why doesn't he have him executed?"

"What, do ye think my father is a peasant?" James asked haughtily. "King Edward would do well to persuade such a high-ranking lord as my father to be on his side!"

"Enough of your blethering, lads," Bishop Lamberton called. "It's time to go."

Alex returned the bowl to its owner. The men dismantled the table while Meg was still stacking the dishes. Within minutes, everything was securely packed away in the trunk at the back of the carriage.

Alex followed James to the front of the carriage. They climbed up to the driver's bench as the men readied their horses.

Meg gave a little wave as she followed the ladies into the carriage. "Dinnae make too much noise up there," she warned, pointing discretely at Lady Eleanor.

With the horses now hitched, the driver swung up onto the bench, the boys sliding out of his way. "Dinnae crowd me," he grumbled as he positioned himself in the center and took up the reins.

Alex and James left the bench and found a place to sit on the chests that were strapped down to the carriage roof.

"Let's rock and roll," Alex said, smiling.

"Aye, we'll do plenty of rocking – that's for sure," James said. "This carriage is none too steady up here. That serving girl didn't like it none. She'll be glad ye're better so she can ride inside the carriage again."

"Hyah!" The driver released the brake and cracked his whip. The carriage lurched forward.

15

BERWICK-UPON-TWEED

The carriage rumbled through Berwick's town gates and turned down a cobblestone street lined with tall row houses.

"What a grand town!" Meg exclaimed, glad to have joined the boys up top for this last stretch of their ride. From her lofty perch, she could see into the windows of the houses as the carriage rattled past.

"Ha!" James laughed. "This is nothing. London and Paris are far grander!"

"You've been to Paris?" Alex asked, surprised.

"No," James admitted. "But that's where my father's wife wants to send me. I'm to go there with Bishop Lamberton so I can get a *proper* education while things settle down."

"Such fine homes," Meg said. "But why are so many empty?"

"The Scots who owned them are all dead," James replied. "King Edward wants the houses given to the English, but the English dinnae want to come up here because they're afraid we're going to get our revenge one day. And they're right!"

The carriage came to a halt before a large home on the town square. A squire dismounted and banged on the door. A hatch slid open and a guard's face peered out, framed by the narrow opening.

"Lady Eleanor is here with Bishop Lamberton," the squire said. "Bring your master at once."

The hatch slid shut, and the squire was left to glare at the door for several minutes before it was flung open. A man came striding out, his robe billowing behind him.

"No one is to enter," he announced, punctuating his message with a decisive thump of his ornate staff.

"Pardon me?" the squire asked incredulously. "Are ye telling me that ye will deny entry to the lady of Sir William Douglas, governor of Berwick, noble lord of vast estates across the kingdoms of both England and Scotland?"

"I regret to inform Lady Eleanor that her Berwick estates have been forfeited by order of the king." The robed man turned to face the carriage. "I'm under orders to keep all and any from entering this house."

Bishop Lamberton dismounted. He looked the richly robed man up and down, then turned his gaze to the empty houses about the square. "It appears ye have done rather well for yourself," he commented. "At least compared with most others who once lived in this town."

"I am alive – can ye fault me for that?" The man shifted uncomfortably.

"Lord Douglas is not likely to remain imprisoned for long. Surely ye realize he willnae take kindly to the treatment being accorded his lady?"

"Things have changed," the man said. "King Edward has

ordered that Lord Douglas be taken to the Tower of London with the next available armed transport."

"Quietly, please!" Bishop Lamberton glanced toward the carriage to see if Lady Eleanor had heard. He rubbed his chin. "That is bad news, indeed. However, we cannot have Lady Eleanor turned out into the streets. What do ye suggest?"

The man reached into an inner pocket and handed Bishop Lamberton a key. "Merchant Frazer's house down by the harbor stands empty. I believe ye'll find it well appointed. Lady Eleanor should be sufficiently comfortable there."

"And where is Merchant Frazer?"

The man paused. "Ye will recall that when King Edward came here last, he was in a great rage and ordered that every inhabitant be killed?"

Bishop Lamberton nodded.

"Well, Merchant Frazer and his family did not leave in time."

"Ah." Looking disturbed, Bishop Lamberton swung back onto his horse.

"I strongly recommend that Lady Eleanor does not linger in Berwick," the man added. "She must make her way to Paris before King Edward learns of her presence and decides to have her join her husband – or Merchant Frazer."

Bishop Lamberton waved to catch the carriage driver's attention, then pointed in the direction of the harbor. The driver turned his horses and coaxed them into a trot. As the group left the square, the carriage curtain fell closed.

———•◆•———

"The Tower of London?" Meg's mouth gaped open. "Is that where, where –"

"They pry out people's eyeballs and pop off their finger-nails?" James snapped. "Yes, that's the place."

"I . . . I . . . I'm sorry, James." Meg rubbed her nose awkwardly. "But they won't do that to your father . . . will they?"

"Many who go there dinnae come back," James said.

They rode the rest of the way along the cobblestone streets in silence. The carriage passed under an arch and headed down a hill toward the river Tweed, the driver pulling the brake to keep the carriage from overtaking the horses. He directed the carriage around several tight corners, and they came upon a riverfront street. Moored a short distance off-shore were North Sea merchant vessels, some with as many as three masts. Their bows pointed into the wind, waves slap-ping at their sides.

The carriage stopped before a grand house overlooking the port. Next to a tall door framed by pillars, an ornately carved wooden plaque stated that this was the home of the merchant Frazer.

Now deceased, Alex thought glumly. He wondered where in the house the merchant and his family had been slaughtered.

"There's Berwick Castle." James pointed up a steep hill that faced the river and town. "See the tower to the right? *That* is where they're keeping my father."

Alex stared. Hog Tower. After all this time searching for his parents, was he really so close?

"There's only one thing to do," James said. "We have to help him escape."

Alex smiled.

———— ·•·• ————

The Frazer house was grand, but it did not have its own stables and coach house. After the guards had hauled the chests from the carriage roof and brought them into the house, the carriage and the horses had to be transferred to a nearby livery stable. Bishop Lamberton gave the squire enough coins to pay for the guards' dinners and bunks at the seamen's inn – with some left over for a few ales. He cautioned him to keep the men together. Sailors poured back ales in the many back-alley drinking holes, and there was always a risk of trouble.

The house's central staircase was wide enough for Alex, James, and Meg to climb side by side. James tried a door at the landing and found it opened into a narrow set of servants' stairs leading back downward.

"This way, James," Bishop Lamberton beckoned from the top of the main stairs. "There's an attic room on the next floor that we can share. This floor will be for Lady Eleanor and her assistants, Meg included. Alex can find himself accommodation in the servants' quarters out back."

James didn't budge. "If the servants' quarters are good enough for Alex, they are good enough for me."

"Do as ye will." Bishop Lamberton shrugged. "But bear in mind, we'll be employing a few servants, and it will be noisy back there with their comings and goings."

Lady Eleanor's attendant, Isabelle, called for Meg to

assist with preparing Lady Eleanor for what the Lady complained was her much-overdue bath. Alex and James disappeared down the servants' stairs, which opened up into a large kitchen. Water for Lady Eleanor's bath was being heated in a pot on a coal-fired stove. Leading off the kitchen were a few small windowless rooms, each with two beds, a table, and chairs.

James stuck his head into each room, stopping at the one nearest the back door. "This will do," he announced. "Let's put my trunk in it so that the servants will see this one's taken."

Alex helped James carry the chest from the entrance hall. "It's heavy," he complained, gripping the handle with both hands. "What on earth have you got in it?"

"I'm to be sent off to Paris," James said, puffing as he struggled with his end. "So I brought everything I thought I'd need."

The boys set the chest down in the center of the room. Taking a key from his inner pocket, James unlocked the padlock and lifted the lid.

Alex raised an eyebrow. The garments inside the chest included finery with a frilly collar and hosiery leggings.

"Oh, that's in case I meet the king of France," James said hastily, spotting Alex's expression, "or one of his dukes or something. My good stuff is down at the bottom."

James casually tossed his neatly folded clothes onto a bed. Reaching into the trunk with both hands, he paused for dramatic effect, then held up a chain mail shirt.

"Nice!" Alex admired the closely meshed loops. "It must have taken ages to make this thing. Where'd you get it?"

"It's from my father," James replied proudly. "He said that a shirt like this has saved his life many times. Do ye want to try it on?"

Alex tugged it over his head.

"That's backward." Exasperated, James motioned for him to turn around. He adjusted the shirt and fastened the loops at the back. "There," he said admiringly. "Neither sword nor arrow can kill ye the-now."

Alex swung his arms experimentally. The shirt flowed with a slight rustle. It was a bit big for him, but not as heavy as he thought.

"My father said I will grow into it. It's very dear, and he isn't going to buy me one every year. Here, try on the rest."

James passed Alex a hooded tunic bearing the Douglas three-starred crest and a belt. Next he brought out leather arm protectors and a helmet with a chain mail fringe.

Soon Alex looked every inch the elegant young knight. He wished he still had his crossbow.

"And now," James began solemnly, "it is time."

He lifted a short, sheathed sword from the trunk. Taking hold of the leather scabbard firmly with one hand, he slid out the sword with the other.

Alex stared with admiration. The blade was keen and sharp, and it had a finely wrapped hilt that would give it a solid grip. Green and red stones glinted from the crossguard.

"Kneel," James ordered.

Alex did as he was told.

"Alex Macpherson the First, friend and battle companion of William Wallace, traveler through time from hundreds of years from now . . ." James rested the flat edge of the sword on one of Alex's shoulders, then on the other. "I hereby declare ye to be Sir Alex, comrade in arms to Black Douglas, famed leader of the War of Scottish Independence. Rise, Sir Alex-to-be."

Alex stood and James clapped him on the shoulder.

"Excellent!" he proclaimed. "We shall do battle together, starting with an assault on Berwick Castle, where we shall bring the enemy to its knees."

"Great. When do we start?" Alex rubbed his hands together.

James frowned. "First give me my things back."

Alex and James were still making invasion plans when, in the early afternoon of the following day, a group of riders stopped before their house. James watched through the front-room window as a squire climbed the stairs to pull the bell rope.

A servant opened the door.

"Earl Warenne to see Lady Eleanor," the squire announced.

The servant bowed deeply as an older man with a deep blue cape dismounted, climbed the stairs, and strode purposefully into the foyer.

"Good of ye to come, Lord Warenne," Lady Eleanor said as she gracefully descended the central stairs, her hands holding her flowing gown. "Do come in."

The door to the front room was opened for the guests. Earl Warenne's eyes narrowed as he caught sight of Alex.

"Lady Eleanor," Earl Warenne said, not taking his eyes off Alex, "ye petition for the release of your husband, Lord

Douglas. Yet, at the same moment, ye harbor a boy who helped bring about the destruction of our army just days ago."

"Really?" Lady Eleanor replied, turning to Alex in astonishment. "How did he do that?"

"He deceived Cressingham into leading his men over a narrow bridge, where they found themselves in a highly . . ." Warenne grimaced, "indefensible position."

James looked at Alex with admiration.

"How very remarkable." Lady Eleanor fanned her face, flustered.

"*Remarkable* is not the word I would use to describe it." Earl Warenne jabbed his finger toward Alex. "*He* brought about the English army's worst defeat in living memory – and when I was in charge!"

"Well, M'Lord, having delivered this miscreant to ye must put us in your favor," Lady Eleanor said smoothly. "Perhaps ye would be so kind as to put in a good word to King Edward for my husband."

"Your husband has a respectful lineage that goes back centuries. How he could put in his lot with an outlaw such as Wallace is beyond me." Earl Warenne's lip curled. "His actions have infuriated King Edward. His Grace wants me to bring Lord Douglas to the Tower of London, and there's nothing I can say that would change his mind. However . . ." Earl Warenne said, giving Lady Eleanor a perfunctory bow, "I thank ye for having brought me this boy. I will do my best to see that your husband comes to no harm.

"Men!" Earl Warenne snapped his fingers. "Seize him."

16

A Present-Day Excursion
at Low Tide

C raig stepped into his sneakers and gave each tongue a sharp tug. He turned off his phone and tossed it onto the bed. It wouldn't work where he was going. He grabbed his knapsack, tiptoed down the stairs, and slipped out the side door into the crisp early-morning air.

A steady hum came from the milking machines over in the barn. His father had just started the milking, so he would be busy for the next few hours. His older siblings, Annie and Willie, wouldn't be getting up for a while. He was on his own.

Craig could see his breath. The sun had yet to break over the hills. Usually he slept in on Saturdays. Now that he was up, dressed, and packed, his plan seemed ridiculously unreal.

Well, if he was going to do this, he had better get going. Soon the tide would reach its lowest point in a month, and it was not going to stay that way for long. Craig shouldered his knapsack and set off down the lane.

When he got to the edge of the cliffs, the rising sun had become a fiery ball just above the ocean horizon. Down below, he saw a coastline at the lowest of low tide, with a lot more rocks and beach exposed than usual.

The wet rocks were slippery and hard to cross. Almost no one ever came here. And why would they? Unless, of course, they knew that – under an overhanging rock accessible only at a very low tide – there was a hidden cavity that led deep under the cliffs to a very surprising place.

Craig picked his way around the shore. He scanned the water's edge. *Where was that overhang?* He had to find it soon, before the tide reversed itself.

Craig shone his flashlight under a slab. Yes, this had to be it! Although smaller than he remembered, the space extended further than his light could reach.

Craig took one last look around the coast. *Good-bye, my time*, he thought. *Good-bye, boring, meaningless school classes; good-bye, stupid farm chores.* He was going to become a knight one day! True, first he would have to become a pageboy, and then a squire, but he was sure Sir Ellerslie would take him on. In time, he would become an accomplished rider, an expert sword-fighter, and he'd join William Wallace in the battles for independence!

His only regret was the pain he might cause his family – other than Willie, who he fought with constantly and who would probably be glad to be rid of him. But Craig was not going to let thoughts of his family stop him – not when a glorious past awaited.

Craig scampered into the narrow tunnel. After wriggling and slipping his way past many constrictions, twists, and turns, he came to the dead end he remembered from the only other time he'd been here. It was when he was with his brother, sister, and Alex. Alex had been searching for his missing parents; Craig and his siblings had hoped these caves would hold clues as to where their mother had gone, following her disappearance the prior year. When they had reached this dead end, they had thought they could go no farther, but then they found the shaft that led straight up and opened into tunnels that took them to the time chamber, deep in the cliffs.

Craig shrugged off his knapsack and shone his light up the shaft. Remarkably, the pitons they had hammered into the sides still looked polished and shiny, as if they were put there just yesterday. He strapped on his climbing gear and began his ascent.

The rocks were slippery, but it wasn't the hardest climb he had ever done. He was one of the few from his school who could handle the toughest section of the indoor climbing wall. Still, each time he inserted his rope into a higher piton and adjusted the slack, it gave him comfort to know there was only so far he would fall before the rope stopped him.

Craig reached the top and hoisted himself into a chamber. He paused, listening. Suddenly lights clicked on all around him.

"Oh, for Christ's sake," groaned a burly older boy. "That's not your little brother, is it?"

Craig shaded his eyes. He recognized that voice. It was Willie's friend, the spray bomber. "Alan? Is that you?"

Squinting into the light, Craig saw others in behind the lights, including one with the familiar long brown hair of his sister, Annie.

"What do you think you're doing here?" she demanded.

Craig shrugged. "I was just off to see how Alex was."

"Well, pesky little brother," Willie growled, "you'll have to do that another day. You see, we're using these tunnels now, so scram."

"Make me," Craig said, throwing his harness to the ground.

"Wait!" Annie held Willie's arm. "What are you going to do – throw Craig down the hole?"

"Not a bad idea," Willie said.

Alan let out a chuckle. "Bring him along," he suggested. "We can test for danger by sending him ahead."

"Let's hope we run into something nasty, then," Willie said.

"Oh, stop it!" Annie stamped her foot. "I'm not going with any of you if you don't smarten up. And, in case you've forgotten, I'm the one who's figured out the professor's formulas on making the time portal work."

"Okay, fine." Willie gave his friend a glance. "But keep Craig out of my way."

"What are you wearing, Annie?" Craig asked, eyeing her skirt.

Annie sighed. "We're wearing these clothes so we'll fit in when we arrive back in time," she said, reaching into her pack. "Good thing I brought this old tunic as well – you would look rather silly showing up in those modern clothes."

"I figured Sir Ellerslie would give me what I need."

"We're not going to Duncragglin. Here." Annie tossed him the tunic. "Hurry up and get changed. We need to get going."

Craig held up the tunic with two fingers. "I'm not wearing this thing. Do you have any idea how itchy and scratchy it is?"

Annie grabbed Craig by the shoulders. "You will put it on or you will go home – we have no time for babies. Alex is imprisoned in Berwick Castle, and he will die if we don't get him out."

"What? How do you know that?"

"I've been doing my homework. I learned from the professor that a foreign boy was blamed for the English defeat at Stirling Bridge. So I went to the library at the University of Edinburgh to read chronicles written back then. I discovered that, after the Battle of Stirling Bridge, a boy was locked up in Berwick Castle's Hog Tower. The professor didn't tell me that part. I think he was keeping it from me on purpose."

Craig stood on one foot to pull off his sneaker. "So what else did this chronicle say about him?" he asked, throwing the shoe down and starting on the other.

"Nothing."

"Nothing? Why not?"

"Because anyone who screwed things up so badly for the English would be tortured and killed straightaway, and there would be nothing more to write about."

Craig pulled on the tunic. "What are we waiting for? We had better get going!"

"Right then." Alan reached into an inner pocket of his tunic and pulled out a spray can. "Shall I mark the way?"

17

HOG TOWER

Alex's cell was small and dark. The only light came from a deep window cavity high up by the ceiling timbers. For a glimpse of the sky, he had to pull himself up using the window ledge. If he tried hard, he could catch sight of the ocean.

On bright mornings, the sun made an outline of the window high up on the opposite wall. Because the walls were thick, the outline narrowed as the sun rose until it disappeared altogether. It never reached Alex's outstretched fingers.

One bucket served as his toilet, another held his drinking water. His bed was a few armfuls of dirty straw. On cold nights, Alex used the smelly blanket he was given.

He received one meal a day – if the thin gruel they gave him could be called food. Alex had no idea what it contained, but he slurped it down. After a few days alone in the cell, he was too hungry to do otherwise.

The visit from the jailer was a daily highlight – of sorts.

His jailer was not the jovial type. At about midday, Alex would hear him clomping up the steps and shuffling up to the cell door. There would be the clinking of keys, a clatter in the lock, and the jailer would shoulder open the stiff timber door. Each time, he would set down a bowl of gruel, pour water from a bucket to top up Alex's drinking water, and leave the empty bucket to serve as his toilet. Then he would take up the dirty bucket and the empty bowl from the day before and leave. Alex never heard him speak, not even when Alex asked if he could have some fresh straw or a clean blanket, or how long he had to remain in the cell, or what was going to happen to him. Nothing – not even a grunt.

Alex considered trying to escape, but the jailer never left the doorway. If Alex did not place his buckets and empty bowl at the door, he did not get topped up and he did not get replacements. For Alex to escape, he would have to force his way past the jailer, who was far too big and strong to allow that to happen.

And so the days passed. Alex wondered if people had grown old and died in cells like these, with everyone except their jailers forgetting they were even there.

Then, early one morning, quite unexpectedly, more than one set of footsteps came toward his cell. Alex sat up with his back to the wall, wondering if this was the day he would face his punishment. If he were lucky, they would kill him quickly.

The key did its usual rattle, and the door swung open. Instead of guards coming to take him away, Bishop Lamberton and James appeared from behind the jailer. Overjoyed, Alex struggled to rise.

"Dinnae get up." Quickly crossing the dingy cell, the bishop knelt next to Alex. "How are ye, lad? Have ye been mistreated?"

"Not really." Alex leaned back against the wall. Sudden movements made him dizzy. "I've made a few friends. See there?" Alex pointed weakly to a spiderweb that stretched between two ceiling timbers. "That's Matilda. I sing 'Waltzing Matilda' to her whenever something lands in her web. That only happens every couple days, though. We've been friends for a while. . . ." Alex paused. "Tell me, how long have I been here?"

"It's been just over a month. . . . We came as soon as we could. At first, they wouldnae allow us."

James knelt next to Alex and pulled open a cloth bundle. "Here, we've brought ye some food."

Alex took a bite of the fresh bread. It tasted *so* good. He offered James a piece, but James shook his head, looking miserable.

"What's the matter?" Alex mumbled through a big mouthful. "Did something happen to your father?"

James shook his head. "He's all right. I visited him yesterday. They keep him in a nicer part of the tower than this."

"Will he be freed?"

"Earl Warenne is taking him to London," James replied, his voice hollow. "But I'm sure it won't be long before he's back. He has a lot to offer King Edward – if he chose."

"And what about my parents?" Alex pressed him. "Have you learned about anyone in this tower who might have a garment with tiny clasps?"

"Aye," James replied, staring down at his feet. "My father has a garment like that."

"Your father?" Alex struggled to rise. "But . . . he's not from the future, is he?"

"I assure ye, he is not." James cringed. "He got it long ago –"

"Where? How? Tell me!"

"He got it from a man who was executed," James blurted quickly, his hands covering his face. "Along with his wife."

"Executed?"

James bit his finger. It was Bishop Lamberton who continued.

"A man and a woman came to Lord Douglas to tell him of a plot to kill King Alexander. After King Alexander died that night – despite the warning – the man and the woman couldn't tell Lord Douglas who killed the king or how it was that they knew he was to be killed. So Lord Douglas ordered that they be executed. And that's how he got their garment with the tiny clasps. Apparently the man was wearing it under his robe."

"They might not have been my parents," Alex protested. "Did Lord Douglas say what they looked like?"

"Lord Douglas described them as a man and wife who spoke in a strange way." Bishop Lamberton put his hand on Alex's arm. "Lord Douglas was not convinced they were guilty, but – given the evidence before him and the pressure from the other nobles – he had no option but to give the orders."

"When?" Alex winced.

"Over ten years ago, soon after King Alexander's body was found at the base of a cliff near Kinghorn. King Alexander died on the nineteenth of March in the year of our Lord 1286, en route to see his queen, just as the man and his wife had predicted."

"Here." James took a blue garment from his bag and thrust it into Alex's hands. "My father asked me to tell ye he was sorry and to give ye this. He said it has bothered him all these years to have given those orders."

Alex slowly fingered the faded jacket. The nylon was smooth. He clenched it in his fists.

"It wasn't my father's fault!" James cried. "He didn't want to have them killed."

Alex felt numb. He pulled on the jacket and adjusted it about his shoulders. It was too large. He brought the bottom ends together and pulled up the zipper.

"Look at that!" James exchanged a glance with the bishop. "My father said it took him forever to figure out how it worked. At first, he kept trying to pinch the clasps together. But ye knew it straightaway. My father said –"

"Do you think I give a damn about what your father said?" Alex tore off the jacket and balled it up. "He can rot in his cell for all I care."

"I'm sorry, Alex." The bishop reached for him. "I'm sure that Lord Douglas –"

"I don't want to hear any more about Lord Douglas." Alex furiously waved off the bishop's hand. "Get out of here – both of you – now! Jailer!" he called, his voice breaking. "Take them away. Make them leave me alone."

The jailer grunted and motioned for the door.

Bishop Lamberton took out his purse and slipped a few coins into the jailer's hand. "Make sure ye give the prisoner some . . . extras," he said, looking helplessly to where Alex lay curled up on the floor.

Alex lay with his back to the door, his thin shoulders heaving and his face in the jacket.

"We'll get ye out of here. Just ye wait and see!" James called as he was nudged out of the cell. "We'll find a way –"

The door slammed. Alex curled into a ball on the dirty straw, no longer caring where he was or what they would do with him. Nothing mattered anymore.

18

THE SUBSTITUTE

The block creaked as the mainsheet slid through it. A large, square sail was lowered. The wind gave it one last snap – then escaped out its billowing folds.

"Easy now – 'at's it, ye good-for-nothings. Bring the sail doon on the port side of the deck." The captain cranked the tiller to swing the boat broadside to the wharf.

The thrust from the wind gone, his fishing vessel drifted silently between tall cargo ships.

"Ahoy, chunky. Aye, ye're the one I mean. Take the aft line and tie us up. Make it a proper hitch this time. And ye, skinny lad over there, if ye're done being sick, do the same at this end once the boat has come aboot."

The wharf was built for bigger vessels than theirs, so it was higher than their boat's deck. Willie waited for the stern to drift up against the timbers and then flung his rope over a post.

"Loop it ag'n," the captain snapped.

Willie thought about doing it wrong just to annoy him, but he was too eager to get off the boat. Three days on a small, smelly fishing boat bobbing down the coast had been excruciating. Every time he'd thought he was done throwing up, he had started heaving over the side again. *Three days!* He couldn't *wait* to get ashore.

Craig shouldered their sack of belongings and heaved it onto the wharf. He was about to climb up after it when the captain held him back.

"Wait just a moment." The captain held out an open hand and curled his leathery fingers. "No one gits off this boat until I git the rest of my payment."

Annie gingerly deposited a number of coins in his palm. "You'll find it's all there," she said.

The captain frowned as he examined the coins. He tamped down on one with his few remaining teeth. "Why have I never seen coins like this before?" he grumbled suspiciously.

"They're worth far more than this passage," Annie assured him. Gathering her skirts, she stepped to the side rail and raised her hand. "Now, gentlemen, if you would be so kind . . ."

Willie and Alan hoisted her onto the wharf, where men were busy loading large bundles of wool onto a cargo boat.

From out of the gloomy twilight mist emerged a hunch-backed man with an official crested hat. "Dockage fee," he barked. "Where's my dockage fee?"

Annie looked back at the captain, who had unhitched his boat and was drifting away from the wharf.

"Hey," she called. "You never said anything about a dockage fee!"

"Paying the dockmaster is your problem, no' mine," the captain called back.

"What about our return voyage?"

Instead of a reply, the captain gave the mainsheet a hard pull. Gusts rolled through the rising sail.

"Good riddance," Willie called after the disappearing boat. "There's no way I wanted back on your smelly old scow anyway."

Annie studied the faint outline of buildings at the end of the wharf. A horrible thought crossed her mind. "This *is* Berwick, isn't it?"

The dockmaster grunted an affirmative. He held out his hand. "Payment," he demanded. "Threepence for dockage."

"Threepence?" Annie was aghast. "That boat was here for no more than three seconds! We'll give you this silver coin and no more."

The dockmaster eyed Annie's fifty-pence coin suspiciously.

"There's nothing wrong with it." Annie stamped her foot. "All right, if you insist, here are two coins. There. Are you happy now?"

"Ye are to pay three coins for dockage!" The dockmaster smacked his fist into his palm. A group of men standing further down the wharf turned to look.

Alan reached into his pocket for a can, wondering what color he should make the dockmaster's face.

A robed man excused himself from the group standing nearby and sauntered over. Taking off his hat, he bowed deeply and said, "Pardon me, miss, but what seems to be the trouble?"

"This dockmaster person here won't take our money." Annie held up the coins. "And we were –"

"Wait, may I see those?" The man peered intently. "How

strange! I've never seen anything like them. And ye would pay him two of these for a mere threepence cost? Why, I'll give ye ten pence for each one."

"Well, thank you, sir," Annie said, happily exchanging coins with him. Then she handed threepence to the dockmaster, who wandered off muttering to himself.

"Bishop Lamberton's my name," the robed man said. "I'm here to assist the good Lady Eleanor Douglas in securing passage for her son to Paris. And with whom do I have the pleasure of speaking?"

Annie introduced them, the bishop nodding to each in turn. "We came from Straith Meirn," she added.

"But your manner of speaking is not like those from Straith Meirn." The bishop tilted his head inquiringly.

Annie hesitated, so Alan spoke up quickly. "We passed by Straith Meirn, but actually we're from over there." He waved vaguely out to sea. "You know how the lowlands are on the other side? Well, past them are the highlands, and past them are the, er, great plains, and, um, that's where we're from."

"Are ye now?" The bishop smiled. "Your manner is very like a boy I've had the pleasure of meeting recently, and he too came from very far away."

"Really? Where was he from?" Annie tried hard not to appear too interested, but her hand trembled as she opened her purse to put the coins away.

"The future – about seven hundred years from now."

Annie dropped her purse. Alan and Willie exchanged glances.

"Where is he?" Craig asked eagerly.

The bishop pointed to Berwick Castle, high over the far end of the harbor. "He has been accused of treachery and would have been hanged but for the information he might have about Wallace's plans."

"We have to help him escape!" Annie cried.

"I'm sorry, miss. His fate is in the hands of God. No one escapes from Hog Tower. Come, I will help ye find some safe lodgings. There's also a boy I'd like ye to meet – Lord Douglas's son, James. He knows Alex well."

———◆———

Alex was unsure how many days had passed since Bishop Lamberton's and James's visit. He thought the number might be three. With each day much the same as the last, it was hard to tell one from the other. Lately, the food had been slightly better. The coins that Bishop Lamberton gave the jailer must be helping. Now he was given a piece of smoked fish or flatbread with his gruel.

Today's meal was not sitting well. Alex's stomach clenched up unexpectedly, leaving his only meal of the day splattered on the cell floor. The jailer was not about to clean it up for him. He had to scoop it with his hands and deposit it into the bucket, scraping his hands as clean as possible on the rim. He sacrificed a bit of his water to rinse his hands.

Hearing footsteps, he studied the wall opposite the window. Surely another day hadn't passed already? It must be overcast. There wasn't enough light to tell the angle of the sun.

The tumblers clicked and the cell door was shoved open. Alex struggled to stand up, but the best he could do was prop himself on one elbow. He blinked, trying to focus.

"Alex!" James knelt next to him, concerned. "Ye're not looking so good."

"You don't look so good yourself," Alex croaked, his throat dry and sore. He tried swallowing.

"I've brought ye some visitors," James said as he helped Alex sit up.

Alex frowned at the two shadowy figures who stepped into his cell. The door closed behind them. He did not recognize the burly youth, but the other seemed familiar. *Could it be . . . ?*

"Willie?" Alex said weakly.

"Aye, it's me," Willie replied, bending so Alex could see him better. "This is my friend Alan. We've come to take you out of here."

"But how?"

"We have everything arranged," Willie answered. "Annie and Craig are waiting at the inn. All you have to do is put on this, er . . . hat." He slipped a black headpiece onto Alex's head and adjusted it carefully.

Alex fingered the dangling material. It felt like hair. "A wig?" he asked, puzzled.

Willie pushed his hand down. "No, of course not. It's just to keep your head warm. Here, put on this coat. Alan!" He motioned for his friend.

"It looks just like the one James is wearing," Alex mumbled as Willie and Alan helped him get his arms through the sleeves.

"Ha-ha, it sure does," Willie said. They coaxed Alex to his feet. "Hold steady."

Alan whipped out a small aerosol paint can and sprayed a red circle on the inside of the cell door. He added two dots for eyes, scowling eyebrows, and a zigzag mouth. "Jailer!" he called, putting the can away.

The cell door opened. The jailer stood aside as they passed, with Willie and Alan holding Alex between them.

"Our friend has taken ill, so we have to hurry," Alan explained, slipping a few coins into the jailer's hand. "Please see to it that the prisoner has enough water."

Willie and Alan were in such a hurry that they almost fell down the spiral stairs. As they held Alex between them, his feet rarely found a step. It was just as well – his legs felt as if they were made of rubber. Left to himself, he would have tumbled all the way to the bottom.

Leaving the castle was a blur. Alex vaguely recalled going through an arched passageway, where guards stepped aside to let them pass, and then they were out in the bright sunshine. A carriage stood waiting, its driver looking down in concern.

"James has fallen ill," Willie said to the driver as he helped Alex into the carriage. "We have to get him back to the house as quickly as possible."

The driver did not have to be told twice. He gave a shout and the carriage lurched forward. Willie and Alan peered anxiously through the rear curtains as Alex collapsed onto the padded leather bench.

"Where's James?" Alex asked.

"He'll be going home a different way," Willie replied, staring back at the castle.

"But if he's ill, why is he not with us?" Alex rubbed his hand on the front of his coat. "And why is he not wearing his warm clothes?" He looked up and caught Willie and Alan exchanging a glance. "You didn't leave him there!" Alex struggled to sit up. "You can't do that! Turn around – go back. They'll kill him."

"Relax, he's in on the plan." Willie pushed Alex back down. "And leave that wig on just a bit longer; we're not done fooling the driver yet. Once we get you to a safe place, we're going to alert Lady Eleanor to what's happened. She'll be able to get James out. Bishop Lamberton will help too. They'll just tell Earl Warenne that James was drugged and was not a willing participant. Everything will be blamed on the jailer, who should have noticed the swap – and on us, of course, but they won't catch us. They don't know who we are or where to find us. Other than your friend Meg, only the bishop knows where we're staying, and he won't tell."

"Did Bishop Lamberton agree to this?" Alex asked, astonished.

"What, a plan where Lord Douglas's son gets imprisoned in Hog Tower?" Willie snorted. "No, of course not, but he'll get over it. Meg's role in all this is to let him know what really happened. She'll be the go-between so we can communicate with him."

The carriage slowed. Alan parted the curtain a crack to look out. "We're there," he warned. "Get ready." The carriage clattered to a halt. Alan took out an aerosol can and sprayed a green smiley face on the inner carriage wall directly behind the driver. He opened the carriage door and leaped to the ground. "Quickly," he said. He helped Alex down, making sure to stand between Alex and the driver.

Willie slammed the carriage door shut behind him, keeping a firm grip on Alex's arm.

The driver looped the reins and prepared to climb down.

"We're all right." Willie waved him off. "Just take the carriage around back."

Willie and Alan helped Alex slowly climb the steps, keeping an eye on the departing carriage. As soon as it had turned the corner, they pulled off Alex's wig and James's coat and threw them next to the front door.

"Now we go into phase two of our plan," Willie explained as they hastened back down the steps. "You go into hiding. Earl Warenne will send his men to search the Douglas house, but they will know nothing about this, and you will not be there."

Willie and Alan dashed around several street corners, hustling Alex along between them. As they descended into the seedy part of the town's waterfront, the alleyways grew narrower. Second-story balconies closed in over top, leaving only small gaps for dirty light to filter through the lines of drying laundry and tattered awnings. A stench rose up from the gutters.

It was not yet dark, and there were lots of people about. A bent old woman dressed in rags held her hand out for money, plucking at their clothes as they passed. Intoxicated sailors sang boisterously as they staggered down alleys with locked arms, bouncing off walls and laughing when one of their comrades fell.

Pretending they too had drunk too much, Alan and Willie slowed their pace and lurched from side to side, Alex still between them.

"No one must notice us," Alan muttered under his breath. "Once Earl Warenne finds out we're not at the Douglas house, he'll have his men fan out across town questioning people – especially down here. In fact, that might be them already."

Several men on horseback clopped past the end of the narrow alley, their heads turning as if searching for something. Alan pulled Alex down several steps into a sunken stairwell, where they pressed into the shadows.

Willie ventured a glance down the alley. The men had kicked their horses into a run in the opposite direction. "They're chasing after some scruffy kid," he whispered. "Let's go!"

They hurried through a maze of alleys until they reached a tavern, a babble of voices and languages spilling out its open windows and doors.

Alan checked all around and then directed the group into a neighboring alley. He rapped on a side door. "It's us," he hissed. "Open up."

A latch clicked, and the trio spilled through the door into a dark stairwell.

"Thank God you've made it!" cried a girl. "Oh, Alex, you're such a mess!"

"Annie!" Alex put his arms around her.

They clambered up the stairs, Annie and Willie supporting Alex between them.

"Stay by the door," Annie called back to Alan. "Craig should be back any minute. He went to watch out for you."

A knock sounded on the door. Alan opened it just long enough to allow a panting bundle of rags to scurry in before slamming it shut again.

"Phew!" Craig flung off his tattered topcoat and came clomping up the stairs. "That was close!"

"Was that you the horsemen went after?" Willie asked.

"Of course." Craig paused, trying to catch his breath. "Your pretend drunk act was so stupid, it wouldn't have fooled them for a second. I had to hit one of their horses with a stone so they wouldn't spot you."

"They could have killed you for that!" Annie gasped, helping Alex into a chair by the table.

"Nah, they would have had to catch me first."

"Well done, you little fart." Willie gave Craig a knuckle roll on the top of his head.

Alex wolfed down the cold lentils, beans, and salted fish that Annie slid across the table to him. His head was swimming. Things had changed so rapidly that he was having trouble making sense of it all. "How did you know where to find me?"

"You've been written about in ancient chronicles," Annie replied cheerily. "Once I read about a boy idiotic enough to bring down the English army and end up imprisoned in Hog Tower, I knew it had to be you."

"Did you find out anything about my parents?"

Annie's face fell. "Only what James told us –"

"What, that they died trying to save King Alexander?"

Annie put her hand on Alex's arm. "At least you know what happened to them. Now you don't have to keep looking –"

"They didn't die!" Alex exclaimed, getting up. He put both hands flat on the table for support. "James's father ordered their execution, but he didn't stick around to see it happen."

"If you say so," Annie began, "but all the same –"

"Now I know exactly where to find them – I just have to go back in time to right after King Alexander's death and save them before they are executed!"

Annie stared, her mouth open. The room fell silent.

"King Alexander died on March nineteenth, 1286. I think I know how to adjust the time chamber to bring us there. . . ." Alex looked around at everyone watching him. "You don't have to come with me," he added.

"You're right, we don't." Annie put her hand to her forehead. "It's just that we've come all this way to save you, and now –"

Willie raised his fist. "Of course we're coming! Right, Alan?"

Alan held up a spray can. "Color my world," he said with a broad smile.

"I'm coming," Craig piped up.

Annie sighed. "All right then. We managed one jail-break. Why not another?"

The boys let out a cheer. High fives were slapped all around.

"Imagine the look on the jailer's face when he realized it wasn't you in the cell," Willie said, grinning.

"Almost makes me wish I was there," Alan said.

"Thanks, guys, for coming to get me," Alex said. "You risked your lives. . . ."

"Nah, we were just having fun." Willie clapped him on the back. "Think nothing of it."

Although buoyant, Alex was exhausted. He gave up trying to finish his lentils, collapsing onto a bed instead. He was asleep before he could pull up the blanket.

19

FOUR AGENTS

"Send in the four agents!"

"M'Lord Warenne, they are very dangerous and, er . . . unpredictable," the aide cautioned. "Are ye sure ye wish to use them on a task like this? It would be like swatting a fly with a hammer, if ye get my meaning."

"Of course I'm sure." Earl Warenne waved his arm irritably. "Bring them to me."

"These are highly paid men," the aide continued. "To send them after a mere boy –"

"That is no mere boy!" Earl Warenne leaped to his feet, his chair falling over backward. "He has brought about the worst defeat in my life. How am I to explain this to King Edward? An army of twenty thousand English soldiers is defeated by a rabble of Scots, all on account of being diverted over a cursed bridge by a boy babbling of food hidden on the other side. 'Have ye had him drawn and quartered?' is what King Edward will ask. And what reply can I give him? 'No, Your Grace, the lad has escaped'?"

The aide shifted uncomfortably. There was nothing to say.

"Oh God," Earl Warenne moaned, holding his head in his hands. "Is this how I will be known throughout history – as a bumbler thwarted by a boy, the coward who fled the Battle of Stirling Bridge?"

Afraid to answer, the aide busied himself by righting Earl Warenne's chair.

"No!" Earl Warenne pounded the oak table with both fists. "Bring me the four agents," he cried. "Now!"

"As ye wish, M'Lord." The aide bowed and backed from the room.

Breathing heavily, Earl Warenne sat waiting, his clenched fists on the table before him. The door flew open, and the aide ushered in four men. They were giants, each taller than King Edward – who was called Longshanks for a reason. A blast of cold air seemed to come in with them. Earl Warenne shuddered.

"Ye called for us, M'Lord?" said the first, a hook-nosed man with a sturdy longbow slung across his back.

"Introduce yourselves," Earl Warenne snapped.

"So no one will discover our origins, we are known only by our aliases," the hook-nosed man replied. "I am known as War because that is what I am good at. My friend here is Conquest, and that is what happens to whatever side he is on. . . ." War coughed, glancing at Conquest. "Well, sorry about that bridge mishap – bit of a misjudgment, that."

Conquest folded his massive arms, his eyes narrowing over his heavy, protruding jaw.

"Never mind that. Mistakes happen," Earl Warenne said hastily. "Who else have we here?"

"My friend Famine, who likes to starve out his enemies."
War motioned to a thin man whose sparse whiskers twitched
at the sound of his name.

"And that last man, behind ye there, who is he?" Earl
Warenne demanded.

There was a thump from a tall staff, and a black-robed
man stepped out from behind the others. Deep within the
robe's hood, Earl Warenne saw a chillingly pale face with
dark sockets.

Stretching back thin black lips, the man said in a hollow
voice, "I am Death."

"We are your humble servants," War added with a bow.
"How can we be of service?"

Earl Warenne regretted meeting these men without his
armed guard present. His voice breaking, he said, "Last night,
a boy escaped my custody here in Hog Tower." Clearing his
throat, he continued with as deep and assertive a voice as
he could muster. "I want him found and brought to me."

War put out his hand, palm down, near his lower chest.
"Is he about this big, with green eyes and a peculiar manner
of speech?"

"Ye know of him?" Earl Warenne asked, surprised.

War nodded. "We've been wondering when he would
show up next," he said. "That boy has an amazing ability to
be in the wrong place at the right time. When we were in
Crawford to hide food for your army, he was there with an
ox driver, causing trouble. Twice he eluded capture. More
recently, I missed my shot at William Wallace during the
Stirling Bridge battle because of his interference. What's more,
we suspect he is the boy we encountered some time ago –"

"Alive," Earl Warenne announced. "I want him to be still breathing when he is brought to me."

"Consider it done." War smiled. "That boy's time is up."

Meg hitched the wicker basket higher into the crook of her arm as she stopped to survey the waterfront. The sun had barely cracked the horizon. It was too early for the handlers to be loading and unloading and too late for the carousing sailors to still be up and about. The streets were quiet. With a final glance over her shoulder, she ducked into the alley next to a tavern and rapped on the first door. There was no answer, so she knocked again, less softly this time. Meg waited a few moments, then kicked the door loudly.

"For God's sake, open up," she called into the crack.

The door unlatched, and Meg pushed her way into the stairwell to find a sleepy, messy-haired Willie blinking nervously at her.

"It's about time!" she hissed. "Didn't ye tell me to be here at daybreak?"

"Sorry," Willie mumbled. "Slept in."

"It's very important we aren't seen, and me having to pound on a door doesnae help matters," Meg grumbled, bustling up the stairs.

"Meg!" Alex swung his feet over the side of his bed.

From around the room, sleepy heads lifted from pillows.

Meg dropped her basket and gave Alex a hug. "We thought for sure ye were going to die in that tower." She whisked the cloth off the basket, using it to dab her eyes. "Look, I've brought some food."

"How's James?" he asked.

Meg flicked the cloth and spread it flat over the table in the middle of the room. "Lady Eleanor is trying to convince Earl Warenne that James was kidnapped and had no part in Alex's escape. She's had to pay him a hefty sum to see things that way, and – last I heard – she expects James to be released today."

Alex breathed a sigh of relief. "That was a crazy thing for him to do."

"We're no' done yet," Meg said, worried. She emptied her basket onto the table. "Soldiers are scouring the town looking for ye, and I heard one of them laughing how ye dinnae have a chance. It seems Earl Warenne has assigned special agents to track ye down."

"Oh, Alex, aren't you *special*," Alan said, laughing from across the room.

"It's no laughing matter," Meg snapped. "These agents are fearsome men – giants each one of them, and they ride huge horses too. They were the ones who tried to kill Alex and his friend Don-Dun."

"Why did they try to kill you?" Annie pulled her night-shirt about her as she got out of bed.

Alex shrugged. "Best I could tell, it was just for fun. That's what they do. On their way to Crawford, they killed the ferryman."

"They leave such a trail of death and destruction that people have taken to calling them . . ." Meg made the sign of the cross and lowered her voice, "the Four Horsemen of the Apocalypse."

"The book of Revelations, my favorite!" Alan burst out

laughing. "Are people saying we're going to have plagues, famines, earthquakes, and spewing volcanoes too? Is God going to reveal Himself and let us know what He thinks? I hope He does, 'cause then I'll give Him a piece of *my* mind." Alan reached into his pocket. "What color should I give Him? How about this one? It sprays a kaleidoscope!"

"Alan, *please*. No making fun of God." Annie put her arm about Meg, who looked as if she expected the earth to swallow them up. "He didn't mean it – did you, Alan?" She glared at him.

"Not me," Alan chuckled. "I'd be the last one to be saying we got a raw deal here. I'm far too thankful for all the good things we have. Take, for example –"

"Right," Annie interrupted. "So, Meg, what do we do now?"

"To help with your quest to find Alex's parents, Bishop Lamberton has arranged for ye all to have passage on a merchant vessel that's headed up the coast," Meg replied. "He said it'll make a stop in Straith Meirn, just for us."

"Oh, no! Not another three days of puking over the side of a boat," Willie moaned.

"Would you prefer ten days of traveling overland through a battle zone?" Annie asked. She patted Meg's hand. "He doesn't mean it – he really is grateful for what Bishop Lamberton has done for us, aren't you, Willie?"

Willie nodded dutifully. "When do we sail?" he asked.

"Tonight. The bishop said he can have everyone smuggled aboard at noon today." Meg picked up her empty basket. "I'm to hurry back to the house before I'm missed. As soon as Lady Eleanor rises, she'll be asking for me."

Alex walked to the window and parted the curtains a crack. Armed men sauntered past at regular intervals, their heads turning from side to side. "Soldiers are searching the waterfront," he cautioned.

"There's naught to worry aboot," Meg said, putting on a heavy accent. "I c'n go where I please. They're lookin' for a youth who speaks strangely and doesnae belong – no' a poor local lass who's missin' a hand."

Annie latched the door behind Meg, and they sat around the table nibbling on the pickled herring and cooked turnip she had brought. Time passed slowly. Peering cautiously through the window, they saw that the soldiers were searching everyone and everything that had been taken onto the wharf, demanding that chests be opened and sliding swords into tall bundles of wool to make sure no one was hiding inside.

The tavern below was coming to life. Workers stomped in for a brief soup and ale break. From the alley came the rumble of a cart, followed by the shouts of men straining under heavy loads. The tavern was receiving barrels of ale in preparation for another night of heavy drinking.

A scraping and clattering sound rose up from directly below the floorboards. "Stand back!" called a muffled voice.

Much to their horror, a hatch lifted out from the floor and fell to one side. Up through the opening popped a head with a bowl cut.

"It's the bishop!" Craig exclaimed.

"Hello, everyone," Bishop Lamberton called out cheerily from the top of his ladder. "I hope I didnae startle ye too much."

"Not at all," Alan muttered as he slowly lowered the stool he'd snatched up.

"Bring everything ye have." Bishop Lamberton motioned for them to come. "We have to get a shipment of ale ready to ship up the coast."

He descended the ladder. The others followed, puzzled. They found themselves in the back room of the tavern, among stacked tables, bar stools, and empty barrels.

The bishop tilted a barrel so they could all see inside. "Looks great, does it not?" he said proudly. "They'll never know ye were in them. There are bricks fastened down at the bottom so that once a person is inside, the barrel will weigh about the same as a keg of ale."

"When a person is *what?*" Willie turned pale.

"There is a breathing hole hidden just below the top rim, and padding around the inside so it won't be so bad when ye get rolled about," the bishop added.

Craig climbed in, crouching so his head was below the rim. "Plenty of room," he announced.

"For you, maybe." Alan examined the barrel.

"I thought ye might be too big." The bishop tossed Alan a set of work clothes that were barely more than rags. "So instead, ye're to be the mute porter. Are ye a good actor?"

Alan shrugged.

"Excellent! That's about all ye'll have to do. Every time someone speaks to ye, lift your shoulders, make strange faces, and let out groaning noises. They'll give up soon enough." The bishop hefted a wooden mallet. "Pick a barrel, climb in, and I'll close it up," he said. "Move along now. I've got to be going. I cannae be seen here, or suspicion will fall on Lady

Eleanor. Waiting outside is a wagon with real barrels of ale and a driver who is in our employ."

Willie clutched a barrel rim and breathed deeply. "I don't know if I can do this," he said shakily. "Can't I be a porter?"

The bishop shook his head. "They are interrogating everyone out there and would find it suspicious if they encountered two mute porters. But here –" He took a small flask from his pocket. "Have a drink of this."

Willie took a sniff. "Phew, what is it?" He held it at arm's length.

"It's what healers give people before pulling out their teeth or cutting off their arm . . . or whatever needs doing. It'll make it so ye dinnae care about being in a barrel. Drink all of it and ye won't even *know* ye're in a barrel."

Willie took a swig and recorked the flask. Putting on a silly grin, he climbed into the barrel. He would have to lower his head to his knees for the lid to close. "How can I take another swig when I'm like this?" he complained.

The bishop handed him a rag. "If at any time ye feel like screaming, stuff this in your mouth. Remember, if they find ye, they'll ax their way into each and every barrel straight-away to find the others."

"How will Meg get on board?" Alex asked.

Bishop Lamberton paused. "She won't be," he said. "Lady Eleanor has quite taken to her, and – just prior to my coming here – Meg told me she has decided to stay on as one of Lady Eleanor's personal assistants."

"She can't do that," Alex cried. "What about –"

The bishop raised his hand. "She is safer with us than with ye," he said sharply. "Remember, being an assistant to a noblewoman is a distinguished position. And tell me, what else do ye think this world has to offer her?"

Alex fell silent.

The bishop placed his arm about Alex's shoulders. "It is what she chose. She cannae be traveling through time with ye – she is terrified of the idea of going back in time to when she was younger, and she's even more frightened at the thought of living seven hundred years from now. She asked me to say she's sorry, but she's staying with Lady Eleanor. She wishes ye well in the search for your parents, as do I."

"Thank you, Bishop. Please wish her well for me also . . . and tell that little Black Douglas to give them hell."

The bishop smiled. "I'm sure he will!"

Taking a deep breath, Alex climbed into a barrel.

"Can you make room for this?" Alan held up four spray cans wrapped in a cloth. "There's no room under these work clothes for me to hide them."

Alex obligingly stuffed the bundle next to him in the barrel.

"One more thing." The bishop held up another flask. He shook it, and from within came a sloshing sound. "It's water. There's one for each of ye to take into your barrels. But dinnae drink it dry. Ye're to give it a shake if guards tip your barrel. It'll help convince them it's full of ale."

Craig poked his head up from his barrel. "Annie! Where are you going?"

"If I'm to be sealed up in a barrel for who-knows-how-long," Annie replied from halfway up the ladder, "I'm using the chamber pot one more time!"

20

THE GOOD SHIP *SCHEVENINGEN*

Alan carefully wheeled a barrel out of the tavern's side door. Each barrel looked alike, and already he was having trouble remembering who was in each one. The wheel cart dropped down a step, and he heard a muffled curse.

That would be Willie.

Tipping up the wheel cart, he deposited the barrel next to the wagon and bent in close. "From now on, keep your yap shut," he hissed. "We are outside now, and there are others who might hear you and wonder why a barrel is talking." The barrel wobbled. Alan suddenly noticed that the barrel was upside down. He tipped it over and set it upright. "Sorry about that!"

The wagon driver stood watching with folded arms. "I was told I would get a deaf and dumb porter, not an idiot who doesnae ken which end of a barrel is up," he said harshly.

Alan straightened. He knew that voice. "Who's the idiot?" he retorted, squinting back at Lady Eleanor's carriage driver. "Who was so easily fooled into driving James to Hog Tower, and then driving everyone but James back?"

The wagon driver flung off his overcoat. "It's time ye were taught some manners," he growled.

"As ye wish, James. Right away, James," Alan mocked.

Careful to keep the wheel cart between him and the driver, Alan backed through the side door of the tavern.

"Bishop Lamberton?" he called. "Can you have a word with the driver please? He seems a bit edgy, for some reason. . . . Bishop Lamberton?"

The bishop was gone.

Alan gulped. He then levered another barrel onto his wheel cart, careful to keep it upright this time. Lowering it gently down the step to the street, he shot a glance at the scowling wagon driver, who looked angrier than ever.

Alan tipped up the barrel, wiped his sweaty palms over his trousers, and extended a hand. "Well, why don't we just let bygones be bygones," he said with a big cheery smile. "We were doing only what was necessary for us to free our friend Alex, and it worked, didn't it? Alex is now in a barrel, and James is being freed by Lady Eleanor."

The wagon driver held out his arm as if to shake Alan's hand, but he cuffed the side of Alan's head instead.

"Ow!" Alan yelped. "What was that for?"

"That was for fooling me." The wagon driver's hand flicked out and smacked the other side of Alan's head. "And that was for the colored circle ye left in Lady Eleanor's carriage. I've rubbed it forever and it's still not gone."

"Sorry about that," Alan muttered, rubbing his sore temples. He kept a wary eye on the driver in case he had another grudge to get off his shoulders.

"Think nothing of it," the driver said. "Now, let's lift these barrels onto the wagon. And from now on, no more talking – ye're to be a deaf-mute, not a smart arse."

A soldier held up his hand, signaling the driver to stop his wagon. The horses snorted and stamped their feet restlessly as the soldier approached.

"What have we here?" he demanded.

"Kegs of ale for the *Scheveningen*," the wagon driver called down.

The soldier climbed onto the wagon and rocked the uppermost barrel. A sloshing sound came from within. He leaped back to the ground and gruffly waved them on.

"That was easy," Alan whispered as their wagon rumbled down the wharf.

"Keep quiet," the driver replied without moving his lips. "We're no' done yet."

"Who's the ugly dude with those soldiers down at the end there?"

The driver twisted Alan's overcoat about his neck until he couldn't breathe. "One more word out of ye and I'll make sure ye'll never speak again – ever. Got it?"

Alan nodded vigorously, his eyes bulging.

The driver released him. "He's one of Earl Warenne's agents – the one they call War. Stay away from him."

Alan continued nodding, rubbing his neck, and puffing.

The driver gave him a shove. "Excellent," he said. "Now ye're looking the part. Keep it up."

Pulling the wagon up to the side of a tall, two-masted

merchant vessel being loaded with crates and bundles of wool, the driver called, "Ahoy, *Scheveningen*, I have your kegs of ale."

"It's about time ye got here." The purser irritably slapped the upper deck rail. "Heavy cargo is to be at the bottom of the hold, and those barrels were to be loaded first. Ahoy there," he called to the other handlers. "Set your crates aside until we get this ale aboard. And stop your complaining. If ye're in so much of a hurry, ye can lend these men a hand."

Grumbling, the other men sauntered over to help as Alan and the wagon driver began carrying the barrels onto the wharf. Alan watched aghast when one of the men tipped a barrel over and rolled it toward the ship.

"Easy with that," the wagon driver barked. "I'd rather we use the wheel cart."

"I ken fine how to handle these things," the man retorted. He set the barrel upright next to the ramp and gave the top a hearty slap. "Ye can cart them up from here."

Alan hastily tipped the barrel onto the wheel cart and pulled it up the steep gangplank to the ship, the driver pushing from below.

"Down the hatch with it," the purser said, hurrying them along. "Watch it now. That's precious cargo ye're hauling about."

Alan and the driver gently stacked barrel after barrel on its side in the dark hold. About to descend the gangplank for the next one, Alan stopped short. War was nosing about the remaining barrels, using a short club to tap each one in turn.

"My good sir – ye are just in time to help us load," the driver said cheekily.

War rocked a barrel back and forth suspiciously. "Take the stopper out," he demanded.

"I cannae do that, sir," the driver replied. "The ale would go bad. I'm under strict orders . . ."

War pulled out a short ax from under his cloak and gave it a swing. The ax head cracked through the oak staves and sank deeply into the barrel.

Alan shrieked.

War wrestled the ax free, and ale gushed out over the wharf. The deckhands groaned with dismay.

War put his ax back under his cloak and turned to the bundles of wool. Unsheathing his sword, he stabbed one through its center. The sword came out clean. Satisfied, War sheathed his sword and jerked his head for the soldiers to follow.

The deckhands rushed to cup their hands under the ale that still glugged from the splintered wood. They splashed it up to their faces and slurped what they could catch. More men joined in, enthusiastically ripping off the broken barrel top and plunging their heads into the barrel to get a drink. Others fought for their turn. Hoots of laughter turned into shouts of anger. Fists flew and bosses came running.

The driver and Alan struggled through the melee to save the remaining barrels, hurriedly wheeling one after another onto the ship's deck.

The purser dabbed his quill into an inkwell and made a scratch on his list. "We have been short-shipped one keg," he said decisively. "It shall not be paid for."

"Goods on the wharf are goods received," the driver protested.

"Only after port inspections are completed."

"That was no port inspection!" the driver exclaimed angrily. He took a deep breath. Putting his hand on Alan's shoulder, he said, "All right, but the lad is to go with the barrels to Straith Meirn – that was the deal."

The purser studied his list, nodding absently. "Aye, that was what the bishop paid for. Now get the rest of the barrels below deck. I need to finish loading this ship if we're to sail tonight."

After the last barrel was safely stowed in the hold, the driver passed a pry bar to Alan. "This is to pull off the barrel tops," he said. "Dinnae open them until ye're out at sea."

"How will I know which to open?" Alan asked.

"Knock on them, search for the airholes, whatever." The driver started up the ladder. "My job is done, and the sooner I'm gone the better."

"Thanks a lot," Alan said sarcastically.

The driver paused, one arm hooked on a rung. "Look, why the bishop has risked so much for the safety of your lot is beyond me – especially after what ye did to James. Nonetheless, I find myself wishing ye well." He extended his hand. "So good luck, wherever your travels may take ye."

Alan shook his hand. "Say bye to James and Meg for us."

"I'll do that." The driver climbed up the ladder. Alan heard his footfalls down the gangplank and his parting words with the ship's purser. There was a shout to the horses and the clomping of their hooves on the wharf, and then Alan was alone – with his barrels.

Alan sat on the upper foredeck and watched as the deckhands stowed the last of the goods and provisions and the sailors readied the ship to sail. The sun was nearing the horizon, and the first mate was encouraging the men to hurry.

"Get moving, lads," he urged. "We have to be out at sea before dark."

The sailors pulled the gangplank and the mooring ropes aboard. The ship's sails were unfurled as it drifted away from the wharf. Wind snapped at the canvas. The ship creaked, heeled slightly to starboard, and picked up speed. The tiller-man spun the wheel and maneuvered the ship around others jostling for position to be the next to tie up.

They were away!

The wharf became smaller. At the far end, Alan spotted a man with a deep hood, leaning on his staff and staring out at the boats. As if feeling Alan's watchful eyes, the man turned, raised his staff, and pointed.

Alan shrank behind an open hatch, a chill running down his spine. The man wasn't pointing at him . . . was he?

The first mate called for a tack. Sailors doubled up to pull sheets through their blocks, the tillerman spun the wheel, and the ship turned to drift directly into the wind. The sails flapped impatiently until the wind caught them from the other side and filled them out again.

Alan peered around the hatch, looking up and down the receding wharf. There was no sign of a man with a staff. He wondered if he had just imagined the whole thing.

Turning to crawl back around the hatch, Alan almost bumped into a pair of legs. Startled, he glanced up at the blue-caped man towering over him.

"Dinnae give me that dumb look." The man nudged Alan with the toe of his polished boot. "I know ye can talk."

Alan stood, giving his leggings an awkward tug to hike them up. "Are you the captain?" he asked.

"Of course I am, ye idiot, so get one thing straight. Your passage may have been paid for handsomely, but what I say goes." The man roughly twisted Alan's shoulders so that he faced the shore. "See that? Your friends are to stay in their barrels until it's out of sight, got that? And keep them off the upper deck. I dinnae want any other ship reporting back that they spotted young ones aboard. Understand?"

Alan curled his lip.

"I'll take that as a yes. Now get below." The man shoved Alan toward the ladder. "If ye've got any questions, ask the mate – I dinnae want to be bothered. Nary a word from any of ye, got that?"

Alan climbed down a ladder to the mid-ship deck, then down another to the lower hold. Shadowy barrels loomed in the darkness. The captain had told him to wait until land was out of sight, but to hell with that. Alan pulled out his pry bar and tapped on barrels until he found one that tapped a reply.

Alan pried off the lid and Craig came crawling out.

"Got to go," Craig squeaked, hopping about uncomfortably. "Where's the loo?"

"You figure it out," Alan said, continuing to tap on the barrels. The next one didn't sound full of ale either, but there was no reply tap. Concerned, Alan pried off its lid. Inside, Willie lay in a motionless ball. Alan hastily grabbed his shoulders and pulled him out.

Willie lifted his head. "Boo," he said. Tucked under his arm was an empty flask.

"You stupid bugger." Alan gave him a friendly cuff. "You didn't save any for me!"

"Shorry about that," Willie slurred. Doing his best to stand up, he fell over.

Murmurs and thumps sounded from the barrels. Leaving Willie still struggling to get up, Alan tapped on barrels until he found ones that replied. A few levers with his pry bar later, he had both Alex and Annie out of their barrels. They stretched their cramped limbs while Alan tapped the lids back onto the empty barrels.

"Thank goodness." Annie took several deep breaths. "Even with the airhole, it gets really stuffy in there."

"Where are my cans?" Alan stuck his head into the barrel that Alex had occupied. "Phew," he said, grabbing the bundle from the bottom. "I'll be needing them."

A scream came from the deck above. Craig raced down the ladder, falling the last few feet.

The angry, pock-scarred face of the first mate stuck through the ladder hatch. "What did the captain tell ye? No going on deck!" He brandished his whip. "I'll be using this on the next one o' ye that comes up."

Craig examined his skinned knee. "I was only going pee over the side," he cried. "Where else was I supposed to go?"

The first mate gestured to the back of the hold. "There's a privy with a bucket and a bag of hammocks ye can sling over the cargo to sleep."

"When will we get something to eat and drink?" Alan demanded.

"Try catching some of the furry things that scrabble about at night," the mate said, laughing. "We're no' serving food on this boat. Ye should have thought to bring something." He stepped back and slammed the hatch shut.

Alan rushed up the ladder and gave the hatch a push, but the first mate had secured it tight. Scrabbling over top of barrels, he clutched the bars of a ventilation hatch. "Hey, ugly jackass! Did your mother drop you on your head when you were born? Did she abandon you in some gutter because you're so stupid and ugly?"

The first mate's whip came snapping down on Alan's fingers. Alan caught hold of the whip and pulled back, using his legs to push against the bars.

The first mate lost his grip, and Alan fell onto a bale of wool. Willie's triumphant shout was cut short by his loud hiccup.

"Give me back my whip!" the first mate screeched, glaring furiously through the bars. From somewhere behind him came the sound of laughter.

"Let us out of here and I'll think about it," Alan spat back.

"Hand it over or I will let ye rot in there!"

"Piss off, mate. That's what you had in mind in the first place." Alan tossed the whip onto a crate. "Go away and leave us alone."

They could hear the first mate stomp across the deck and turn on the men. "What have ye been doing, ye useless stumps? Turn us more to starboard and tighten the sails, or I'll have ye flogged!"

"With what?" a sailor snorted, raising another burst of laughter.

"Up the mast with ye," the first mate commanded. "And there ye'll stay for a double watch. Anyone else who gives me trouble will be keelhauled in the morn!"

Grumbling, the men went about their tasks as the first mate stormed up and down the deck.

"They *will* feed us, won't they?" Craig asked.

"I'm not sure I'd want to eat anything they gave us," Alex answered. "The mate would probably spit on it or worse, though I suppose if we got hungry enough –"

"Just how long is it before we're in Straith Meirn?" Craig interrupted.

"About three days – if the winds are good."

"Well, I suppose we have water –"

"And there's lots of ale down here!" Alan piped up.

"Oh, don't talk to me about ale," Willie moaned, holding his head.

"Serves you right for drinking all the spirits the bishop gave you," Annie said.

They made use of what little daylight was left to hook up the old hammocks they found rolled into a bundle.

Craig eyed the frayed netting doubtfully. "I think I'll sleep on a bale of wool," he said.

"I wouldn't do that if I were you." Alex adjusted the loop on his hammock so it hung tighter. "Rats will come out at night and nibble on your toes if you're not up off the ground."

Craig wriggled between Annie and Willie. "Okay, budge over, you two," he said, reaching to hang one end of his hammock on a rafter hook. "I get the middle."

The hammocks were strung none too soon. Night fell and an almost compete darkness settled into the hold.

Craig squirmed to get comfortable in his gently swaying hammock. "It kind of keeps you level while the boat goes side to side, doesn't it?"

"That's a good thing," Willie moaned, taking deep, gulping breaths.

"If you have to throw up, do not, I repeat, do not do it here," Annie cautioned, "or I'll make you lick it up."

"What did I do to deserve a sister like you?"

"You're lucky, that's all. Now go to sleep!"

The talking died down. They fell asleep to the creaking of the masts and the rhythmic slap of waves against the ship.

21

A TEMPEST

Alex woke the next morning to the sound of wind howling in the rigging. He felt the ship shudder, its bow crashing deeply into a wave before rising sharply to ride over it.

As it slammed into another wave, the ship jolted. Alex was amazed that the bow could absorb such a violent impact. Water trickled down the inside of the boards.

"It's not so nice out there," Annie said.

There was a groan from Willie. "Why, oh why, does this boat have to go up and down so much?"

Annie raised her finger threateningly.

"Okay, okay." Willie rolled out of his hammock and staggered toward the rear of the hold. Moments later, they heard him retching.

Listening to the loud pounding of the waves and occasionally getting up to stretch or go to the privy, they spent the day in their hammocks. It was hard to move around without being thrown into the cargo.

Water started spraying into the hold through the barred hatches, and it sloshed under the floor slats.

"The storm is getting worse," Alex commented. "Waves are breaking over the deck."

"If it keeps up, won't the hold fill with water?" Annie asked, alarmed.

As if in reply, someone slammed shut the hatch covers, plunging them once again into complete darkness.

"Great!" Willie moaned as he fumbled forward from the back of the hold. "It just keeps getting better and better, doesn't it?"

No one felt hungry that day. Annie doubted if even the crew and the captain had an appetite. She wondered if anyone was up the mast keeping watch.

"Do ships ever run into each other out here?" she asked into the blackness.

"Of course," Alan's disembodied voice replied. "Especially in weather like this."

Time passed, and they could no longer tell whether it was night or day. Eventually they drifted off to sleep.

They were awakened by the crashing sound of the deck hatch being thrown open and the tramping of men coming down the ladder. Stormy light illuminated their surroundings for the first time in many hours. Startled, Annie saw that the floor was under a lot of water, rushing from side to side with each roll of the ship.

"All hands," a sailor cried. "We need to bail."

Alan waded through the knee-deep water to help man the buckets, with Willie and Alex close behind. Working with the sailors, they filled buckets and passed them up to those on deck.

"Have we hit something?" Alex asked above the roar of waves and wind.

A sailor plunged his bucket into the water and handed it up. "This old scow's no' built for storms like this," he said, catching an empty bucket tossed from above. "She's coming apart at the seams."

The bailing seemed hopeless, but they continued for hours. Everyone took turns pitching in, and after a while, it felt like their arms were going to fall off. To make matters worse, they had to fend off floating crates and empty barrels that had come loose from their bindings and were surging back and forth with the water.

Suddenly the ship rode up a large wave and heeled almost completely onto its side. For an eternity, the ship hung there, as if undecided on whether to capsize or turn back. Seawater gushed into the open hatch, and more crates burst loose from their tie-downs.

The ship rolled back from the brim, but the hold was now more than half full of water. Sailors abandoned their buckets and scrambled up top as water continued to flood the hold.

Annie was hit by a crate and knocked underwater. Craig pulled her back up, and they were swept to one side of the hold. Alex, Alan, and Willie rushed to help. Fending off the drifting cargo, they brought both Craig and Annie to the ladder. They fought through a torrent of water that poured down the hatch and reached the deck just in time to see the ship's one lifeboat pull away, full to capacity with the crew.

"Come back!" Annie shrieked, clutching the ship's rail with both arms to keep from being swept overboard.

The wind snatched her voice and flung it away. There was no response from the men. Sailors pulled at their oars, and the gap between the lifeboat and the wallowing ship widened. The captain stood with his back to his ship, his blue cape billowing as he gave orders, his scrawny first mate at his side. The lifeboat disappeared behind a wave, only to reappear yet further way.

Tattered canvas flapped furiously from broken spars. The ship rolled sluggishly, the lower deck nearly level with the heaving ocean.

"We're sinking," Annie said.

Alan kicked aside a broken hatch and disappeared below deck, emerging moments later with an empty barrel. "Drop it over the side and tie it to the railing," he called to Willie over the howling wind. "I'm getting the rest."

With Alex's and Craig's help, Willie tied the barrel to the rail with loose rigging from a broken spar while Alan went below for another three barrels. After a hard battle, they finally had them securely lashed together in the water next to the lower deck. Alan pulled out his pry bar and levered up the lids.

"Get in," he yelled. "I'll send you off."

Willie peered into a barrel. "You've got to be kidding," he groaned.

"Get over it," Alan said roughly. "Once the storm has passed, you can bang open the lids from the inside and wait for rescue. A ship is bound to see you before long. Hurry now, before it's too late."

Alan held the barrels steady as each person climbed in.

"The weight on the bottom of these barrels will keep them upright," he said, "but hold your shirt over the breathing hole to keep water from splashing in."

"What about you?" Annie asked, crouching down in her barrel.

"I'll think of something."

Alan hammered the lids on with his fist, loosened the rope from the rail, and gave the barrels a shove. He couldn't climb on top and stay with them, as his weight would be too much. The breathing holes needed to stay well above the water.

The barrels slowly drifted away, disappearing and reappearing with each rise and fall of the huge waves.

Alan went back to the hatch to see if there was a crate or anything he could salvage to use as a raft, but he couldn't go below anymore – the hold was completely full of water.

The ship's stern was settling lower and looked as if it would sink first. Alan climbed onto the upper foredeck and searched for a broken mast, a loose hatch cover – anything he could use for floatation – but everything that wasn't tangled up in rigging had been swept overboard.

He leaned out over the rising bow and spotted the barrels a good distance from the ship. They rode high in the waves and appeared to be in no danger of capsizing.

Alan smiled. The storm would end, and they would be found. For him, though, it was another matter.

Hanging on to the broken rigging with one hand, he took out a spray can and tried spraying a black signature. It clung to the wet deck for only a few seconds before being washed away.

The stern settling ever lower, he climbed up to the bow-sprit and peered out over the churning seas. There he waited for whatever came next.

———◆———

Long, miserable hours passed in the stifling darkness of Alex's pitching barrel. The air had become so stuffy, it was hard to breathe. Water sloshed about the bottom, having seeped in despite the shirt Alex stuffed into the airhole.

Panting, Alex had to resist the urge to punch the lid. Once it was off, he wouldn't be able to close it again. He persuaded himself it would be better to wait for the calm, or for when the barrel was finally so full he had no choice.

But what if he left it to the last minute and found the top wouldn't come off? What if he pounded with his fists and it wouldn't open? The thought of drowning inside the tiny space terrified him. And what about Annie, Craig, and Willie? Did they have it as bad as he did – or worse?

Alex hit the lid with his palm. To his surprise, it not only popped off easily, the wind caught it and blew it away. He pulled himself up and gulped in huge breaths of fresh air. Spray blew from the tops of the waves and lashed at his face. The barrels rose and fell. Looming before him was the black outline of a cliff.

Alex pounded on the sealed barrels. "Everybody out. Now! Hurry!"

First Annie's, then Craig's lid came up. Together they pried at Willie's barrel until they got it open.

Terrified, they watched the waves crash against the rocks, each hitting with a force that would crush a house. The spray from breaking waves burst over them.

As they were swept into an inlet, cliffs towered above them on either side. With each surging wave, they drew closer.

Annie pointed frantically, but her shout was drowned out by the roar of the waves.

Shielding his eyes from the spray, Alex saw that their barrels had snagged against a rope that extended across the inlet.

"Grab hold of it!" he shouted, lunging half out of his barrel to reach the slimy green rope.

Willie threw the loose end of the rope tying the barrels over this new rope and pulled. Alex did the same with other bits of the rope. Together they fumbled to secure their barrels to this new lifeline. A huge wave rose up under them, pushing their barrels toward the cliffs. The rope tightened.

The storm raged, waves surging under them, threatening to dash the four against the rocks. Each time, the rope held them back. Alex checked the knots they had made, tightening them where he could. There was nothing else to do. Finally, exhausted from a long sleepless night, he slumped down in his barrel and rested his head against his knees to wait for the storm to subside.

22

THE MONKS OF LAUFIDLIN

Alex stood up and twisted first one way, then the other, glad to be alive. They were still in the same inlet as the night before, but instead of being tossed about on crashing breakers, the four barrels now rode waves that lapped peacefully against the shore.

"Rise and shine, everyone," he called, pulling on his shirt.

Heads came up over the barrel rims, turning to gape at the cliffs around them. They studied the thick, sturdy rope that saved them the night before, still tied to either side of the inlet.

"Someone must use this to tie their fishing nets or to moor their boat," Willie guessed.

"Hello?" Annie called, her hands cupped to her mouth. "Anyone here?"

There was no reply.

Alex swung his legs out of his barrel and slipped into the water. The others followed. They swam along the rope and pulled themselves up onto the rocks.

After trailing the shore to where the cliff was easier to climb, they began their ascent, shivering from the cool breeze. Clambering over its crest, they reached a steep, grassy slope where startled sheep trotted away from the intruders.

Alex looked back. Between them and the distant horizon, there was nothing but calm water.

"Too bad about Alan," Willie said sadly. He shaded his eyes to stare out over the bright ocean.

"Maybe he's on a raft," Annie said.

"He's a pretty tough guy," Alex added. "He'd have thought of something."

"Think so?" Willie asked hopefully.

"Guys . . . he's dead," Craig said.

"Craig!" Annie made an urgent motion behind Willie's back.

"Maybe he's right." Willie said sadly.

They resumed their climb up the slope, their wet clothes steaming in the warm sun.

Annie raised her hand. "Does anyone hear that?"

"Hear what?" Craig asked.

"Shhh!"

They stood quietly listening to the rustle of the wind in the grass and the squawks from distant gannets.

"Was it just the wind blowing over the rocks?" Alex asked.

"There!" Annie pointed to the top of the hill.

Men in long white gowns were framed against the blue sky. They chanted in unison, their arms rising and falling with the tempo.

"Did we do another time travel when I wasn't looking?" Craig asked incredulously.

"Maybe we should hide," Annie said. "They're getting closer."

Alex hesitated. "Where? Back in our barrels?"

The chanting men continued down a winding path. Then they stopped and stood silently with their heads bowed for several minutes, their hands about the wooden crosses that hung from their necks.

"Nice haircuts," Craig whispered. It was as if each monk had drawn a line from ear to ear over the top of his head and then shaved all the hair in the front.

"That look might just catch on in our time." Willie grinned. "It would go well with face piercings."

The pudgy man at the head of the procession let out a deep "amen," which was repeated in unison by the others.

Alex approached him uncertainly. "I'm pleased to meet you, sir," he said, bowing his head. "Our ship was wrecked in the storm last night, and we were wondering –"

The pudgy man waved for silence and motioned for Alex and his friends to follow him. No one said a word.

"Why don't they speak?" Annie asked apprehensively.

"Maybe they're dumb," Willie said.

"All of them?" Craig asked.

"Let's not be rude," Alex said. "I'm sure they can hear."

Seeing no option and hoping the men might have something to eat, they followed the leader. The other men waited until they passed, then closed in behind them. The pudgy man led them up and around several grassy hillocks to a stone chapel in a sheltered valley. He escorted them through a side door. They were brought to a room where a gray-haired man sat writing with a quill behind a large oak desk littered with many sheaves of paper. He too wore a long white robe, but his cross was silver, not wood.

"Thank ye, brother. Ye may go," the man said, carefully dabbing his quill before returning it to its holder. The pudgy man bowed and backed from the room.

"We were on our way to Straith Meirn to find my parents when our ship went down in the storm," Alex explained. "We would be grateful if –"

"How ye came to be here is of no importance," the man interrupted. "We asked God for more lay brothers, and here ye are." He folded his hands on the desk. "Let me tell ye the rules. Here on the Isle of Laufidlin, ye shall not speak, except in prayer. Together with our other lay brothers, ye shall rise with the bell for the first service of the day, after which ye can return to bed until ye are summoned for our prime service at dawn. Our High Mass is mid-morn, after which we have two more services – one after our first meal, the other after our second. When ye are not at these services, ye will be working the fields. Transgressors will be held to account by the abbot, and that is me."

The abbot paused for his words to sink in.

"On this, your first day, ye may rest. Observe the other lay brothers, and learn what it is ye are to do – because from this day forward, ye shall be one of them, a worker in our fields. This, God has ordained by answering our prayers."

Alex opened his mouth to speak, but the abbot slapped his desk and raised a finger.

"One word is one lash. Ten words is ten lashes. From now on, the only sound ye will make is when ye join in our chants. Is that understood?"

Alex bobbed his head, catching himself in time not to say, "Yes, sir!"

"Good. Now ye may go."

The abbot clapped his hands, and the pudgy man entered the room. The abbot took up his quill. "Simon, give them their habits and show them their beds," he ordered, giving his quill a quick dip into the inkwell. "The rest they are to learn through silent observation, humbly before the eyes of God."

Simon pointed to Annie.

"Yes, I know one of them is a girl," the abbot said irritably. "But who are we to question the wisdom of God? We can use the extra hands." The abbot scratched a few lines of ink on a scrap of paper and bent over his work, signaling that the matter was closed.

Simon motioned for them to exit. Once outside, several more half-bald men – large ones – joined them.

"Where do you think you're taking us?" Willie demanded. "I don't know what your abbot has in mind, but we are on our way to Straith Meirn and have to be going."

Simon raised a finger to his lips.

"I've had it with this silence stuff – just point us in the right direction and off we'll go." Willie shrugged. "Fine, don't answer. We'll find our own way." He turned to leave.

Simon tilted his head slightly. Two big men took hold of Willie, one on each side. Alex leaped to protest, and men took hold of him and Annie too. They attempted to grab Craig, but he dodged under them and sprinted away as fast as his little legs could carry him.

Simon stamped his foot and waved for one of the men to give chase. The man hiked up his long white habit and jogged stiffly after Craig.

"Let go!" Willie squirmed and kicked, but the grip on his arms only tightened.

The men led them to a dormitory with a protruding porch. Simon took down a coiled whip from the wall. He gave the men a nod, and they ripped Willie's shirt from his back and tied his hands to a post.

"Stop!" Alex fought to squirm free, elbowing the man who held him. Then a fist landed on his stomach with an explosion of pain. Alex gasped. The men tied his hands to another post, and he felt bursts of pain over his back. Spots swam across his darkened vision. His hands were untied, and he was pushed down into a chair. Someone held his head back and reached around from behind to hold a sharp knife before his eyes. Alex kept very still as the knife scraped against his scalp.

Finally they let Alex go. He slumped forward. His hair lay scattered on the dirt floor around him.

Someone threw a bundle into his lap. Alex slowly pulled it open. It was a white habit. He looked up. A man gestured for him to put it on. Reluctantly, Alex pulled it over his head, standing to let it fall down about his legs. He turned to see Annie beside him – dressed all in white, her head shaved, and her face wet from tears.

"Don't worry. It'll grow back," Alex said. Ignoring the man who shook his whip threateningly, he put his arm around her shoulders.

———◆———

Craig ran like a rabbit, occasionally throwing a glance over his shoulder to see the big bald ox of a monk lumbering after him, his habit ridiculously hiked up about his waist. Craig was faster, but he did not know where to go. He ran past a field where bent monks looked up from their weeding in surprise.

Reaching the top, Craig stopped, gasping for breath. Back the way he came, the rolling hills and cliffs led down to where they had swum ashore. Ahead, the hills became increasingly rocky until, far in the distance, they dropped off to the sea.

Craig groaned. He was on an island. No matter how long he ran, he could never get away from the monks. Craig decided he needed to reach the barrels and paddle one away. It might not be the speediest boat, but on a calm sea, he could get it to the mainland. Once he got there, he would find help to rescue his friends.

Craig first had to fool his pursuer into thinking he was going the other way. The monk was trudging up the hill, close enough now for Craig to see his confident grin. Craig threw a rock at him. A look of alarm spread over the monk's face. He ducked, straightened, and shook his fist.

The next rock caught him on the shoulder. The monk staggered and flung his arm over his face. When he looked up again, Craig was gone.

Craig skipped from boulder to boulder so fast that he almost flew. Just when he thought the monk would have no hope of catching him, his foot slid out from under him and he tumbled into a deep crevice.

Dazed, Craig reached up to feel his head. His hand came away red with blood. He tried to stand, but pain shot up his leg.

Craig wriggled deeper into the crevice to be hidden from above. Each bump was sheer agony. He pressed himself into its furthest reaches, his body shuddering uncontrollably. He bit his sleeve to keep from crying out. The ground below was wet and sticky. He felt as if he were floating away on a gentle sea. *Don't worry, guys, I'm coming back*, Craig thought, clinging to hope. *I'll bring help. . . .*

———◆———

Alex was awoken by the sound of a bell.

It was dark, yet around him came the shuffling sounds of monks rising from their beds. The dormitory door opened, allowing in enough light for him to see the monks tidying their bunks.

Alex got out of bed. Someone shoved him, and he fell into line with the monks as they drifted out into the night. It was impossible to tell Willie and Annie from the other white-robed figures.

Their procession entered a candlelit chapel. The monks solemnly filed into the pews and sat down. The abbot stood at the head, a flickering candle giving his face an eerie glow. He let out a melodic chant. The monks replied in chorus. Alex could not make out a word. He suspected they were chanting in Latin.

Alex felt a jab in his ribs. The monk next to him motioned for him to sing, so Alex did his best to join in. There was a lot of repetition. Many notes were held long enough for him to mimic them.

The abbot fell silent. He knelt and the monks followed suit. They clasped their hands and bowed their heads. Alex did the same, not wanting to receive another jab. The monks stayed motionless in prayer for what seemed like an eternity before the abbot finally said, "Amen."

The men rose and silently filed back to the dormitory. Soon the room was filled with the sounds of deep breathing and snores.

Alex felt as though he had just fallen asleep when the bell sounded once more. Again he stumbled to the chapel to join in more chanting and silent prayer. This time, the abbot rose to speak.

"Listen carefully, brothers," he began. "And what ye will hear coming up from far below are the agonized screams of unworthy souls burning in hell for time without end." The abbot paused.

Alex listened hard, but all he could hear was the stifled breathing of the monks around him.

"One wrong word and ye too can become one of the damned, my brothers, so pray to God for the strength to maintain your silence." The abbot's gaze trailed over the monks, lingering briefly on Alex. "Only the worthy may enter the kingdom of God. Life is but a trial. Give your every moment to Him. Work for Him until your fingers bleed. Prove to Him that ye are worthy."

His fists raised high, the abbot ended his sermon to the loud chorus of "amen" from the men.

"Now, go forth and work for the glory of God."

The men obediently rose and shuffled from the chapel.

Craig tried to sit up, but it felt as if his head were being used as a drum. The pounding subsided only slightly when he put his head back down.

He probed about with his fingers. A cloth had been wrapped around his head. Exploring further, he found that his leg had been bound to a board.

Rock walls around him slipped in and out of focus. The memory of falling into the crevice came flooding back.

Dim light entered the mouth of the cave, where a motionless figure was outlined by the night sky. Pulling himself onto one elbow, Craig saw it was a man wearing a tattered tunic, with long unkempt hair. The man was sitting straight upright, his legs tucked under him.

"You're not one of the monks, are you?" Craig asked nervously, his head slowly clearing.

The man watched Craig for several long moments before giving an almost imperceptible shake of his head.

"Do you live on this island?"

The man gave a brief nod. He reached forward and placed a bowl in front of Craig.

"Don't you speak?" Craig asked, waving away the awful seaweed smell that wafted up from the bowl.

The man cleared his throat. "Aye, I speak."

"Who are you?"

The man took a long time to reply. "I am no one."

"What is it you're doing here?"

"Contemplating God."

Craig groaned. Just when he could really do with some help, who does he come across but some wacko hermit.

Craig forced himself to have some of the seaweed and mushroom broth, then lay back onto the reed mat, grimacing from the effort. Despairing, he wondered how long it would be before his leg was well enough for him to get away from all these crazies and find help.

———•◆•———

Alex hacked at the ground with his long-handled cultivator, sweat dripping from the end of his nose. For weeks he had worked these fields, able to converse with Willie and Annie only in whispered snatches when passing each other. Still there had been no sign of Craig. He bent to pull up another weed and tossed it between the rows. It would be collected later, along with the many others he had pulled.

Trying to ignore the pain from all his popped blisters, he worked quickly to catch up to Willie, who was weeding the next row. "We've got to get off this island," Alex muttered, careful to keep the nearby monks from seeing his lips move. "How far away do you figure the mainland is?"

Willie stretched his aching back and had a good look out over the sea. A monk motioned for him to return to work. Willie twisted from one side to the other and bent to retrieve his cultivator. "It's four or five miles," he murmured.

"We could swim it." Alex hacked at another weed.

"I don't know. . . ." Willie wiped his brow. "I'd hate to be halfway and find out we couldn't."

"We'll rest by doing a back float now and then," Alex said under his breath.

"What about Craig?"

Alex paused. "He must have gotten to the mainland somehow," he replied, frowning at a stubborn weed. "It's been weeks and there's no sign of him. Once we get to shore, we'll start a search. There have to be people there who can help us."

"We'd better pick a calm day."

"Night. The longest time we can be away without being noticed is from bedtime after sundown to when they get up in the dead of night for their god-awful chanting session."

"Swim in the dark?" Willie groaned. "What does Annie think of this plan?"

"I'm going to ask her next. I'm sure she'll like it."

Alex finished his row and started on the one next to Annie.

"Are you crazy?" she whispered. "We can't swim in these habits. We'd be dragged down and die before we got a hundred yards!"

"But . . . we'll leave the habits behind," Alex improvised.

"Does it look like I've brought my bathing suit? Just what do you think I will be wearing when I crawl out on the other side?"

"Underclothes?"

"What! You mean, that flimsy linen thing they gave us? That long sleeveless bag of an undershirt? Great. So now I get to run around half naked, freezing cold, while we're looking for someone to help us."

"But we can't stay here," Alex pleaded. "We have to find Craig."

Annie took a deep breath and turned away.

"Tonight?"

Annie reluctantly nodded her agreement. Craig had to be found. Wherever he was, he might desperately need their help. And besides, Annie hated this place. She often caught monks staring at her, and it made her very nervous.

23

THE LIVING SAINT

Weeks passed slowly for Craig.

Once a day, the hermit took out Craig's chamber pot and fed him a seaweed-mushroom broth, always in that order. He then changed the cloth bandage on Craig's head, rinsing out the one he had removed so it could be dried and reused.

The hermit spent his days sitting cross-legged at the entrance to his cave, his lips moving soundlessly. He was not interested in conversation. When Craig asked him his name, he replied that names did not matter. Asked where he was from, the man said only, "Here, there, everywhere," then trickled sand from his fingers.

Bored, Craig would babble on – mostly to himself. The man didn't seem to mind. He just sat there regarding Craig with a detached look.

One day, Craig told the man about the time chamber. "Spirits were all around me, plucking at my clothes," he said, his eyes wide as he recalled the terrifying episode. "Some of them were only bits of people, like an arm with a hand that was still moving, or just a head that floated about while it talked to me, saying things I didn't understand. . . ."

"Go on."

"Dead people were flashing before my eyes, faster and faster. Then it got brighter until – pop – the spirits were gone and I felt like I was in a cloud of cotton candy." Craig shuddered. "It's all like a strange dream, except when I wake up, I'm in a different time."

"Take me to this place," the man said.

"Do you want to go to another time?"

"I seek a place where time does not exist."

Craig grimaced. That was just the sort of thing he would have expected the man to say. "If I promise to take you to the time chamber, will you help me and my friends get off this island?"

The man nodded.

"Yes!" Craig pumped his arm happily.

The next day, the man came into the cave with a few sticks lashed into a crutch.

Craig tucked it under his arm. "It works," he said, wincing as he took a few steps.

The man disappeared deep into the cave. When he reemerged, he had changed from his ragged tunic into a long black habit that was tied about his waist with a clean white cord. A simple wooden cross hung from his neck.

"Were you a monk before you, er . . . went off the deep end?" Craig asked.

"Come." The man led Craig out of the cave and headed up a hillside, his staff thumping the ground before him.

"Wait!" Craig cried, hobbling after him. "Shouldn't we go at night? I don't want the monks to see me."

It was too late. Several monks spotted them. They'd been herding sheep, and – much to Craig's astonishment – they dropped to their knees and folded their hands. They remained motionless, their heads lowered, even as the hermit walked past with Craig in tow.

"Well, you certainly caught them by surprise," Craig panted, doing his best to keep up. "I guess they didn't recognize you. . . . Oh, no, where are you going now?"

The black-robed man followed a well-worn path straight down the hillside to the stone chapel. Monks had run ahead to announce their imminent arrival, and the abbot stood waiting for them, his white robe fluttering in the gentle breeze.

The abbot dropped to one knee and bowed his head. "Welcome, most holy Friar Baldwin," he said, rising to extend his hands in greeting.

Craig's jaw dropped. *Friar* Baldwin?

Friar Baldwin accepted the abbot's kiss on both cheeks.

"Ye've been gone less than a year. What has brought ye back from your holy meditations so soon?" The abbot shot Craig an angry glance. "Have ye been disturbed?"

"A boat," the friar said. "We will be going to the mainland."

"Leaving us so soon?" The abbot looked dismayed. "But we are still copying your previous meditations, the ones that have brought so much fame and glory to our humble order, and we thought ye would write the next chapters upon returning from your deep contemplations."

"My contemplations have not concluded. God has given me a message, and I am now on a new path."

"A message?" The abbot looked bewildered. "Will this path return ye to our chapel in the near future? We will provide ye with a quiet study for ye to write your learned ruminations –"

"I will bring the others with me also."

The abbot hesitated. "Others?"

"The two boys and the girl who God brought to this island with my disciple."

"Oh, Lord." The abbot raised his hand to his mouth.

"Where are they?" Friar Baldwin glanced expectantly at the monks who were flocking to the chapel to see his holiness.

"Gone," the abbot said barely above a whisper.

"Gone?" The hermit raised a holy eyebrow. "Where?"

"Our Lord has taken them."

Craig felt his stomach drop like a stone. His throat suddenly dry, he opened his mouth, but no sound came out.

"Just last night, they answered the Lord's call." The abbot bowed his head. "Silently they rose from their beds and walked into His arms. Brother Simon noticed they were missing. He roused the other monks and went looking for them in the dead of night. They searched the island and found only their habits upon the shore. They had given themselves to the sea."

Craig smothered a giggle.

"The boy is not well," the abbot said. "Let us take him from ye so ye can journey unimpeded."

"My dear abbot, ye dinnae understand." Friar Baldwin smiled. "The boy is not joining me on my journey – I am joining him on his."

The abbot shrugged helplessly. "As ye wish. Our only hope is that ye return soon and continue your very inspired writings. Perhaps it would be best if one of our monks accompanied ye?"

"No." The friar held up his hand. "All I ask of ye, my good abbot –"

"I am at your bidding, my good friar." The abbot bowed his head respectfully.

"A boat, if ye please."

"Right away."

The abbot clapped his hands and the monks sprang to attention. They set out for the shore.

Craig hurried to keep up, not wanting to be left behind. He would not be surprised if the friar forgot he existed when Craig was not within his sight.

"I have seen many people's reactions upon learning that loved ones have answered the Lord's call," the friar began. His staff thumped the trail alongside Craig's crutch. "But never before has laughter been one of them."

"That's because they're not dead," Craig said, smiling. "They swam over to the mainland."

"Swam . . . all that way?" The friar mimicked a frantic doggy paddle, his nose up in the air. "Like this?"

"No, they probably switched between the sidestroke and the breaststroke."

"The breaststroke?" Friar Baldwin's eyes lit up. "And it keeps ye afloat? I'll have to learn how to do that one day."

"It's easy!" Craig put his crutch down and gave a demonstration. "You just part your arms like this while kicking your legs at the same time."

"Somehow that's not at all like I imagined." Friar Baldwin sighed. "Ye say they can make it all the way to the other side doing that?"

Craig nodded.

"Well, I'll be damned."

—————•◆•—————

The boat was upside down at the base of a steep slope. Sheep scattered as the monks approached. They took hold of the gunwales and hoisted the boat off its cradle. After marching it smartly down the flagstone path to the water's edge, they lowered one side and rolled it over in a well-rehearsed maneuver. They slid the bow into the water and placed a narrow ramp on top of the boat's stern.

Friar Baldwin stepped into the boat, oblivious to the difficulties Craig was having behind him. Waving his arms for balance, Craig hopped up the ramp and nearly fell into the back of the boat. He plopped himself down and swung his bad leg over a bench, finally making it to the bow, where the friar had motioned for him to sit.

A half dozen monks scampered in and took up oars. Simon came aboard last and sat on the bench at the stern. He readied the tiller, shooting Craig withering glances when the friar was not looking.

"Come back soon," the abbot pleaded. "We are counting on ye."

It was as if the friar had not heard. The abbot gave a reluctant nod. The ramp was raised and the boat was shoved off. The oars bit deep and the monks strained their backs. Simon lowered the tiller and set course for the mainland.

Craig searched the mainland coastline, wondering where Annie and the others would have gone. He hoped they'd found someone to help them and were not still cold and wet.

The monks rowed the boat around a bend and into a sheltered bay with a small fishing village. Simon steered for the harbor and the boat coasted to a tall pier.

A group of travelers rushed toward them.

"Can ye tell me, is this boat for hire?" one asked. "We are looking for passage to an isle that is somewhere near here."

"Are ye from the monastery?" another asked eagerly. "Have ye seen the holy man?"

Friar Baldwin held up his hands. "Who is this holy man ye seek?"

"What? Ye dinnae ken the holy hermit, the most revered Friar Baldwin of Laufidlin?" one cried out. "How can this be? He's a living saint, for goodness' sake! Do ye ken how many other living saints there are? None, that's right! He's known throughout the kingdom as the wisest man alive. Nobles and their scholars debate his every word."

"But isn't this hermit just a man of flesh and blood?" Friar Baldwin asked. "What makes ye say he's a living saint?"

"He's been known to be in two places . . . at the same time!" the pilgrim replied in a hushed tone.

"Two of him?" Friar Baldwin clapped his hands in delight. "How marvelous! God certainly moves in mysterious ways."

"Oh, stop wasting time on him," another pilgrim cut in. "Ahoy," he called to Simon. "Can ye take us to the Isle of Laufidlin?"

Simon nodded, holding up three fingers and tapping his palm to indicate the cost.

"Those baldies must be Laufidlin monks," a pilgrim said excitedly. "Aren't they the ones who never speak?"

The pilgrims gathered up their bundles and paid Simon, brushing Friar Baldwin aside in their eagerness to get aboard. The boat rocked and settled dangerously low in the water.

"Who was that silly monk back there?" one asked, squirming next to Simon.

Simon shrugged.

"He cannae speak, remember?" another admonished. "But who cares? We'll be seeing the holy man soon."

"And maybe his other self too!" cried another. "How wonderful if they both were there."

"Row, row, row," the pilgrims chanted as the boat pulled away from the pier.

The monks strained against the oars, and the boat slowly gathered momentum. Simon elbowed a pilgrim aside to pivot the rudder. Chattering happily, the pilgrims headed out to sea.

"Follow the children," the friar called, giving them a friendly wave that no one bothered to return. "For they know the way." Then he turned and walked toward the town.

"Where are we going?" Craig called after him.

"It is time for my meditations."

"Meditations!" Craig cried in dismay. "We need to find my brother and sister, and Alex. We can't be hanging about meditating."

The friar did not reply. Craig hobbled after him, furious.

At the outskirts of the fishing village, they came to a chapel. A monk saw the friar and turned to summon the abbot, tripping over the hem of his robe in his haste.

"My dear Friar Baldwin," the abbot said, welcoming the friar with open arms. "It has been far too long since ye've last graced our order with your presence. Just name what we can do for ye and it is yours."

"A meal and a bed for the lad, if ye please," Friar Baldwin replied. "And see if the lay brothers can find three young ones who came walking out of the sea."

"From the sea?" the abbot echoed, incredulous. "Has there been a miracle? Have these young ones been walking on water?"

"No, they did the breaststroke," the friar explained. "Something I intend to practice one day, God willing."

"But isn't the stroking of breasts . . . er . . ." The abbot awkwardly flapped his hands.

"Prohibited?" Friar Baldwin offered.

The abbot nodded vigorously.

"Not when ye are in the sea. Now, my dear abbot, if ye would excuse me. It is time for my meditations."

24

COLD HOSPITALITY

Shivering in the dark and cold, Annie rapped on the door of a small thatched cottage. A surprised murmur and rustling came from within. The door creaked partway open.

"Who comes knocking at this hour?" demanded a short, disheveled man with a high squeaky voice. His hand trembled as he held his oil lamp high. A round woman peered out from behind him, nervously clutching her nightclothes.

"I'm terribly sorry to disturb you, sire," Annie said. "But we're cold and badly in need of a place to warm up."

The man tilted his head, regarding his visitors with suspicion.

"Walter, think of our souls, man. Can ye no' see they are monks? Look at how their heads are shaved, for goodness' sake." Exasperated, the woman pushed the man aside. "Come in, come in."

A large black pot hung over a fire pit in the center of the tiny one-room cottage. There were beds on one side, a table on the other.

"Here, wrap these about ye," the woman said, handing them blankets straight off the beds. "What are ye good monks doing out at this hour, running about in your undergarments?"

"We were on our way over from Laufidlin when our boat capsized," Annie lied. "We hung on to it for hours, until it finally drifted to shore."

"Capsized in calm seas?" the short man asked, surprised. "How did that happen?"

"Oh, later with that, Walter," the woman said. "Have ye got the fire going yet? We need t' start warming the stew and heat this place up a bit."

Walter knelt on the dirt floor and sprinkled bits of peat moss over the coals. Puffing gently, he coaxed the flames until they licked the bottom of the pot.

"They're young t' be lay brothers, are they no'?" he asked, dusting off his knees. "Our son wasnae accepted as a brother at the Niewhame monastery until he was eighteen years of age."

"The abbot said he had a sign from God," Annie explained. "We were shipwrecked during the storm a few weeks ago. When we washed up on Laufidlin in barrels, the abbot recruited us on the spot."

"First shipwrecked, then capsized." Walter shook his head. "Ye are an unlucky lot, are ye no'?"

"Walter, enough questions! Can ye no' see how exhausted these poor bairns are?" The woman patted a bed. "Here, have a lie down. It's almost time for Walter and me to be about our farmwork anyway. We'll head out for an early start in the fields and give ye some peace and quiet."

She prodded her hesitant husband to get ready for work, threw her coat over her shoulders, and strapped on her boots. "We'll be back in a few hours," she said as she pushed him out the door. "The stew in the pot will be ready by then."

The two of them left the cottage just as the fields started taking on the pale colors of dawn.

"What do you make of that?" Alex asked, peeling off his wet undershirt.

"I don't think they believed a word we said," Annie replied, carefully keeping her blanket wrapped about her as she hung her undershirt before the fire. She climbed into a narrow rope bed.

"Well, no wonder," Alex snorted, climbing into the other. "You're such a lousy liar. Why on earth did you tell them we capsized?"

"They would never have believed we swam – no one back in this time knows how to do more than doggy paddle. And if I told them we escaped, they'd get really suspicious."

"Guys, guys, in case you didn't notice, we have a serious problem here." Hands on his hips, Willie paused to get Annie's and Alex's full attention. "Look around you. That's right – two beds, two blankets, and three of us."

Annie clutched her blanket and glared. "That is your problem, Willie, not mine. Do not think for a moment that when I'm in my birthday suit, I'm sharing either my blanket or my bed with you."

Willie turned to face Alex.

Alex groaned. "Pass me my wet undershirt, would you?"

Well into the morning, the cottage door opened and sunshine came streaming in. The farmer's wife stood beaming at
the travelers, who blinked out from under their blankets.
Alex hastily pushed Willie's arm off him, elbowing Willie to
get him back on his own side of the narrow bed.

"Look who I brought." The woman delightedly ushered
in a white-robed monk. "This is our son. He's from the
Niewhame monastery, which is the same order as Laufidlin,
except they're no' so strict with the no-speaking rule."

A young bald man beamed down at the startled youths.
"I'm pleased to meet ye," he said with a slight bow.

"Go on, show them what ye brought," his mother said.

The monk proudly held up three white habits.

"You're too kind," Alex said flatly.

"We can have ye back in Laufidlin in no time," the monk
said, handing them each a habit. "There's a boat that goes
over at least once a week."

"That's wonderful." Reluctantly, Alex pulled the habit
over his head. The hem fell to the floor.

"We dinnae have any your size," the monk said apologetically. "Maybe ye can fold it double where ye tie it about
your waist."

The woman nudged her son aside. She lifted the lid of
the pot that hung over the flickering fire. A puff of steam
drifted up to the ceiling. Digging in a ladle, she gave the
contents a stir.

"Stew's ready – pass me a bowl, would ye, roly-kins?"

"Mum, my name's Tedru!"

"Tsk, tsk. Only six months in the monastery, and look at
ye pretending to be all grown-up." The woman pinched his

cheek. "Well, no matter how long ye stay there, ye'll always be my little roly-kins poopie-pie."

His hands full, Tedru was unable to protect himself as his mother jiggled his cheek affectionately.

Alex did his best to keep a straight face. Willie didn't even try, grinning from ear to ear as Tedru, red-faced, passed him a bowl.

"How do ye like it at Laufidlin?" Walter asked, pulling up a stool. "I hear they're no' as lax as Tedru's monastery."

"It's terrible." Willie took a hungry slurp from the bowl. Wiping his mouth with the back of his hand, he added, "We certainly won't be going back there anytime soon."

"But ye have to go back," Tedru said. Coughing, he lowered his bowl. "Ye cannae just walk away from your vows!"

"Vows? We did a lot of chanting, but I don't remember any vows." Willie shrugged. "Anyway, it's that evil monastery we're walking away from."

"Evil monastery?" Tedru's mother gasped.

Tedru dropped to his knees, his face raised to the heavens. His lips moved in prayer.

"We'll no' have blasphemy in this house!" Walter threw open the door and glared. "Out with ye."

"Give those habits back." The woman clawed at the garments. "Ye're no' fit for wearing them!"

Alex, Annie, and Willie tripped over each other in their haste to exit.

"Demons!" the woman shrieked. "We'll gather our neighbors and have ye purified by fire!"

"Ye willnae get far." Walter shook his fist.

"Well done, Willie," Annie gasped as they ran up a hill, habits hiked up to their knees.

Willie tried to catch his breath. "How was I to know . . . that they were . . . going to turn into a bunch . . . of howling-mad banshees?"

"Did you see the horns sprouting from the woman's head?" Alex said, laughing.

"Can't you guys take this seriously?" Annie cried. "Don't you know what *purified by fire* means? They want to have us tied to a stake and burned alive!"

"That's bad," Willie said.

"Keep running," Alex replied.

———◆◆———

The voice came from nowhere.

"Craig, lad, it is time ye were awake."

"Friar Baldwin?" Craig groggily propped himself on one elbow. "Is that you?"

"Shhh, do not wake the monks." Friar Baldwin's face hovered eerily over a candle flickering within a perforated cup. "It is time we resumed our journey."

"But it's the middle of the night," Craig whispered. "Shouldn't we wait until morning so we can see the way?"

"No."

Craig felt for his clothes. He barely had time to lace up his boots before the candle receded. Craig followed it past beds of sleeping monks, through the front vestibule, and out the tall dormitory door.

It was dark out. Craig knew he was on a path only by the flagstones under his feet.

"Why so early?" Craig adjusted his crutch under his arm and set off after the candle.

"A monk approached me after the midnight service. He spoke of three young monks who had come ashore from Laufidlin."

"Where are they now?" Excited, Craig hobbled to catch up.

"They're in God's hands."

"What's that supposed to mean?"

"They are to be burned at the stake for blasphemy."

"Oh my God!"

"But that's not their biggest problem," the friar continued.

"What could be worse?"

"They have entered Flinders Bog." The friar adjusted the bag he had slung over his shoulder. "No one goes into Flinders Bog – at least not those of sound mind."

"What's so bad about this bog?" Craig asked, struggling to keep pace. "Tell me!"

"Those who enter rarely return," Friar Baldwin began, his staff tapping on the flagstones. "Flinders Bog is a valley of death where hell has risen up to stake a presence. It is filled with bad air, rotting trees, and brackish waters thinly covered by moss. Evil lights lure men into its depths, where nothing is what it seems. Vines are devils' fingers, land is water, and water is land. One misstep and ye are taken."

"That's terrible! How do you know so much about this place?"

"Oh, I lived there for a while." Friar Baldwin shrugged. "What better place to contemplate God than on the threshold of hell? It isn't such a bad place once ye get used to it, but for your brother, sister, and that other boy . . . let's just hope we get there in time."

Finding it too slow with a crutch, Craig threw the sticks away and hurriedly limped after the friar.

25

FLINDERS BOG

"I'm not sure this was such a great way to go." Willie brushed aside a vine to climb from one fallen log to another.

"We lost all those crazy farmers, didn't we?" Alex was careful to test the squishy ground before taking each step. He didn't want to break through again. The last time, his leg dropped into a smelly, goopy mess right up to his thigh, and Willie and Annie had to pull him out.

"Yes, but now we're lost too." Willie irritably kicked a rotting branch that was in his way. "We're getting nowhere, and soon it will be dark."

"I think we're still heading north," Alex said, struggling to see which way shadows fell. He slapped at the maddening midges that kept landing on the back of his neck. "If we just keep going, we're bound to end up somewhere."

Willie gave an exasperated cough. "There's no way we're making it out of here before dark. Just where are we going to sleep in this mucky hellhole?"

"How do I know?" Alex snapped. "Do I look like I have all the answers? At least we're not tied to a stake with a whole lot of firewood under our feet."

"I'm hungry, I'm tired, and I'm thirsty," Willie whined. "We can't drink any of the swamp water, and I'm cold."

Alex felt a knot deep in his gut. Willie was right. There was no place to lie down in this swamp. They were already cold – what would it be like once it got completely dark and they had to stop? The best they could do was huddle together, shivering, and wait for morning. It would be an awful night. He didn't want to think about it.

Alex pressed ahead as fast as he dared. The colors had faded to gray, and he was having trouble seeing where to place his feet.

"What's that?" Annie pointed to a pale light flickering in the distance.

"I wonder if it's someone who might help us," Willie said.

"Hello, hello," they called, stumbling through the darkening forest toward the light. As they drew nearer, it vanished.

"Wait!" Willie yelled, dismayed. "Come back!"

"I'm feeling dizzy." Annie clutched a tree for support.

"Me too," Alex said. "I feel like I'm floating. Maybe we've been breathing too much swamp gas."

"Guys, we *are* floating – watch this!" Willie flexed his knees and the ground heaved. It was as if the entire spindly forest were on a floating mat. Even the larger trees around them bobbed up and down, making *gloop* noises as the ooze below them slopped about.

"Don't do that." Alex grabbed Willie's arm. "We could fall through."

They waited for the bouncing to subside, unsure which direction to go.

"There's another light," Annie said quietly.

Willie squinted. "You mean, the one that's being held up by a swamp ghost in a long black robe?"

Alex rubbed his face. "We have definitely been breathing too much swamp gas."

"Come," the black-robed apparition called.

"Did you hear it say 'come'?" Willie whispered.

"Yes."

"Great. Now we're hearing things too."

"Oh, for God's sake," the apparition snapped. "Follow me. And step only where I do. The ground is not safe."

"Sounds like a real person to me," Alex said uncertainly, unable to see a face within the dark hood. "I guess we should follow him – what have we got to lose?"

"Our lives?" Willie whispered.

The black-robed man turned away and held his lantern high. In single file, careful to step in the footsteps of the person in front, they followed the apparition down a snaking path through the boggy woods until, finally, they came to a small clearing with a lean-to. A head peeped out.

"Craig!" Annie cried in astonishment. "What are you doing here?"

With a whoop, Craig came bounding out.

"Where the hell have you been?" Willie asked. He grabbed his little brother and affectionately rubbed his hair.

"Friar Baldwin's been looking after me," Craig replied. Ducking away from Willie, he explained how he had broken his leg and had been cared for by a holy friar who's considered a living saint and wants Craig to take him to the time chamber because he expects to find God there.

"What, find God?" Willie shot a glance over to where the black-robed man was kneeling, his head lowered. "You've got to be kidding!"

"What's he doing?" Annie asked, concerned.

"Praying. He does that a lot," Craig said. "Sometimes it lasts only a few minutes; other times it goes on for days."

"I don't think we want to stay here that long," Annie said. She watched as the friar mumbled through his prayers. "Isn't there a way to get him to snap out of it?"

"Can't say I ever tried," Craig said. He opened the friar's bag and pulled out folded tunics. "He brought these, figuring it would be best if you changed out of your habits. There's clean water for washing up in the barrel. Save some for drinking, though."

By the time everyone was done washing and changing, Friar Baldwin had finished his prayers and was starting a fire. He tipped some live coals from a small ember pot onto a carefully arranged bed of dry moss. It wasn't long before he had a cheery blaze casting a flickering light up toward the gnarled branches all around them. He made a tripod out of lashed sticks, hung a pot over the flames, and scraped in a few chopped mushrooms off a board.

"Thank you for rescuing us, Friar Baldwin," Annie said politely, smoothing the coarse tunic down over her legs.

"Suffer the little children," the friar said, nodding as he stirred the pot. "And forbid them not, to come unto me."

Willie leaned in close to Craig. "What's that supposed to mean?"

Craig shrugged. "He takes some getting used to," he replied quietly.

"I think he's talking about going to the time chamber," Annie said.

"What? How do you know?" Willie asked.

"He's quoting the scriptures. The 'come unto me' part is about going to God, and Craig said the friar believes the time chamber is where God will be found."

Willie took a seat on a raised log. "Well, I don't like the 'suffer' part," he said. "He can do all the suffering he wants – I'm not interested."

"The 'forbid them not' part works for me," Alex said. "To reach Duncragglin, we've got to get through Dundee and go further up the coast. We could sure use his help getting there. Did you tell him we're going back in time to rescue my parents?"

"I did, but I'm not sure it sunk in," Craig replied. "He's quite stuck on the 'finding God' thing."

Showing no sign that he had heard anything they said, the friar ladled the contents of the pot into bowls and passed them out.

Annie blew away the steam. "It looks like the friar made this entirely from what grows around here," she said, poking her finger into her bowl. "There are bits of moss, lichens, mushrooms, and some lumpy bits. What could they be?"

"Snails," Craig reported glumly. "I watched him collect them from under rotten logs."

"Maybe we should think of them as escargots," Annie suggested, forcing a smile. "They're a delicacy in France."

"Call them what you want," Willie said. "They're slugs. One thing's for sure: if you like eating them, you will never go hungry around here. You can see their slimy trails practically everywhere you look in this wet, rotting hellhole."

"Slurp them down without chewing," Alex suggested. "Then they won't go *pop* in your mouth."

Willie gulped.

"There you go." Alex smiled. "That wasn't so bad, was it?"

26

DUNDEE

It took a full day of hiking through meandering trails for the bogs to give way to highlands, with cleared fields, cattle, and farms, and then three more to reach the gates of Dundee, where they found the town in an uproar.

"What goes on here?" the friar asked a group of merry-makers who staggered past, holding each other about the shoulders and swinging their mugs of ale.

"The English garrison has surrendered," one replied gleefully.

"Wallace is – hic – on his way," hiccupped another. "The English are – hic – desperate to be gone before he gets here."

The man beside him took a deep drink of ale and wiped the foam from his beard. "We shouldnae just let them go," he said, pausing to let out a deep belch. "They've been stealing from us for years, taking our women, and keeping us poor."

"Flay them," demanded another. "Skin them alive."

Chanting "Death to the Southerners," the men lurched along, clutching their mugs and gathering up stones.

The friar and his followers entered the town, carefully avoiding crowds. The main street leading up the hill to the fortress gates was packed with singing and dancing townspeople. Some waved sticks. Closer to the castle, the mood grew uglier. The crowd hurtled taunts and jeers at the English soldiers, who were silently watching from high up on the castle's parapet.

Annie stopped and stared. "Do you see what I see?"

Alex followed her gaze. His jaw dropped. "It can't be. . . ."

A painted yellow smiley face beamed at them from across the castle's tall oak doors.

"Alan?" Annie said.

"This might have been done by one of his ancestors," Willie suggested. "Maybe he comes from a long line of taggers."

Annie rolled her eyes.

A trumpet blew and a hush fell over the crowd. A robed man stood facing them with his arms raised, his back to the castle doors.

"I am Alexander Scrymgeour, royal standard-bearer of the kingdom of Scotland," he called out. "And I bring ye good news. With this surrender of Dundee Castle, the English have been driven from all of Scotland – except from Berwick and Roxburgh at our southern borders. Scotland is once again for the Scots!"

The crowd burst into loud cheers, waving hats in the air. Men and women danced with joy, linking arms and kicking up their legs.

"In the name of King John Balliol, William Wallace has appointed me constable of Dundee Castle," Scrymgeour continued. "The English have surrendered this castle on the condition of safe passage – and that is what they will receive."

A deathly silence greeted his words, giving way to angry muttering.

"Hang them!" someone called out. A coil of rope was thrust into the air. The crowd roared its approval.

Scrymgeour waved impatiently. "Do not make me fight to protect the English," he warned. "Attack them, and my men will come to their defense. The garrison has surrendered, but it has not disarmed. Let them pass, or there will be much bloodshed."

Scrymgeour gestured to his men, and the soldiers advanced, splitting the crowd into two and pushing them to either side of the street. The trumpet blew again.

Scrymgeour turned to face the castle. "Open the gates," he shouted.

The English had disappeared from the castle parapet. Winches clicked, chains rattled, and the heavy portcullis was raised. The huge doors swung open, dividing the smiley face into two.

For a moment, there was silence. Then the English came marching out, led by men wearing doublets over chain mail with swords at their sides. They displayed no banners, had no horses, and looked neither left nor right. Tight-lipped, they progressed stiffly down the street.

The crowd cursed them angrily, but threw no stones. The English passed through the tight, protective cordon of Scrymgeour's men without incident.

"Aren't there more English than that?" Willie asked in surprise. "How could so few control this whole area?"

The English troops marched steadily toward the harbor, where a ship had been readied. The crowd did not follow. Instead, they kept watching the castle.

More men came straggling out, their heads hanging low as they glanced fearfully at the waiting crowd.

"Why did they not come out with their leaders?" Willie asked. "Why are the soldiers not protecting them?"

Annie grabbed Craig and pulled him away from the crowd. "Because these ones are not English," she said over the roars of the townsfolk.

"Who are they? Irish?"

"No. Scots."

"We better leave," Alex urged. "Something tells me this is not going to be a friendly reunion."

Stones flew and cries of pain filled the air. Some of the cowering men were pulled from the procession and beaten. Others were summarily dragged away by men who threw coils of rope over their shoulders. The men still in the procession huddled together, many on their knees, some bleeding from where the stones had hit.

In the midst of the mayhem, the friar appeared. He had removed the cross from about his neck and held it up for all to see. "Let any of ye who have not sinned cast the next stone," he challenged.

"Stand aside, Friar," called a man from within the mob. "These men deserve to die."

"They are traitors!" called another.

"If these men are traitors, then so are many of our nobles." The friar turned in a circle as he spoke so the townsfolk on all sides could hear. "These men are your brothers. Show them the errors of their ways – forgive them and take them back to your homes."

The stones stopped flying – but mostly because the crowd was now so tight, it became hard not to hit one another. Angry but thankful fathers cuffed their wayward sons, and crying mothers took their boys in their arms and led them away. Those from the castle not claimed by their families did their best to blend in with the townsfolk.

"Our friar has saved some lives here," Annie said, relieved that the beatings had stopped.

"Not all." Willie nodded toward the castle gates, where a row of men hung twitching from the ends of their ropes. Another was still being hoisted.

Annie turned away with a shudder. Glancing at the remaining men, she suddenly gripped Alex's arm. "Could it be . . . ?" she began.

There, among the last of the Scots to leave the castle, was a burly, bristly haired boy. Alan. He looked thinner. Seeing Annie and the others, he thrust both fists into the air and let out a giant whoop.

They ran for each other, pushing and shoving their way through the jostling townsfolk. There were hugs and high fives and backslaps all around as they came together, with questions pouring from everyone at once.

"One at a time." Alan laughed. "You didn't think one little sinking ship could bring about the end of me, did you now?" He explained how the ship had wallowed in the waves but didn't actually go underwater. When the storm passed, an English ship transporting soldiers came in for salvage. "Earl Warenne's four agents were on that ship," Alan said. "Soon as

I was dragged on board, they were onto me, wanting to know if a young lad answering to the name of Alex was on board the ship. I said, 'Aye, he was washed overboard early in the storm. He's down with the fishes.' They looked at each other, kind of disappointed. Then the beefy one, called Conquest, said, 'Well, that's that then. Let's head back and collect our fee.'"

"So they're gone?" Annie asked hopefully.

"Not sure. That hooded dude, Death – you know – the one with the hollow eyes? He wasn't convinced Alex was dead. Said he couldn't feel it in his bones. They wanted to slap more answers out of me, but some English officer dragged me away and put me to work polishing boots."

"You were a boot boy!" Willie laughed.

"Yeah, well, I spat on their things while I worked – even though it made the boots shine all that much brighter." Alan grinned. "The biggest mistake they made was to have me help cook now and then."

In turn, Willie, Craig, Alex, and Annie explained to Alan how they'd escaped from an island monastery and came to be traveling with a friar.

"That's a nice haircut they gave you," Alan said to Annie, ruffling the bristles on her head. "But it would be better if you shaved it up the sides a bit and dyed it red."

"Then I would look like your last girlfriend." Annie pushed his arm away. "Especially if I had a row of piercings over my eye."

"And what would be wrong with that?" Alan retorted. "At least I know what I want in a woman."

Annie gave him a shove.

Alex coughed. "Excuse me, you two, but has anyone seen our friar?"

They searched the street. Taverns were filled to over-flowing. Men crowding the doors were passed ales from within. Mugs clanked together in celebration. Cries of "Scotland!" and "Freedom!" filled the air, but nowhere did they see a black-robed friar.

It was Craig who finally spotted him. "There!" he said, pointing. "By the castle."

The friar was kneeling before the hanged men, his head bowed.

"Oh, no. He's not doing the prayer thing again, is he?" Willie moaned. "We could be waiting for hours for him."

"Maybe we should join him," Craig suggested.

Willie snorted. "You go right ahead. I'm not kneeling in the muck, that's for sure."

Feeling less than sure of himself, Craig wandered up behind the man he'd spent weeks with on the island – the man who had set his broken leg, fed him, and told him things he did not understand . . . the man he thought was a complete nutter.

Craig dropped to his bare knees in the mud. He folded his hands and bowed his head, just like the friar, and wondered what he should be thinking. *O Lord*, he began, *please don't make so many bad men.* He paused. That didn't sound right somehow. He wondered why the friar troubled himself over bad men at all.

"And please help me find whatever good there might be in the bad," Craig mumbled.

The friar opened one eye. "Now ye're getting somewhere," he said with a big smile.

———— ◆ ————

"Alex, let me understand this properly." The castle lord,
Sir Ellerslie, paused, leaning back in his tall council chair.
He looked haggard and pale. Alex and his friends had
recently arrived at Duncragglin Castle from Dundee. "Your
friends came back from the future to rescue ye from Berwick's
Hog Tower."

Alex nodded, giving his friends a smile of encouragement.

"And now ye intend to go back eleven years to rescue
your parents."

"Yes, sir!"

Sir Ellerslie turned to Friar Baldwin. "Your Holiness," he
began wearily. "Please tell me again. Why is it that ye wish
to accompany them on this journey?"

"*Part* of the journey," Friar Baldwin corrected him. "They
wish to emerge from this place into another time – I intend
to stay in between the two."

"And why, pray tell, would ye want to stay in a place I've
heard described as hell?"

"Through hell one finds God," the friar replied.

"I suspected as much." Sir Ellerslie sighed, taking the
hand of his wife, who was seated next to him. "What do ye
make of all this, my dear?"

"It seems that Alex has found where he needs to go."
Sir Ellerslie's wife squeezed his hand. "We knew this would
happen one day."

"Aye, even though we hoped he would stay and grow into a strong knight of Scotland here in our time, we knew he would likely go back to his own time, which we understand to be over seven hundred years hence. But never did we envision he would wish to go further back, to a time when we were first married. Think of it, my dear. What if one of us encountered Alex then?"

"I have no recollection of doing so." Sir Ellerslie's wife looked puzzled.

"I have seen many things I'll never forget." Sir Ellerslie stared off into space.

His wife leaned in, concerned. "What are ye telling me? What is it ye recall?"

"I was at the trial of the man and woman whom Alex calls his parents." Sir Ellerslie bent his head. "There's more," he whispered. "A strange lad spoke up on their behalf. He had been brought in with a number of thieving hill men, and, and . . . I told the magistrate to have him hang with the rest!"

Nervous glances shot back and forth.

"No!" Sir Ellerslie thumped the arm of his chair. "That way lies madness. Ye are alive the-now, and I cannae allow ye to go back to a time where ye are dragged into the Straith Meirn town square to be executed. Ye are to stay here – in this time – forever."

Sir Ellerslie stood up and charged out of the room, leaving a startled gathering to stare after him – everyone, that is, except the friar, whose eyes were closed in prayer.

27

SIR WILLIAM

O n a balcony overlooking Duncragglin Castle's great hall, Alex pulled back a corner of the plush red curtain and watched. A hush fell over the dense gathering of some of the most important men and women in all of Scotland, some seated at the long table and others standing. One of the many nobles in attendance, Robert the Bruce, had pulled out his sword.

"Kneel," he commanded.

William Wallace dropped to one knee. "My Lord," he protested, "I am not worthy of this great honor."

His protestations were drowned out by applause.

"No one could be more deserving," Robert assured him, speaking loudly. "Who was it who sacrificed so much to help Scotland in her hour of need? Who united so many of us divided Scots and led us in our greatest victory of all time, turning back the might of the English army at Stirling Bridge? Nae, not merely turning it back. Destroying it, crushing it, and leaving England humiliated before the eyes of the world!"

"It was him," Wallace said, pointing to Sir Andrew Moray, the noble who had joined him in the battle and been hit by an arrow.

Sir Andrew shook his head. "I was there with my men – as were some other nobles, including Sir Ellerslie here, our kind host." Sir Andrew motioned to a pale and tired Sir Ellerslie, who sat at the head of the table. "But ye led them, Wallace. Ye held us Scots together, making us stand our ground as the English advanced over that bridge, raising your sword to personally slay the cursed Cressingham, treasurer of the king of England."

Sir Andrew coughed, covered his mouth with a handkerchief, and doubled over. He crumpled the handkerchief before tucking it away, but Alex, from his high vantage point, saw the inside was red with blood. Sir Andrew's assistants leaned in, looking concerned.

Sir Andrew waved them away. "It was my privilege to be there," he said weakly. "The honor is yours."

Again, men and women cheered, thumping the table and stamping their feet in approval.

Robert motioned for silence. "There is more. As ye are aware, we have been without a sitting king for far too long. John Balliol is in exile. It is well-known that many dispute his claim to the throne."

An angry murmur rippled through the hall.

Robert raised his hand to quiet the room. "We asked King Edward to help us choose King Alexander's successor, and what has he done? He has given us John Balliol, a Toom Tabard, an empty coat, stripped of all vestments of royalty. And why? So he can rule Scotland himself. We need a king who can unite us against this Hammer of the Scots. And until we have this king, Scotland needs a guardian, a man who can hold this great country together as we sort out our differences. We need a man who can help us form a united front against England, and I say that man is William Wallace."

A great roar rose to the rafters. Alex let the curtain fall back to block out some of the noise.

"What's happening?" Craig asked.

"William Wallace is being proclaimed guardian of Scotland."

"I knew that would happen," Craig said.

"Of course you did!" Willie exclaimed. "We learned it at school."

"It's time to go," Alex said. "The guards are all gathered around the entrance to the great hall to hear what Wallace has to say. It's now or never."

"I'll get the friar." Craig turned toward the chapel.

"No," Alex said. "We can't take him with us."

"But we *have* to take him," Craig pleaded. "I promised him I would. Why can't we?"

"Think about it – we're going back only eleven years. When *we* go back in time, we stay the age we are. If someone from this time came with us, they'd end up in the same time as their younger selves – and then what? There would be two of them. Everything would be all screwed up. Come on, let's go!"

"Wait!" Craig cried. "There *are* two of him – the pilgrims said so. That's one of the reasons he's considered a living saint."

Alex stopped. "There *are* two of him?"

"Yes, I'm afraid that's true," said a voice from the stairwell.

Alex whirled about. "Friar Baldwin! When did you get here?"

"Having seen as much of the world as I have, it takes a lot to surprise me," Friar Baldwin said. "But today, I must admit, it happened. For years I've heard there was someone very like me doing the same sort of things. All this time, I thought it was just the imagination of highly impressionable pilgrims. Well . . ." He glanced over his shoulder. "There's someone I'd like ye to meet." Friar Baldwin stepped aside to let a man come forward.

To their great astonishment, the group came face-to-face with – another Friar Baldwin.

"Hello, everyone," the second friar said. "It's been a long time."

Alex stared first at one, then the other of the two friars. They were almost identical – except, with them side by side, he could see that one was older.

"Because I've gone back in time, I've had the great advantage these past eleven years to know that I would live to see this day," the older friar said. "And to have this glimpse of the man I once was."

"And it is good for me to see the man I will become," said the younger friar, bowing to his older self.

"Oh, no!" Alex put his hand on his forehead. "Things have become seriously mixed up."

"At least the friar takes it well," Annie whispered. "I'd be totally freaking out right about now."

"Well, since there's two of them, I guess that means one of them is coming with us," Craig piped up.

Alex thought fast. "Friar Baldwin . . . I mean, the older Baldwin, sir, if you please, we need you to come with us as far as the dungeons, so you can help cover our tracks."

"Aye, I do recall doing that," Friar Baldwin said. He opened his robe to reveal a rope tied to his belt. "We used this to reach the caves."

"Brilliant!" Alan exclaimed. "No one will think you went anywhere because, of course, they will see your older self – although you will appear suddenly aged."

The friar nodded. "They will take that as another of my miracles and be further convinced that I'm a saint."

They descended spiral stairs and crossed an empty courtyard. Everyone was still at Wallace's proclamation. Remembering the way from when Annie, Willie, and Craig had last left this time, they passed through an alcove and down the steep, spiraling stairs to the dungeons below.

Alex poked his head into a musty gate room. It was illuminated only from what little light made it down a ventilation shaft. No one was there. Sir Ellerslie told Alex that during this time of war, there was no use having imprisoned men sitting about awaiting trial. Rather than lock up wrongdoers, Sir Ellerslie simply had them join his army, where they had to shape up – or else.

"Are the gates locked?" Alex asked anxiously.

"Not that I remember," the older friar replied. "But it was eleven years ago. . . ."

Sure enough, when Alex tried opening the iron gates to the dungeons, he found that they swung freely. It was unnerving to be in the presence of someone who knew exactly what was going to happen for the next few minutes.

The two friars lit torches and passed them out.

They all headed into the damp dungeons with their cramped cells. A steady drip echoed noisily. Hearing squeaks, they caught glimpses of rodents scrambling out of their way.

Coming to a door, Alex paused to take a deep breath before shouldering it open. He thrust in his torch. Other than the cobwebs, it was as he remembered it. The torture chair stood ready for its next victim. Iron manacles hung from the wall. In the center of the room was a vertical rack with a big ratcheting wheel, used to pull a person in two impossible directions.

The younger friar sighed. "God works in mysterious ways," he said.

The older friar put his shoulder to the rack and slid it over the flagstones. He dropped to his knees, wriggled his fingers into a crack, and tipped a stone on edge, revealing a dark opening below. "The way to the time chamber," he announced triumphantly.

"How did ye know this was here?" The younger friar peered down in amazement.

"I've been here before, remember? When I was ye."

The younger friar threw up his hands. "Oh, right. Ye *are* me."

Alex shook his head. This two-friar business was giving him a headache. A thought struck him. "Hold on!" he cried, turning to the older friar. "Before we go any further, tell me – will I rescue my parents?"

"I wish I knew." The older friar spread his hands apologetically. "The time chamber threw us through the gates of hell, and I lingered there for an eternity before I awoke on a mountainside in a previous time. This is the first I'm seeing ye since then. But there's one thing I do know. . . ."

"Yes?" Alex asked eagerly. "What is it?"

"God's will will be done."

Alex groaned. "You are no help at all."

Both friars laughed simultaneously.

Alex tied the rope around his waist and sat at the edge of the opening. "Ready?"

The older friar nodded.

Alex slid off the edge and felt the rope take his weight. The friar played it out, and before long, Alex was at the bottom. One by one, everyone was lowered.

"God bless all of ye in your quest," the older friar said, his voice drifting down to them.

"And ye in yours," the younger friar called back up.

They heard a scraping sound, and the flagstone was dropped back into place. There was no turning back.

They followed the tunnel, their torches casting flickering shadows along rough rocky walls. It opened into a large crescent-shaped chamber filled with intricate carvings. Pillars resembled the trunks of trees, with branches that soared up high to form the chamber's vaulted ceiling. Stone birds stared down at them from delicately chiseled twigs. The entire chamber looked like it had once been a living forest, which had suddenly been petrified and buried deep underground.

Opposite them was a wall covered with stone vines and

branches. Strange creatures, large and small, peered through the leaves.

Alex had been here twice before, and it seemed different each time. It was as if the carved animals changed places. The only thing that hadn't moved was the monstrous head of stone, smack in the center of the wall.

The friar rubbed his thumb over the cross that hung about his neck, his lips moving soundlessly.

Alex walked over to the wall and pressed on the nose of a stone iguana whose telescopic eyes looked in different directions. He knew many of these carvings had moving parts, some by twisting, others by pushing or pulling, and that they all worked together like combination dials on a huge safe. How they were set would determine where they emerged in time.

"Are you sure you know how to go back just eleven years?" Annie asked.

"Of course!" Alex cracked his knuckles. "Didn't you see me keep notes on how the professor brought you back to the future the last time? First, I've got to turn the head on that bull-stag thing that's holding the globe on its shoulders, then I give the moon just a slight clockwise twist so it's at a different angle to the stars. Every click is a year. After that, all I need to do is pull down on the bird's head so its beak goes –"

"He was off," Annie said.

"Off?" Alex paused. "You mean, he didn't get it right?"

"It took us two tries."

"Oh."

Alex scaled the wall's carvings to reach the creature with the globe. An antler that he used as a handgrip clicked into a new position. He didn't mean for that to happen. He shifted to position himself on a creature's head, twisted the moon ever so slightly clockwise, and put his hand on the bird's head. He stopped. This couldn't be right.

Alex climbed back down and tried pulling the antler back to where it had been, but it was stuck.

Taking a deep breath, Alex closed his eyes and thought hard about where he wanted to go. *The king has recently died. Lord Douglas ordered that my parents be executed. Sir Ellerslie gave the commands to executioners, who were mounting the steps to –*

"No!" Acting on impulse, Alex scrambled back up the wall and simultaneously yanked on a ring in the bull's nose and pulled down on the bird's head so that its beak dipped into the hole at its feet.

The rumbling started. The floor shook, and there was a crash. Stone dust billowed through the chamber, clouding the flickering torchlights.

Coughing, Alex fell to the floor and covered his face with his sleeve. As the dust settled, he saw that the jaw of the huge grinning head of stone had lowered to the ground, its mouth gaping open.

Alex motioned for everyone to come in close. "We've got to stay together," he cautioned. "It might close with some of us on the outside."

"We're to go down Satan's gullet?" the friar asked. "How very interesting. Shall I go first?"

"Thank you, Friar. Be my guest."

The friar paused. "My older self had said that I would not see ye again until this day, so I will take this moment to wish ye well with your quest to save Alex's parents." The friar raised his hand and made the sign of the cross. "God bless ye and go with ye on this difficult journey."

"Amen!" Alan exclaimed, raising his hand to give the friar a high five.

Annie pulled Alan's arm down. "Thank you for all your help," she said, bowing politely. "It has been a privilege to meet you."

"And thanks for saving my life!" Craig piped in.

The friar ruffled Craig's hair.

"Guys," Alex said, clearing his throat to get everyone's attention. "This thing can close up at any moment – we have to go."

With the friar leading the way, they all climbed into the cavernous mouth and up the stone tongue. They came to the top of the throat and the space narrowed, forcing them to crawl on their hands and knees.

"Any second now," Alex warned, his heart beating rapidly. "We're past the pivot point."

The stone slab under them abruptly dropped, and the tongue behind them rose up. The jaw boomed shut, hard. They slid down the remaining slope and were flung out over an abyss, their arms flailing helplessly, torches spinning from their grasp.

They fell, yet the wind did not rush past them. Instead, they drifted through a kaleidoscope of flashing lights and swirling colored mist.

Shrieks and moans came from all around. Alex couldn't tell which sounds were from his friends, which came from him, and which were from whatever or whomever was rising up to greet them. Not able to see past the end of his arm, he grabbed Annie's hand to keep from losing her. She felt cold, and he pulled her close – only to discover he was clutching a severed arm. Screaming, he pushed it away. Frantic, he looked for Annie and the others, but all he saw drifting in and out of the swirling mists were the ghastly gray faces of the dead. They were laughing, cackling, calling him, reaching their shrouded arms for him, plucking at his clothes.

Alex kicked and squirmed. It was as if he were in a mass grave of decaying bodies that had all come alive. There was no getting away from them. He curled into a whimpering ball, covering his head with his arms.

Suddenly an updraft pushed him toward a shimmering brightness. He was no longer drifting, but soaring, racing, ever accelerating. It grew so bright he could no longer see. The top of his head felt like it had burst open and everything had come streaming out.

28

Hill Men

Willie heard a strained, heavy panting and the crunch of footsteps running on loose shale. A man dressed in rags dashed by. Willie leaped to his feet, his head still spinning. Hoofbeats and shouts surrounded him.

Annie lay nearby. She rolled onto her side and held her head.

"Over here!" Alan called. "Quickly!"

Willie helped Annie to her feet, and they scrambled the short distance to the brambles behind Alan. After they wriggled on their bellies under the thorny branches, Craig helped to pull them into a hollow near the center. Alan crawled in after them, rearranging the branches to hide the way they came.

"Where's Alex?" Annie asked.

No one knew.

They parted the tangled branches to peek out. More raggedly dressed men were sprinting down a nearby slope, leaping over bushes. Men on horseback were in close pursuit, clubbing anyone they caught. The ragged men soon gave up, clustering helplessly as the men on horseback circled. Scattered about the hillside were men who lay still and others who held their bleeding heads as they tried to get back on their feet.

"Those four big men on the horses," Alan pointed, "aren't they the ones Earl Warenne hired to track Alex down?"

"But that's eleven years from now," Willie whispered. "They can't have followed us back in time, can they?"

"No, I think they're just eleven years younger," Alan replied.

The riders demanded that the men gather their injured. A small prone figure lying facedown on the open hillside was seized by the back of the tunic and dragged over the rocky ground.

"That's Alex!" Annie cried, clapping her hand to her mouth. "They'll kill him!"

"Why would they?" Willie asked. "They won't know who he is. They've never met him before, remember?"

A team of horses pulling a prison wagon stopped nearby. The men on horseback prodded the ragged band of men into the back of the wagon, ordering them to carry the unconscious in with them. Alex was slung aboard.

One of the hill men suddenly scooped up a fistful of dirt and flung it into a horse's eyes. The horse reared and skittered back, the rider struggling to retain control. The man sprinted away, sailing over bushes and rocks in huge leaps. A single horseman went in pursuit. He tucked his club away and unsheathed a long gleaming sword.

Yelping with fear, the man ran an erratic path that took him ever closer to where Annie, Willie, Alan, and Craig lay hiding. The rider was steadily closing the gap. Just when it seemed as if the man were about to scramble under their bushes, the rider thundered alongside. The man fell to his knees, the tip of a sword protruding from his chest. The man looked down at it as if wondering what it could possibly be doing there. Then, just as suddenly, the sword tip disappeared.

The rider wheeled his horse about and gave his companions a wave with his bloodied sword. Then he galloped away, leaving the man still on his knees, staring dumbfounded at the small gash in his chest.

No one else tried to escape. The remaining captured men climbed into the wagon with Alex. Annie and the others could do nothing but watch as the driver flicked his whip and the wagon rumbled away, the riders clopping along at its side.

Annie wriggled out from under the bushes. The kneeling man blinked at her.

"Are ye an angel?" he asked.

"You'd best lie down." Annie took him gently by the shoulders and eased him to the ground.

"I havenae been such a bad man," the man babbled, tears filling his eyes. "I didnae want to join the robbers. I tried to look after my family – really, I did – but the Lord took them away, and when I lost my land, what was there for me to do?"

Annie pulled up the man's shirt and pressed it against his chest where blood was bubbling from the gash. There was no stopping the blood trickling out from under him.

The man clutched Annie desperately. "I had two boys and a wee girl. I would have had another, but my wife died when our fourth was born. Oh, I miss them so."

"Would you like to see them again?" Annie asked, her bottom lip quivering.

The man trembled. "Aye, I would, aye, aye. . . ."

Annie put her hand on his forehead. "Close your eyes and think of them."

As he did, a slow smile came to his face.

Spasms racked his body, and then he was gone, the smile still on his face.

———⊶◆⊷———

Alex was lying facedown. Bands of light fell over a blood-ied arm that lay before him. Wiggling his fingers confirmed his suspicion – it was his arm. He felt his head. Its insides felt a lot bigger than the outside, but it seemed to be in one piece.

Why was he being jostled about? Dimly, he realized he was in a moving wagon. Lifting his head, he saw that he was not alone. All around him were men in filthy rags, heads resting on knees, unkempt hair hanging over folded arms.

"Look who's wakin' up," one grunted.

"Shame," another said, making loud smacking noises. "I was just takin' a fancy to 'm."

"Shut it back there!" The wagon-driver turned and shook his whip at them.

Alex scrambled to his knees. "Let me out!" he called to the driver. "There's been a mistake."

"Tell that to the magistrate," the driver replied over his shoulder. "And ye'd best come up with something good or ye'll hang along with all the other thieving vermin we round up and haul out of the hills."

"Hang?" Alex clutched the bars. "What magistrate – where?"

"Straith Meirn – now keep your mouth shut. We've got a long ride ahead of us, and I dinnae want to hear any more yammering back there."

Alex looked past the driver. To his horror, he recognized the four big armed men on horseback riding alongside the wagon. *They couldn't be . . .*

"Who are they?" he asked in disbelief.

"Those riders?" The driver laughed. "Just some bounty hunters the townsfolk have hired to help us round up vermin. Now get away, or I'll call them over and have them shut ye up."

Alex hid his face. *The riders couldn't possibly know who I am*, he reasoned, taking deep breaths to stay calm. *This is eleven years before I met them.*

He risked a glance. The riders looked younger than when he had last seen them outside the mill where Don-Dun was held captive. They seemed timeless somehow. The thin one caught Alex staring, and his sparse whiskers twitched into a smirk. Alex quickly turned away.

A dirty man sat with his mouth open across from Alex. "Unless ye've got friends in high places, the magistrate will soon have ye swinging," he cackled. "That old bag of guts is out to get us."

"It doesnae matter none." An older man waved a withered hand. "We dinnae have much of a life anyway, what with all the livin' in caves and sleepin' under pigskins. There's no home for the likes of us, and no home to be made either."

"Oh?" protested yet another man, who lay back on one elbow, his legs crossed. "Well, I kind of like my life – 'specially when I get to stick it to one of them nobles." He thrust an imaginary knife and laughed, the stumps of his few remaining teeth sawing back and forth.

Alex turned away from the man's foul breath. At the other end of the wagon, a frightened-looking boy sat staring into the dirty straw. Covered in grime, he didn't seem much younger than Alex.

"Hello, what are you doing here?" Alex asked, sliding over.

The boy hissed at him.

"Leave 'm be," a man next to him said.

"Is he your son?" Alex asked.

"Gib?" The man shook his head. "Who's to say whose son he is? We captured his mother during one of our raids. Neylles was her name. She died giving birth. With no one taking care of him, it's a miracle he's lasted as long as he has."

"What's that ye're saying?" Another man thumped his chest. "I fed him – shared what little I had."

"Aye, but only when ye were taking him out to lie on the road in one of your robberies."

"Worked, did it no'?" The man flipped his greasy hair back over his shoulder. "They always stopped their carriage. Ha! Stupid nobles. How many did we kill?"

"Enough for the town to raise a bounty." The man pointed an accusing finger. "We're going to hang on account of ye, Dungbag Dirk."

"Dungbag!" Dirk's fist shot into the air. "Now *there's* a name to be remembered by! For years to come, minstrels will tell tales of Dungbag and his dogs."

———•◆•———

Children dashed out from around the backs of huts, calling loudly for their friends to join them. Bits of fresh dung were thrown at the passing captives, the children squealing with delight whenever they scored a hit.

Women tending cooking fires straightened and stared, their arms folded. Men stood at the roadside, shouting insults. A growing crowd followed the wagon, hurtling filth and stones. Alex was glad that armed men rode alongside.

The wagon rumbled into a small cobblestone square sur-rounded by shuttered storefronts. In the center, tents and awnings sheltered the few remaining merchants who had yet to pack up. It was near dusk, and most had left their wares secured under tarps for the night.

The wagon approached the end of the square, where a stone building cast a long shadow. The wagon creaked and swayed as the driver guided his horses into a neighboring alley and pulled up on the reins. The wagon stopped. He wedged the brake and leaped to the ground. The horsemen dismounted and drew their swords, the villagers gathering at the end of the alley.

A trapdoor was flung open, revealing a set of stone steps that led into the ground alongside the building.

The driver unlocked the padlock and swung open the back of the wagon. "Get moving," he barked.

A roar went up as, one by one, the captives reluctantly climbed out. Villagers reached past the cordon of armed men to poke with their sticks and fling stones.

Dirk dropped out of the wagon and landed heavily on both feet. Swatting away a stick, he snorted defiantly and spat. Stones bounced off his back as he stomped down the stairs.

Alex was jostled with the others as they leaped from the wagon and ran for the stairs. A stick caught him on the side of the head, and he was pushed to the ground. He crawled the last few feet under a rain of blows and tumbled down the steps, the last of the hill men stepping over him in their scramble for shelter.

He landed in the cellar, where the only light came from a tiny shaft. Holding his throbbing head, he paused while his eyes adjusted to the darkness.

A big man pointed with his club. "I am your jailer," he announced. "Go through that door at the end – now!"

The captives stumbled along an uneven dirt floor, ducking their heads to keep from hitting the joists. The jailer closed a gate behind them, securing it with a massive padlock.

"Where's our food?" Dirk demanded. "It's been more than a day since we've eaten."

"Food?" The jailer snorted. "Not a chance. It would just end up in your drawers when ye hang."

A rumble of protest erupted from the hungry prisoners. Dirk rattled the gate. "Damn it, man. Bring us bread, at least."

The jailer motioned through the bars with his club. "See them buckets? That's water, and it's all ye're getting." He let out a short barking laugh. "That way, all ye'll leave is a puddle."

"There's a place in hell for people like ye," Dirk roared as the jailer turned away.

"Let's hope our place in hell is better than his," a prisoner muttered.

"Just shut it." Dirk gave him a push. He gestured with his arm about the damp and dingy cellar chamber. "See this?

This is hell. And our life? More hell. So dinnae talk to me about what hell is to follow – we've already had our share." Dirk paused, squinting into a dark recessed corner. "Hello. Who have we here?"

A haggard-looking man in a dirty robe stood up. "We are guests of Lord Douglas," he said stiffly.

Craning his neck to see behind the robed man, Dirk stabbed with his finger. "I mean, who have we *here?*"

"This is my wife, Lady Macpherson." The man motioned to the woman lying on the straw. "Please pardon her for not returning your greeting; the murky water they give us has made her unwell."

Macpherson? Did I hear that right? His heart pounding, Alex strained to make out the man's features in the dim light.

The man before him had a swollen, black eye, red gashes across his face, and a scruffy beard. He looked nothing like the father he vaguely recalled from when he was five, nor the smiling face in the old pictures. But just how many Macphersons would Lord Douglas have imprisoned at this time?

"Oh, there's no need for formal introductions." Dirk rubbed his hands together and licked his crusty lips. "Stand aside, Lordy."

The haggard man's arm darted out, and Dirk fell to the ground.

The other men stared, bewildered. The man had hit Dirk so quickly that half of them didn't see it happen.

"George, what is the matter?" A woman's weak voice quavered from the shadows.

George knelt and held Marian's hand. "Not to worry, my dear Marian."

Marian and George Macpherson. Alex could hardly believe it! They had to be his parents. After all this time, he had really found them!

George glanced up at the scruffy boy who stood staring with his mouth agape. "What is it?" he demanded.

"Er, nothing," Alex replied hastily, turning away.

"You have a strange manner of speaking," George said suspiciously. "Where are you from?"

"I couldnae say, sire," Alex replied, doing his best to mimic the current manner of speech. "But it's very far doon the coast. Will the lady be all right?"

George's brow furrowed. He glanced sadly at the pale woman next to him. She had gone back to sleep. "Who's to say, lad," he said. "Tomorrow will tell."

Alex looked back at his tired father, who held his mother's hand. He just couldn't bring himself to tell his father who he was. How could he tell him that his only son – a boy who had grown more than eight years older in his absence and had come through time to find him – was now to be executed at his side, along with a collection of filthy, murderous hill men? His father would be deranged with grief. And how would his mother, sick and weak, take to learning her son was to hang? She would die with a broken heart.

Alex turned away, devastated. Slumping into a corner, he buried his face in his arms.

What little daylight that reached them through the tiny shaft was fading. Soon they would be in complete darkness.

29

SENTENCING

The magistrate shifted irritably in his raised chair and surveyed the scene before him. Villagers gathered in the square. Women huddled in their shawls to ward off the crisp morning air as children chased each other in and out of the throng.

The magistrate sighed. He hated getting up so early, but the villagers wanted to be present for these proceedings. They had to work in the fields all day, and sundown was their favorite time for the hangings. That left only the early morning for these trials.

What a collection of prisoners he had to try today: everyone from hill men to foreigners suspected of having had a hand in the king's death. The four bounty hunters the local villagers had hired did a good job rounding up suspects. They were an intimidating bunch, spreading fear by calling themselves the Four Horsemen of the Apocalypse and going by the names War, Conquest, Famine, and Death.

And now, as if there weren't enough prisoners here already, brought in just this morning was yet another: a big, bony local lad wearing a silly white hat.

"Bring them out," the magistrate barked.

A long line of prisoners shuffled from the alley, their shackled feet chained from one prisoner to the next. Despite being hurried along by guards, they advanced slowly, in jerky steps that were often cut short.

"Ellerslie, did ye have to chain them together?" the magistrate grumbled, settling back to pick some dirt from under his nails. "Are they so dangerous that all these guards, plus those four big men who headed up their capture, were not enough?"

The young noble at his side shrugged apologetically. "We dinnae want them running off."

"What did Lord Douglas say about the foreigners?" The magistrate watched as a chained man struggled to help the female prisoner walk. She looked unwell.

"That they were to be hanged. Prior to his fateful ride to see his queen, the king had ordered that, should anything happen to him along the way, the foreigners were to be executed. So Douglas said that is what we are to do."

"Aye, the king is dead, but we have yet to say 'Long live the king' to another." The magistrate leaned in close. "Are ye sure we willnae offend some neighboring power by executing these two?"

"Better that than to offend Lord Douglas. I say, off with their heads." Ellerslie gave an enthusiastic swing of his arm.

The magistrate twisted in his chair. "Really? Ye prefer that to a hanging?"

"Let's do both." Young Ellerslie nodded gravely. "First we

hang them, then we cut off their heads. That way, we can display their heads by the town gates. Lord Douglas would like that."

The magistrate raised an eyebrow. "Quite keen to please Lord Douglas, are we?"

The young noble flushed. "He is my benefactor, sire, one who has promised that I will be a knight one day, if I keep up my good work."

"I'm sure ye will make a fine knight." The magistrate clasped Ellerslie by the shoulder and smiled at him. He pointed to the broad-shouldered boy with the floppy white hat who, although only in his teens, stood taller than the rest. "Tell me, is that the young lad who I hear killed the son of the English constable of Dundee? What happened there?"

Ellerslie shrugged. "The constable's son was always out picking fights with local boys – this one he lost."

"Did I hear right, that the boy was captured while in disguise?"

Ellerslie laughed. "Aye, a local innkeeper put him in a gown, slapped that floppy white hat on him, and had him sit behind a spinning wheel. He had his pursuers fooled for a while, and he might have gotten away with it if he wasn't so damned big."

"What's his name?"

"William Wallace."

"Never heard of him. . . . Who are his parents?"

"No one of any note."

The magistrate sighed. "What a shame – such a fine, strapping young lad. Ah, well, this will be the last anyone hears of William Wallace."

The stumbling prisoners were finally prodded into a row between the magistrate and the growing crowd of villagers. The magistrate straightened.

"Tell me your names," he barked, "starting with the short man at the end."

The first hill man mumbled his name.

"Louder!"

"Gawter!"

"Where are ye from?"

The man looked off to the hills. "Away over," he replied.

"Well, Gawter from away over, do ye ken that ye stand accused of being one of a band of robbers who have plundered travelers and defiled their women?"

Gawter nodded.

"Do ye?" the magistrate asked sharply. "Speak up, man."

"Aye!"

"And what say ye to these charges?"

Gawter hung his head. "What else was there for me to do?"

"Guilty!" The magistrate smacked his wooden hammer down on the armrest of his chair. "At sundown today, ye shall hang by your neck until dead. Next! What's your name?"

The villagers exchanged glances, rubbing their hands in anticipation.

"Dungbag," Dirk replied defiantly.

"What kind of name is that?"

"It is the name your women cry out when I have the pleasure of them."

An angry roar erupted from the crowd. War hit Dirk

over the head with a short club, dropping him to his knees.

"Enough!" The magistrate rose halfway from his chair. "Dungbag, I sentence ye to hang by the neck until not yet dead and to have your entrails removed and burned before your sorry eyes."

Drool dribbled from Dirk's mouth. Dazed, he did his best to spit in the magistrate's direction, but he only managed to get it down his shirt.

"Next! What's your name, boy?"

His inquiry was greeted by silence.

"Speak up!"

"His name is Gib, your honor," Alex said nervously. "He is innocent. The others forced him to –"

"His innocence or guilt is for me to decide," the magistrate snapped. "Gib, where are ye from?"

Gib stammered something incomprehensible.

"Are ye the lad who we've heard stops carriages by lying on the road?" Ellerslie demanded.

Gib nodded.

"He is from noble parents," Alex protested. "Neylles was their name. He has been held by these men since –"

"Silence!"

Pain burst through Alex's head, and he dropped to his knees. Stars flashed through his vision as he dimly glimpsed Conquest stepping back into line with the other guards.

"Neylles, eh?" The magistrate leaned toward Ellerslie. "Didn't some Neylles go missing some ten years back?"

"Aye, but they had no child."

"Still . . ." The magistrate stroked his chin. "We'll leave that one for now. Next!"

The roaring still loud in his ears, Alex felt a prodding in his back.

"It appears he has been struck mute." Ellerslie gave Conquest an angry glare. "Kindly refrain from hitting the prisoners until after they have been declared guilty."

Conquest shrugged.

"Were ye with the others?" the magistrate asked.

Alex tried raising his head, but it nodded back down from the pain.

"Guilty," the magistrate declared. "Ye will be sentenced once we've heard from the others. Next!"

"I am George Macpherson," Alex's father said calmly.

"And who is that ailing woman at your side?"

"Marian, my wife."

"Ellerslie, read out the charges," the magistrate ordered.

Ellerslie held up a scroll. "George and Marian, of unknown origins, said to have the Scottish surname Macpherson, are charged with complicity in the king's death."

A murmur arose from the villagers. This was not a run-of-the-mill charge.

"What say ye?" the magistrate demanded, watching the Macphersons closely. The woman did not appear aware of her surroundings, but the man was sharply attentive.

"Not guilty." George Macpherson's words rang out clearly.

"On the evening that the king died, did ye not seek to speak to him?" Ellerslie asked. "And did ye not gain the audience of Lord Douglas, to whom ye said the king would die if he rode that night?"

George nodded.

The magistrate leaned forward. "If ye had no knowledge of a conspiracy to kill the king, how is it that ye knew that the king would die?"

George remained silent.

The magistrate settled back in his chair. "It is as I thought. The king was found dead at the bottom of a cliff. He was an accomplished rider and knew the trail. It defies belief that he would have simply fallen, particularly when someone knew of his imminent death. That makes ye guilty of either sorcery or conspiracy, and the sentence for both is the same: death. Do ye have anything to say?"

"We are innocent, M'Lord," George replied quietly.

"It troubles me, but I have no choice." The magistrate raised his gavel.

"Wait!" Alex called. "They were trying to *save* the king. They are from –"

His words were cut off by another blow from Conquest's club. This time, he ended up face-first and motionless in the dirt.

Ellerslie glared at Conquest. "What did I say ye're not to do?"

Conquest shrugged and tucked his club away.

"The lad thinks everyone is innocent," the magistrate mused.

"Have him hang with the rest," Ellerslie said hotly.

"Aye, I'm tired of this." The magistrate swept his hand over the line of prisoners. "The whole lot of ye . . . guilty. I hereby sentence each of ye to death at sundown, here on this square."

The boy with the floppy white hat suddenly raised his manacled hands and shook his fists. "Freedom!" he bellowed, much to the astonishment of the villagers.

"Aye, but not for ye." The magistrate banged his gavel. He got to his feet, glad the proceedings were over. "Now, let us get on with our day."

———————

Alex had a splitting headache. He gingerly felt the goose egg on the top of his head.

He had been sentenced to hang this evening, along with the others. Sir Ellerslie of the future had told the truth when he said he was present when the magistrate ordered Alex's execution. Could it really come to this? After all these years of searching, would he die with his father and mother in some remote time?

He peered through the dim light of the cellar prison to where the teenager with the floppy hat sat with his back to the wall, playfully flicking pieces of straw at Gib. Was he really the William Wallace he came to know more than a decade later?

A wet cloth was pressed against his head. Alex looked up and saw his father kneeling next to him, his brow creased with concern.

"How's your head?"

"Hurts."

"Not surprised. Water?" George gestured to the bucket.

"No, thanks."

George squinted. "Where are you from?"

"Away over."

"No, you're not. You're from the future, aren't you?"

Alex's eyes widened.

"How did you know I was trying to save the king?" George demanded. "Where were you going to say I was from?"

"Away over."

"Don't give me that. Who are you?" George crumpled Alex's tunic in his fist and pulled his face in close. "Tell me!"

"Your son?"

"Nooo!"

"It's true." Tears welled up in Alex's eyes.

"What's your name?"

"Alex. I grew up in Canada with Uncle Larry, but came back to Scotland during the summer holidays and found my way into the tunnels under Duncragglin ruins. . . ."

Stunned, George let go of Alex's tunic. Gently pulling Alex close, he gave him a hug. "Don't tell your mother," he said into Alex's ear. "The shock would be too much."

"I'm sorry I couldn't save you," Alex said tearfully.

"That wasn't your job, you silly lad. You were to grow up and have your own life, not go about digging up the past."

"But the past wasn't finished. How could I go on until it was?"

"Well, it's finished now, son." George held Alex at arm's length. He looked defeated. "I'm sorry I've brought everything to this. It really wasn't my intention, you know. . . ."

"Of course not. You were going to save King Alexander."

"That's right."

"Because if you did, Scotland wouldn't have lost its independence, and it wouldn't have had all those wars trying to get it back."

"Stupid, wasn't I?" George leaned back against the wall.

"No, not at all. It made for a great adventure, didn't it?"

George looked at Alex sharply.

"What's life without a little adventure now and then?" Alex added.

George smiled. "You *are* my son," he said. He glanced about the cellar prison. "Do you think there's a way out of here?"

"Sure." Alex pointed to the teenager, who was laughing as he fended off a retaliatory attack by Gib. "For one thing, we know he's getting out."

George studied the big teenager. "Do you really think he's the same William Wallace?"

"Absolutely! The Wallace I met was eleven years older and had a beard, but it's him all right."

"You've met William Wallace!" George's jaw dropped.

"Oh, yes. He rescued me off Stirling Bridge after I convinced Lord Cressingham to cross it, and sometime before that, I gave him suggestions on how to attack Duncragglin Castle."

"Oh my God." George put his hands to his head. "Let me get this straight. You've been back here at various times influencing the course of history. And each time, events turn out in a way that fits with the history we know in the twenty-first century?"

"Well, the history you know, maybe. I wasn't the best student."

George shook Alex by the shoulders. "Do you know what this means?"

"What will be will be?"

"No! It means that I can do something important back here after all. I didn't manage to save the king, but I can still save Wallace."

"Really?"

"Yes!" George's fist shot up, startling everyone around them. He leaned in close. "Without Wallace, Scotland would never have regained its independence. He was the spark that put everything in motion. I must make sure he stays on that path!"

"Okay. So what do we do?"

George leaped up, grabbed the bars, and rattled the gate loudly. "Help!" he yelled.

The big jailer came plodding down the gloomy corridor. "Stop all this noise," he demanded, banging the bars with his club to make George back off. "What's this all about?"

George dropped to his knees, folding his hands in front of him. "Help me please," he sobbed. "They're going to kill me and take my wife."

"Who?" Curious, the jailer peered into the cell.

George pointed to the startled hill men.

"Take his wife?" Dirk took his hand off his bloodied face, his crusty lips parting into a lewd smile.

"See? They'll attack us at any moment. My wife has fainted from fright. You have to get us out of here! Please!" His face pressed against the gate, George reached as far as he could through the bars, his wavering fingers just short of the jailer's doublet.

The jailer turned to leave. "The whole lot of ye will be dead in a few hours. No one will care if some of ye die a few minutes earlier."

"Wait! I have gold."

The jailer paused. "Ye've all been searched. How can ye have gold?"

"I kept it down below." Fingering something hidden in his palm, George nodded toward a bucket. "I cleaned it in their drinking water. Want to see it?"

The jailer thumped his club against the bars to warn everyone to stay back. He bent in close.

George grabbed the jailer and pulled him into the gate. Seizing the doublet on either side of the jailer's neck, George twisted his wrists and pulled with all his might. The fabric tightened. The jailer made tiny squeaking noises. His face turned red and his eyes bulged. In less than a minute, the jailer went limp.

George let him collapse at the base of the gate. He unclipped the jailer's keys and fiddled with the lock. Tumblers clicked, and the gate swung inward. The prisoners leaped to their feet.

"Stay where you are!" George snatched up the jailer's club and blocked the gate.

The men milled about in confusion. Dirk slowly got to his feet. "Ye're no' going to try to stop us, are ye?"

"No, we're all getting out. But I'm not having you all stampede out of here and ruin everything." George gestured to a short hill man. "You!"

Gawter looked side to side and pointed to himself. "Me?"

"Yes, you. Pull the jailer in here and take off his clothes."

"What's your plan?" Dirk demanded.

"William Wallace will dress like the jailer – he's the only one tall enough. We'll stuff some straw up his garments to bulk him up. Once he's outside, he can see where the guards are stationed and find an escape route for the rest of us."

"What kind of a plan is that?" Dirk spat. "How will the whole lot of us get out of this town in full daylight? They'll be on us before we make it to the town gates."

"I have a suggestion." Wallace raised his hand. "We take the flint the jailer uses to light the torch at night and start a fire down here so that smoke goes up the vent. Then every one of ye makes a lot of noise. I'll run out dressed as the jailer and call for the guards. When they follow me back in here, we overpower them, take their surcoats and weapons, and ride out on their horses."

"Easy as that." Dirk stared at him in disbelief.

"Ye could all be waiting in the room just inside the cellar door," Wallace explained. "The guards will be coming in from bright sunshine and won't see a thing. We let most of them pass and then leap on the last of them. When the first ones turn around, they'll be facing ye down a narrow corridor and won't have a chance."

"Let me understand this," Dirk said slowly. "Are ye suggesting that rather than escaping, we take command of this town?"

"Exactly!" Wallace nodded.

"Are ye thinking what I'm thinking, lads?" Dirk licked his crusty lips. "The townsfolk will be defenseless – every last man, child, and *woman*!"

The men rubbed their hands together, a renewed sparkle in their eyes.

"What are we waiting for, lads," Dirk bellowed. "Let's start a fire and make some noise!"

"Not so fast!" George waved his hand for everyone to quiet down. "First Wallace and I need to go out and find out where the guards are. For this to work, we will need to attract as many of them as possible. Otherwise, there will be too many of them left outside for us to overpower, and we won't have enough weapons."

"Wait just one second." Dirk stepped in their way. "What's to keep ye and Willie-Dilly here from just slipping out of town and leaving us in this jail?"

George pointed to where his wife lay on the straw. "My wife will remain here, so you can be assured I'll be back."

Dirk smirked.

George thrust Dirk up against the wall and held him there with his club. "If you so much as lay one hand on her, I will kill you – slowly – got that?"

Dirk nodded.

George pushed him away. Glancing at Wallace, he said, "Let's go." And then the two of them were gone.

Alex carefully arranged the straw under his mother's head.

"Could I have some water please, George?" she said, her eyes closed.

Alex filled a clay mug. He helped his mother sit up.

"Where's George?" she asked, blinking in confusion.

"He had to go out on an errand," Alex replied, gently steadying the cup as she tipped it up with shaky hands. "He asked me to look after you until he's back."

Marian took a sip. A dribble of water trickled down her chin.

"Would you like a wet cloth for your forehead?" Alex asked, dabbing her chin with the cloth his father had given him. "You feel very warm."

"Yes, thanks." Marian lay back on the straw. "I must still have that fever. It's been so many days now."

Alex soaked the cloth in the bucket and returned to his mother's side. He placed the wet cloth over her forehead.

"That's better." Marian adjusted the cloth down over her eyes.

There was a moment of silence, when Alex thought his mother had gone back to sleep. Suddenly she pushed the cloth back up. "Wait a minute. How could George be out on an errand? The last I remember, we were prisoners."

"He . . . er . . . was taken to see the magistrate."

Marian watched Alex intently.

"The magistrate, um, sent for him," Alex continued.

"Why do you seem familiar?"

"I, er . . . well, I don't . . ."

"You don't sound like you're from here. In fact, you sound like you're from where I come from. And your voice is just like George's." Marian frowned. "Tell me, truthfully, do I know you from somewhere?"

Alex stared back at her helplessly, unable to come up with a single thing to say.

"You're my son, aren't you?" Marian said.

Alex nodded, tears in his eyes.

"Oh, my boy." Marian wrapped her arms around Alex and pulled him close. "Why did you ever come here? You're as bad as George."

"We have to get you home," Alex said.

"Yes, home," Marian mumbled, stroking Alex's hair. "My son has come to take me home. I can't believe it. I can die happy now."

"No dying, Mother," Alex said fiercely. "We'll get you to a doctor. You'll be better in no time."

"Yes, better," Marian replied weakly, her eyes closing.

"Sleep now." Alex adjusted the cloth over his mother's eyes. "Soon we'll have some traveling to do."

30

HANGING TIME

"Here they come." Alan's voice was hollow.

"Where?" Craig stretched onto tiptoe, craning his neck to see over the crowd.

The jailer led a line of prisoners out from the alley, armed guards on both sides. Black sacking had been pulled over their heads and tied about their necks. They stumbled blindly, pulled along by the tugs on the chains from the prisoner ahead.

The crowd cheered wildly.

"Isn't there something we can do?" Annie pleaded to no one in particular. "Anything?"

The prison cellar had been heavily guarded for hours, ever since that big jailer had run around calling for help. Smoke had drifted out of a cellar vent, and all the prisoners had raised a big commotion. It seemed that the building would burn down with them in it.

The guards had run with buckets. The smoke stopped. They regained control and made sure it stayed that way, remaining with the prisoners these past hours as they awaited their execution.

The executioners were ready with their ropes and knives. So were the villagers, having hurried from the fields to watch the spectacle.

Annie covered her face with her hands. To have come all this way, only to stand within a bloodthirsty, cheering crowd and watch Alex die a terrible death . . .

She felt her knees grow weak. Light-headed and dizzy, she leaned on Willie for support. Surprisingly, he put his arm around her. It was the first time he had done so in as long as Annie could remember. His face was pale, and he stared at the gallows. She thought about when they first traveled back in time, when Willie was nearly hanged during the battle for Duncragglin. Sadly, this time, there would be no William Wallace to save the day.

Alan took hold of the back of Craig's tunic. "Don't even think of trying anything," he ordered. "There's no point in us all dying."

"But we have to do something," Craig said. "We can't just stand here and watch him die."

"You're right. We can't." Alan steered Craig away from the crowd.

"Where are we going?" Craig asked.

"We're going to wait somewhere else until all this is over," Alan replied firmly. "Then we'll meet up with Annie and Willie and go home. There's nothing else for us to do."

"No." Craig stopped, folded his arms, and stared at the ground. "I'm waiting right here. Don't worry. I won't do anything."

A crier mounted the scaffold. "Hear ye, hear ye," he began. "We are gathered to witness the hanging of –"

"Get on with it," demanded someone in the crowd.

"String them up," added another.

The crier started reading the prisoners' names from a scroll. Jeers erupted from the crowd when he read out the name Dungbag Dirk.

Annie scanned the row of prisoners, each with a black sack tied over his head. Alex would be the smallest of the group, but the only short prisoner looked far too round to be Alex.

Puzzled, Annie glanced back to the building with the prison cellar. She decided they must be performing the executions in two batches.

The first prisoner was pulled, kicking and squirming, up the gallows' steps. A priest made the sign of the cross as a rope was placed around the prisoner's neck. The prisoner made muffled noises and continued to fight, even as the rope tightened.

"Shouldn't these men be given a chance to say their last words?" someone suggested.

"Not these vermin." The chief executioner signaled to his men. They gave the rope a hard pull, and the prisoner rose up off the platform, his legs flailing wildly. The men secured the rope and threw another over the horizontal beam.

"Come on, bring up another," the chief executioner said impatiently. "We can do five at a time up here."

"Which one's Dungbag?" came a cry from the crowd. "He was to be de-bowelled while still alive!"

"Aye, thanks for reminding me." The executioner yanked the hood off the man who was hanging from his neck, his feet still kicking.

A gasp went up from the crowd. There, hanging before them with his eyes bulging and his face red, was not one of the prisoners, but the bounty hunter who went by the name Conquest, a gag tied over his mouth.

"Leave him up there," a guard on horseback ordered, raising his hat. The crowd let out a roar. "Aye, it's me, Dungbag." Dirk laughed, notching an arrow to his bow. "And I'll shoot the first one of ye that makes a move."

The other guards drew their weapons and circled the gathering. Now that the guards were closer, the villagers could see that they were the hill men dressed in the guards' clothes. The jailer leading the prisoners took off his cap and gave the crowd a wave.

"I am William Wallace!" he announced.

"On with the executions," the hill men chanted.

"That's not what we agreed." Alex's father waved his sword angrily. "You there, cut that man down."

The executioner's knife flashed, and Conquest fell in a crumpled, gagging heap.

"Where is the magistrate?" George demanded. "Bring him here – and Ellerslie too."

"They've gone," the chief executioner replied, nervously eyeing the encircling hill men.

"Gone where?"

"Aberdeen. They left soon after the proceedings this morning."

"Damn!"

"So much for your plan to hold them hostage as we leave town," Dirk sneered. "It looks like we'll just have to take some women instead."

"Don't be a fool!" George hissed quietly. "The villagers won't put up with that. Things will get out of hand.

We'll take some other men instead. We'll promise to leave them unharmed outside town if they let us leave and don't follow us."

"They might no' care about some other men, but they'll care about their women," Dirk retorted. "About ten or so should do it. Round them up, lads – pick the pretty ones!"

Dirk ordered the women to come forward, but the village men closed in around them. The hill men pulled out a few women, using their swords to prod back the men who blocked their way.

A village man clung to his young wife as a hill man yanked her from the crowd. "No, take me," he cried.

"Fine." With a hard thrust of his sword, the hill man ran him through.

The village man fell to his knees. His wife screamed, flinging her arms about him. The hill man gave him a kick, but before he could free his sword, the other villagers were on him. Knives came out, and the hill man went down in a rain of bloody blows.

Other hill men came to his aid, but a villager had retrieved the sword. Together with other villagers, he fought back furiously. Another hill man went down, and the villagers gained another sword. Shouts mingled with cries of pain.

"Hold them back!" Dirk spurred his horse forward and cut down a villager in his path. An attacker came in from behind, but Dirk swung his sword in time to hold him off.

In the pandemonium that followed, it was every man for himself. Villagers scattered. Still chained together and unable to see what was happening, the hooded prisoners stumbled about, pulling in opposite directions.

Dirk chased after a group of fleeing villagers. He caught a young maiden and pulled her up onto his horse before those with her could stop him. Kicking his horse into a gallop, he thundered out of the square with the maiden draped in front of him.

———— ◆ ————

George galloped back to the cellar prison. Gawter was readying the prisoner wagon as Alex helped steady the snorting beasts. Marian lay in the back of the wagon, her head rising from the straw to weakly peer through the bars.

"Things have not gone to plan," George panted as he drew up his horse. "We have to be away as fast as we can."

Alex leaped into the wagon. With a "hyah" and a flick of the reins, Gawter urged the horses to gallop.

They took side streets to avoid the chaos in the square. The iron-rimmed wheels clattered over the uneven cobblestones, bouncing the wagon with every sharp bump.

Villagers pressed back into doorways to get out of the way of the careening wagon. A group of youths who were running up ahead had to tumble to one side to keep from being run down.

"Stop the wagon!" Alex shouted, seizing the brake through the bars.

"What are you doing?" George demanded, pulling up his horse as the wagon skittered to a halt. "We have to hurry out of here before they catch us."

"Those are my friends!" Alex flung open the cage door at the back of the wagon. "In here!" he yelled, waving them over.

Alex helped his winded friends clamber aboard. Gawter

had the wagon moving again before Alan's feet were off the ground. Alex and Willie grabbed Alan's arms and slid him face-first into the wagon.

"Where's Annie?" Alex said.

"He's got her," Craig panted.

"Who?"

"One of the escaped prisoners," Willie gasped. "On horseback. He grabbed her and rode off before we could stop him."

"What did he look like?"

"I don't know – it was so fast. He was the one doing all the ordering."

"Oh my God!" Alex threw himself against the bars. Dad!" he called. "Dirk has my friend Annie!"

"Just how many friends do you have back in this time?" George asked. He rode in closer, straining to hear over the loud rumble of the wagon wheels.

"We have to stop him!"

"Don't worry. We'll meet him at our rendezvous," George replied calmly. "It's by the lookout on the cliffs just north of Duncragglin. That's where we're to release the hostages and head into the forest."

"But what if he doesn't go there? What if he just rides off on his own with Annie?"

"I don't think he'd do that," George said, frowning. "But if he does, what can we do about it?"

"You can ride ahead and stop him – you're faster than this wagon."

George shifted in his saddle. "But I've got to help William Wallace –"

"Forget about Wallace!" Alex was ready to explode. "He can look after himself. Can't you see? Saving Annie is the most important thing that any of us could possibly do right now."

"Gawter," George called reluctantly. "Take care of these young ones while I'm gone. Head straight for the rendezvous point. If you get there first, hide the wagon in the bushes and wait. I'll be as quick as I can." George urged his horse into a fast gallop and disappeared up ahead.

The wagon clattered out of town.

"If Dirk wanted to go straight back to his camp, which way would he go?" Alex called.

Gawter nodded inland. "He'd take the first trail into the hills."

"That one there?" Alex pointed to where a narrow trail forked off to the right.

Gawter shrugged. "Could be."

"Take it."

"What, with this wagon?" Gawter said. "What about –"

Nudging Alex aside, Alan reached through the bars with his aerosol can and sprayed red down the back of Gawter's hand.

"Blood?" Gawter shrieked, frantically trying to wipe off the paint. "What manner of sorcery is this?"

"You heard what Alex said. Take the trail."

Gawter tugged sharply on the reins, and the horses veered right. The wagon lurched over deep ruts. Gawter worked the brake to keep the wagon from pushing the horses in the dips. Inside the caged wagon, everyone had to hang on to the bars. Alex did his best to protect his mother.

They climbed up the narrow trail and over a rocky hill-side into a forested dale. Their progress was slow. Dirk would have to be taking his time for the wagon to catch him. Fearful that they were going the wrong way, Alex wondered at what point they should head back. It was possible that his father had overtaken Dirk and freed Annie by now.

The horses wheeled around a sharp bend, and they suddenly spotted Annie standing under a tree, her hands tied to an overhead branch.

Gawter drew up the horses. Alex was about to fling open the prison wagon when Dirk stepped out from behind a tree and held the sharp edge of his sword to Annie's throat.

"Stay in the wagon," he said. "Or I will slice off her head."

Alex froze. Willie gaped, his mouth open, but no sound coming out. Alan fingered his aerosol can nervously. Craig covered his eyes.

"Gawter, lift up your seat and ye'll find a box with a padlock," Dirk said calmly. "Take it, and lock them up."

Gawter obediently took out the padlock. "Sorry, lads, but orders is orders," he said as he clicked the padlock into place.

"All I wanted was to be alone with this fair maiden and enjoy her company for a while." Dirk sheathed his sword. "And now the whole lot of ye had to spoil it."

"Not me, Dungbag," Gawter protested. "I was just bringing them to ye so ye could be rid of them once and for all."

"Aye, well done." Dirk nodded. "Let's do that then, shall we? Pile some brush up around the wagon. I have the flint and tinder in my pocket."

"No!" Annie recoiled. "You can't just burn them alive."

"No?" Dirk gave her a big smile.

"You, you . . . monster!" Annie shrieked as Gawter stacked brush up against the wagon. "You will burn in hell forever if you do this."

Dirk spread his arms. "With the life I've had, eternity in hell awaits me. I might as well enjoy myself while I still can."

Gawter unhitched the horses and tethered them well away from the wagon. He returned with more armloads of kindling and slid them under the wagon.

"Please don't do this!" Annie cried.

Gawter knelt by the wagon and scraped the flint against the striker. Sparks sprinkled over the dry tinder. Tiny flames quickly grew larger.

Suddenly a boot stomped on the fire, spraying sparks into Gawter's face. Gawter looked up into the point of a sword.

Dirk spun about in surprise, hastily drawing his sword. "Why, it's young William Wallace!" Dirk rested the tip of his sword on the ground. "What brings ye here?"

Wallace prodded the kneeling Gawter with his sword. "Unlock the wagon," he said. "And be quick about it."

Gawter fumbled for the key.

"Stop right there, Gawter." Dirk raised his sword.

Gawter's eyes darted from Dirk to Wallace. He threw the key at Dirk, crawled under the wagon, and covered his head.

"My, that's a big sword ye've got there," Dirk mocked as he pocketed the key. "Think ye can handle it?"

Wallace brought his sword around and faced Dirk. His fingers flexed on the hilt.

Dirk lunged.

Wallace deflected Dirk's sword and pushed him aside.

Dirk's next blow came quickly, but Wallace was in time for that one too. They grappled briefly, their swords locked, before Dirk sprang back.

"No' the first time ye've handled a sword, I see," Dirk panted. He took off his cap and bowed. "Just so it's no' your last, how about we call this whole thing off? Ye can go your merry way with your wagon full of friends, and Gawter and I will head back into the hills."

"Fine," Wallace said. "Off ye go then." Keeping a wary eye on Dirk, he cut Annie loose, his sword slicing into the overhead limb as he severed the rope.

"Watch out!" Annie cried.

Wallace lashed out with his leg, and Gawter plunged his dagger into Wallace's thigh from behind. Freeing his sword from the overhead limb, Wallace swung it blindly. Gawter flung up his arm. The heavy sword severed his hand and bit deeply into his neck.

Dirk leaped forward. Annie used the rope that had bound her hands as a whip, wrapping the end about his sword arm. Before Dirk could free himself, Wallace buried the tip of his long blade into his side. Dirk staggered backward, his jaw hanging open.

Wallace reached out for the support of a nearby tree and slid to the ground, holding his leg where Gawter's dagger still protruded. Dirk sat in the clearing, his legs splayed out before him. He held his sword loosely, flat on the ground, and stared in disbelief at the blood soaking through the guard's surcoat that he wore over his tunic. Gawter was not far off, on his knees, clutching his neck with his one remaining hand. His severed hand lay palm up in the dirt.

"Are you badly hurt?" Annie asked.

All three men looked up at her.

"Aye." Dirk nodded miserably. "I think he's cut into my bowels."

"Badly, aye." Gawter stared at his severed hand. Blood trickled from between the fingers of his other hand.

"I may need only a stitch or two," Wallace replied cheerfully.

"Damn," Dirk spat, blood dribbling from his chin.

Alan sniffed the air. "Why is it I smell smoke?"

"Fire!" Annie pointed to the flames licking the underside of the wagon.

"Don't just stand there. Get us out!" Willie rattled the bars.

"The key . . ." Annie tried to remember where it went.

"Looking for this?" Dirk held up the key with a bloodied hand.

Annie reached for it, and Dirk grabbed her ankle. He shuffled painfully to prop himself up on one elbow.

"Do ye forgive me?" he pleaded.

"No!" Annie wrestled the key from his grip and kicked his arm to make him let go of her ankle.

"For God's sake, Annie!" Willie screamed.

Annie dashed for the wagon. It was almost completely engulfed in flames. Reaching right into the fire, she managed to insert the key into the padlock, but couldn't get it to turn. She hastily rubbed her singed hands over her clothes before trying again. This time, she took firm hold of the hot metal lock and cranked the key. It clicked open.

Alan burst through the gate, turning back to help Alex

with his mother. Catching her under her arms, Alan dragged her from the flames, the others leaping from the wagon after her. They rolled on the ground to beat out the flames.

Panting to catch their breath, they watched as the wagon turned into a flaming torch. The horses snorted and stamped from where they were tethered.

"How is everyone?" Annie asked anxiously.

Craig looked down at his singed clothes. "Hard to say," he replied. "It hurts here and there."

"Are you all right, Mum?" Alex asked.

Marian smiled weakly. "Fine," she said. "Don't you worry about me."

"What about you?" Willie took hold of Annie's arms to see her hands. He shook his head in dismay.

Wallace ripped off a part of his shirt and covered his wound, tying it off at the side. He clutched the tree and pulled himself up. "I need to be going. My mother will be fair worried about me," he said, wincing as he took a step. "She's good with a needle and can put in a stitch or two to help this heal."

Alex brought Wallace his horse. "Before you go, there's something I need you to remember," he said, holding the reins steady while Wallace carefully swung his injured leg over his horse's back.

"Name it," Wallace said, taking the reins and pulling back as the horse stamped and circled.

"One day, many years from now, there will be a big gathering of Scottish nobles, and you will be made guardian of Scotland."

Wallace laughed. "Aye, and is that the day ye become king of whatever land ye're from?"

"I'm serious – hear me out," Alex said. "This is very important. When you become guardian, you are to tell Sir Ellerslie what happened here today. Tell him that I did not die, and that my friends and parents didn't die either. Can you do that?"

"So when I'm guardian, and ye're king, he's going to be a *Sir* Ellerslie, is he now?"

"I know you don't believe it, but just remember what I told you, will you please?"

"I'm not likely to forget ye crazy bunch." Turning his horse about, Wallace smiled and waved. "Good luck to each and every one of ye!"

His horse burst into a gallop, and William Wallace was gone.

31

DUNCRAGGLIN

George brought up his horse and stared in disbelief at the team of plodding horses that Alex led out from the morning mist. Annie and Craig were on one horse, Alan and Willie on the other. Hitched behind them, where a wagon should have been, was a two-pole litter that creaked and clattered over the bumpy trail. His wife lay bundled up inside.

"What on earth is Marian doing in that thing?" he asked. "And where's Gawter?"

"He's toast," Alan said.

"And deservedly so," Willie called out from behind him.

"Toast?" George frowned. "Did you encounter Dirk?"

"We smoked him, didn't we, lads?" Alan said, laughing.

"After Wallace left," Alex explained, "we threw their bodies on the fire. Gawter's hand too. We didn't have shovels to bury them, and we didn't want to leave them for the wolves. By the time we finished building this litter for Mum, it was late, so we had to stay overnight."

"You threw Dirk and Gawter on the fire?" George repeated, aghast. "Are you sure they were dead?"

Alex looked at Alan.

"I think so." Alan shrugged. "Anyway, they are now."

"What happened to *you*?" George asked, suddenly noticing both of Annie's hands wrapped in cloth.

"They're badly burned," Alex answered. "We have got to get her back to our time to see a doctor – and Mum too. The sooner the better."

George examined the litter supporting his sleeping wife. "You did a great job building this," he said. "But it doesn't look made for speed."

There was no better way to transport Marian, and they plodded along at a frustratingly slow pace. The road meandered over and around the coastal hills, sometimes in sight of the ocean, other times deep in the woods. They passed a procession of merchants and traded a sword for some bread and smoked fish. A mountain stream provided cold clear water for washing and deep long drinks from cupped hands. Even Marian managed a sip and a few nibbles. Annie kept her hands in the cold water until it was time to go.

When it was still miles off, Craig spotted Duncragglin Castle, its battlements rising above the shoreline cliffs.

The group passed through the main gates unimpeded. This was not a time of war, so soldiers did not stop and question those who came and went.

George led the horses to the stables.

"A penny for boarding and brushing," the stable hand called out.

"I don't want boarding – I want them sold." George hitched the reins to a post.

"Do ye now?" The stable hand strolled around the horses, eyeing them up and down. He stopped next to the litter and scratched his head. "What is this?"

"My wife has fallen ill and needed transport," George replied stiffly. "You can cut it up for firewood if you like. How much for the horses?"

While they haggled over the price, Willie and Alex helped Marian get to her feet. She was shivering despite the blanket about her shoulders.

George steered them toward a table in the open market beside the stables. Marian collapsed onto the hard bench, her head resting on her arms.

George went in search of a few supplies. He spent a half-pence on several torches and a length of rope, and he used the rest to buy them something to eat.

"Need help, Annie?" Willie offered.

"That's okay." Annie carefully pressed her plate between her bandaged hands.

Alex was encouraged to see his mother take a few bites. If only her fever would go down. He rested his head against one propped arm, his elbow on the table. They were almost there. All they had to do was get into the dungeons and –

Alex froze. Sitting at a nearby market table were the four big men. The one who called himself Death raised his mug for a sip, his face shadowed in a deep hood.

Alex quickly turned away. "The bounty hunters!"

"Where?" George glanced around.

"Don't look!" Alex hissed.

"How did they get here before us?" Annie asked, dismayed.

"They must have gotten ahead of us when we went after you and Dirk," Alex guessed.

"Have they seen us?"

Alex risked a glance. "If they have, they're not letting on."

Leaving the four bounty hunters finishing their drinks, they slowly got up and slipped away into the market crowd.

Upon reaching the castle's drawbridge, George straightened the guard's surcoat he still wore from their escape and assertively marched everyone past disinterested guards. Once beyond the raised portcullis, they sped through the empty entrance hall as fast as they could with Marian supported between them.

Alex led the way through a side alcove to the steep spiral stairs leading down to the dungeons below. The gate was unlocked. They slipped inside, careful to not be seen. George paused to fire up the torches.

The guardroom at the bottom of the stairs was unmanned. The dungeons were empty. Alex led them past rows of cells until they came to the torture chamber. They pulled away the heavy rack and pried up the flagstone. George made a loop in the rope and tossed it to Alan.

"You lead the way," he said. "Take a torch."

Alan rappelled down the shaft, George playing out the rope above. Craig pleaded to go down with Willie by clinging to his back, but George insisted they go separately. Annoyed, Craig made no attempt to rappel and had to be lowered like a sack of potatoes.

"Shhh." Annie raised a finger to her lips as George raised the rope once again. "Did you hear that?"

Listening carefully, they heard a distant sound of footsteps.

"Is it them?" Annie whispered anxiously.

"That's probably just a guard doing a patrol," George said reassuringly. "Don't worry. Just go down the shaft and join the others." He placed the loop under Annie's arms and helped her over the edge. "No need to use your hands," he said. "I'll let the rope out carefully."

With Annie safely at the bottom, Alex and George paused to listen. The footsteps were getting louder. They heard the echo of distant voices.

"It *is* them, isn't it?" Alex said, his heart sinking. He looked despairingly from the open shaft to his shivering mother. "They're too close – they'll catch us for sure."

"No, they won't." George put his arm about Alex and took him aside. "But we're going to have to do this in two goes. You go on ahead with the others while I lead these guys astray."

"No! We have to stay together," Alex protested.

"We have no time to be arguing." George held up his hand firmly. "I will remain behind to close up the shaft and hide the tunnel. Once that's done, I'll stay hidden until these men have gone, then I'll find a way to go after you. But don't wait for me – it might take a while. Get your mother to a hospital as soon as you can. Now go!" George threw the rope over Alex's shoulders and gave him a hug. "I love you, son. I'm sorry I've messed up so badly. I didn't mean to leave you an orphan. Please forgive me. I'll see you again as soon as I can."

There were many things Alex wanted to say, but there was no time. His father pushed him along. He slid into the shaft and was quickly lowered. His mother came next. Alex untied her, the rope was dropped, and the flagstone slid back into place.

That was it.

"Come on. What are you waiting for?" Craig called.

"Coming," Alex mumbled, helping his mother catch up.

"Where's your father?" Craig asked.

Alex explained.

"He'll find a way later," Annie said hopefully.

"Of course he will." Alex tried to sound convincing for his mother's sake.

There was nothing for them to do but hasten through the tunnels to the large chamber with carved walls.

When they reached the crescent-shaped chamber, Alex took a deep breath and set about moving the carvings. Worried, he tried to remember how they were supposed to be positioned to advance to their time.

The rumbling started and the stone jaw dropped. They hurried deep into the opening, crawling where it narrowed.

"Brace yourselves to keep from sliding," Alex warned, his arm tight around his mother. The jaw rose to shut behind them, and the floor dropped under their feet. Down the slope ahead they saw the swirling, dimly illuminated mists. Moving closer, they heard the cackles of the damned rising up from the pit of time.

Alex tossed his torch into the pit and helped his mother to the edge. "Ready to go home?" he asked.

She smiled and gave him a feeble nod.

He looked at the others' scared faces.

Then, hand in hand, they jumped.

EPILOGUE

"That's it then, *Sir* Wallace." Sir Ellerslie put his arm around Wallace's shoulders. "We're now officially in your capable hands."

"I still cannae believe it." Wallace shook his head.

The celebrations that had gone on into the late evening were finally winding down. Nobles and knights took their leave, summoning their entourages as they left the grand hall. Sir Ellerslie thanked guests for coming. Wallace did his best to acknowledge everyone's parting congratulations.

"God's blessings go with ye," a friar said, giving a bow. "And a warm farewell from all your good friends."

The friar shuffled away, smiling, and Wallace gestured to the crowd in the hall. "Tell me, Ellerslie, who among this gathering would ye count among *your* good friends?"

"Not many, but I suppose there are a few –" Sir Ellerslie hesitated, frowning after the departing friar.

"What is it?"

"Strange, but that friar looks older than I remember him."

"We all look older – it has been a long night." Wallace bade farewell to a few more guests, accepting their hearty well-wishes. "To think it has come to this," he said, waving as the last of the guests left the hall. "Would ye believe that this very day was foretold when I was but a youth?"

"Foretold?" Sir Ellerslie paused. "By whom?"

"Och, well, do ye remember the time ye were an eager squire working on behalf of the magistrate in Straith Meirn – the time when bounty hunters brought in a wagonload of hill men? Well, ye willnae ken this, but as an unknown rough lad who had recently killed the son of the English constable of Dundee, I was among those ordered to hang that day."

"My God – was that ye?" Sir Ellerslie exclaimed.

"Aye, but fortunately, the whole lot of us managed to escape before the noose was placed about our necks."

"Including the boy and the man and woman who spoke strangely?"

"Aye, them too."

"Thank God."

Wallace gave Sir Ellerslie a curious glance. "Been feeling badly over it, have ye? Well, the tale doesnae end there. After escaping, we had a brief struggle over a young maiden, and I suffered an injury to my leg. I found myself in the midst of the strangest gathering of youth. One, a remarkable young lad, said to me that one day I would become guardian of Scotland, and when that day came, I was to tell ye that he didnae die, and neither did his friends or parents."

"Good Lord! Do ye ken what that means?" Sir Ellerslie dashed from the great hall, taking the spiral stairs two at a time. He searched several rooms, bursting through doors and flinging aside curtains. "They're gone!"

Wallace came up behind him, panting lightly from his sprint up the stairs. "Who's gone, Alex and his friends? Where would they go?"

Sir Ellerslie stared into the distance. "I cannae tell ye, William," he said, "how glad I am to learn that the boy and his parents didnae die that day."

"Aye, fine. But what's that got to do with Alex being gone?"

"Think, William." Sir Ellerslie clasped Wallace's shoulder. "That boy who foretold ye would be guardian – have ye seen him since that day?"

"It was many years ago – I scarcely recall what he looked like, other than his strange manner of speech and . . . oh my God!" Wallace smacked his forehead with the palm of his hand. "Of course!"

"Aye." Sir Ellerslie said. "That was him all right."

HISTORICAL NOTES

In 1297, James's father, Sir William Douglas le Hardi, was taken from Hog Tower to the Tower of London, where he died.

Betrayed by a Scottish knight, William Wallace was captured near Glasgow on August 3, 1305, and taken to London, where he was tried for treason and brutally executed. A plaque that the English later put up near the site diplomatically states that he "fought dauntlessly in defence of his country's liberty and independence in the face of fearful odds and great hardship" and that "his example [of] heroism and devotion inspired those who came after him to win victory from defeat and his memory remains for all time a source of pride, honour and inspiration to his countrymen."

After his return from Paris, in 1306, James met Robert the Bruce and became his right-hand man in the War of Independence.

King Edward I, the Hammer of the Scots, died in 1307 during a march toward Scotland to quell a rebellion led by Robert the Bruce and James. James's terrorizing battle tactics led James to become widely known as Black Douglas.

Principal Characters

Fictional Characters from the Present

- Alan: a spray bomber and modern-day Scottish rebel
- Aunt Fiona: Alex's great-aunt, who has little time for anyone
- Macpherson family: Alex and his elusive parents, George and Marian, who he has sought through time
- McRae family: Annie, William, Craig, and their father
- Professor Macintyre: a professor of archaeology from the University of Edinburgh

Fictional Characters from the Past

- Baldwin (Friar): a hermit philosopher believed to be a living saint (loosely based on Saint Baldred, who, sometime in the eighth century, lived in a cave on the Bass Rock, a small island in the Firth of Forth)
- Donald (Don-Dun) Dundonnel: a Scottish traveling produce merchant
- Dungbag Dirk: a leader of thieves and vagabonds who live in the hills
- Ellerslie and his wife: Scottish nobles who reside in Duncragglin Castle

- Isabelle: handmaiden to Lady Eleanor Douglas, James's stepmother
- Meg: an orphaned girl taken in by a Scottish innkeeper

- Alexander III of Scotland: the king of Scotland whose untimely death in 1286 threw Scotland into many years of turmoil
- Alexander Scrymgeour: the royal standard-bearer of Scotland
- Andrew Moray: a Scottish noble who fought with William Wallace in the Battle of Stirling Bridge
- Edward I of England: the king of England who was also known as Longshanks due to his extraordinary height for the time (over six feet) and as the Hammer of the Scots on account of his brutality toward his northern neighbor
- Eleanor Douglas: James's stepmother, the wife of the Scottish noble William Douglas le Hardi, Lord of Douglas
- Hugh de Cressingham: the treasurer of the English administration in Scotland
- James Douglas (Black Douglas): the son of the Scottish noble William Douglas le Hardi, Lord of Douglas
- John Balliol: the king of Scotland who became known as Toom Tabard (or "empty coat") due to his ineffective leadership and because the arms of Scotland had been torn from his surcoat during his abdication in 1296
- John de Graham: a Scottish knight who fought with William Wallace

- John de Warenne: the sixth Earl of Surrey, a powerful English noble
- Robert the Bruce: the Scottish noble who became king of Scotland in 1306
- William Douglas le Hardi: the Scottish noble who supported William Wallace and was the father of James Douglas
- William Lamberton (Bishop): the chancellor of Glasgow Cathedral who was later appointed bishop of St. Andrews by Pope Boniface VIII
- William Wallace: the son of a lower-level Scottish knight who rose to be guardian of Scotland

BIBLICALLY BASED CHARACTERS

- War, Conquest, Famine, and Death (collectively known as the Four Horsemen of the Apocalypse from the book of Revelations)